BIG DAYS IN
ASHTHORPE MAGNA

Maurice Abney-Hastings

Pen Press Publishers Ltd

Published in Great Britain by
Pen Press Publishers Ltd

25 Eastern Place
Brighton
BN2 1GJ

ISBN 978-1-906206-88-8

Illustrations by Dianne Williams

Printed and bound in Great Britain by
Cpod, Trowbridge, Wiltshire

What they say about it:

"This is England, good and bad, in a nutshell"

"Anybody who knows rural English towns will recognise Ashthorpe Magna"

"Surely it exists – if it didn't before then it will by the time you have read it!"

"Maurice's best work yet"

"God, are we really that bitchy?"

"I'm sure that I'm in it, but I don't know which character!"

"If you really want to understand what goes on behind the scenes in Middle England,
read *Big Days in Ashthorpe Magna*"

If you wish to make comment or request a signed copy of the book please feel free to contact the author at
Maurice@ashthorpemagna.co.uk
or telephone (01789) 763628

www.ashthorpemagna.co.uk

Acknowledgements

This is a novel, but a novel about a quintessentially English town, with quintessentially English people (with the odd French thrown in for good measure!). Is the place real? Are the people real? Are the stories real? Who knows! Certainly some are purely a figment of my own imagination, some adaptations of stories told to me by others and some are based on things I have seen and heard over a long lifetime.

Many people have helped with both stories and ideas, and to all of you, my thanks, and apologies for any who I may have missed.

My daughter, Louise, has steadfastly edited every chapter – this on top of two children, a job, and finishing an OU Degree in English; thanks Lou! Di Williams has been fantastic undertaking illustrations, and in particular the book cover which sums up so much of the essence of the work. Thanks also to Neil Howell who is very much the jester of the town in which we both live, and his humour comes through in George's Corner at the end of each chapter. John Aulton who came up with the true story about the Vicar's Shorts. Many other friends and acquaintances helped, either inadvertently or deliberately – Mike and Dale, Carol from Venue Xpresso, Bill Bayley, and my chum Andy Mills a real, live chairman of the Chamber of Trade and Commerce, Peter Pritchard, and George Higgins who "plays himself" in the book. Many, many others came up with odd little comments, which added to the realism.

Thanks to my son James, who has the unenviable task of preparing the copy on disc for publication, and scanning in all the illustrations, and to my youngest daughter Lucy who came up with the name of Ashthorpe Magna – or had she really been there? My other two daughters, Penny and Tory, have been less involved on a day-to-day basis, but have always been willing to make comment, usually starting "Oh, Dad…" Tory's husband, Jöel has also given his time and skills in helping with putting the illustrations onto disc for printing – this gave Di, friend Peter and I an excuse to visit him at his home near Castelnaudary in South West France!

Ashthorpe Magna may not be immediately obvious on maps or atlases, but to all who have been involved, it is as real as the towns we live in. If you look hard enough you will find it.

Maurice Abney-Hastings
South Warwickshire – November 2006

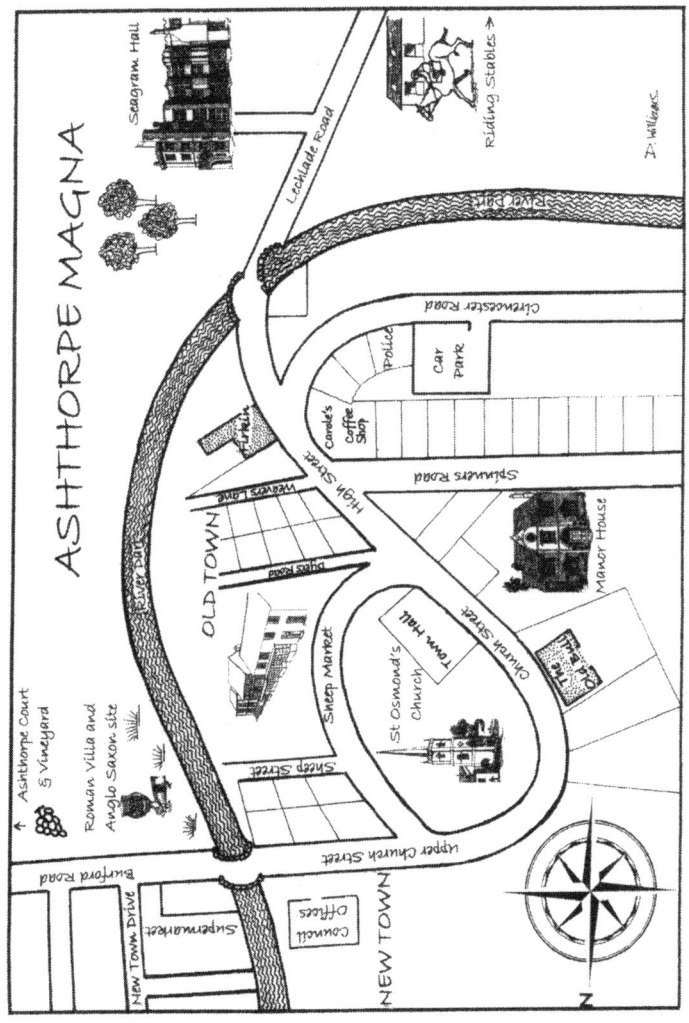
ASHTHORPE MAGNA

Chapter 1

Ian Rose was a new journalist on the Saturday *Telegraph*. Having achieved a 1st Class degree at Oxford in English Literature he had decided on a career in journalism, and had been allocated to the travel department of the popular broadsheet newspaper.

The Travel Editor summoned him in;

"Ian, we keep hearing things about a town in the Cotswolds called Ashthorpe Magna, but not only have I never heard of it, I can't even find it on my map. Be a good chap and get down there to see what is going on."

Ian sat in his battered Austin Mini on the road running from the main Lechlade to Cirencester route, and looked down the hill to the river valley below where he had been told that he would find Ashthorpe Magna. It was shrouded in mist, although where he sat and the area behind was bathed in bright sunlight. The mist started to roll back, and slowly to his left he saw a large Tudor mansion gradually emerge, and to the front the spire of a church, and roofs of other buildings started to poke through the haze. He headed for the town.

"Farmers' Bloody Market!" The booming voice of the Bailiff of Ashthorpe Magna reverberated around the ancient pillars of the Town Hall.

"That bloody weasel-faced Mayor has proposed a Farmers' Market here in front of the Town Hall."

The Reeve of the Court Leet, deputy to the Bailiff, visibly trembled as the sheer bulk of the Bailiff seemed to engulf him. Other Court Officers faded into the background, only too aware of the wrath of the Bailiff. After all he was at least 6 feet 3 inches in height with a not dissimilar girth and a weight of at least 22 stones.

"That bloody little ferret of a Mayor proposes a Farmers' Market!"

This one little piece of information was to rock the foundations of the medieval township nestling into the foothills of the beautiful English Cotswolds in a manner probably never seen since the Roman establishment of Ashthorpe. Despite the glorious early summer evening outside, a gloom settled over the interior of the hall. As the Bailiff pounded up and down the oak floor of the upper floor, The Bailiff's Hall, the 16 officers stood in huddled groups muttering between themselves in an effort to predict what would come next.

The previous month the Town Council had attended a meeting at their purpose-built Council Chambers to be addressed by an official from the South-Western Tourist Board under whose auspices Ashthorpe Magna fell by only a few miles. They had been excited to learn that many thousands of pounds would be available to Councils for the promotion of tourism in the region; the government of the day in its final fling of popularity claimed the credit for these monies although the fact was that the huge sums came from the European Union as a bribe, or even conscience money, for the dramatic overpayments from the United Kingdom for many years. The British MEPs had provided a constant barrage in Brussels until even the most hardened critic of the UK was fully aware that whilst the French and Spanish were net beneficiaries of EU funds, it was the Brits paying in the largest per capita contributions. Through the iniquitous tourism subsidies to our neighbours their tourist figures were hugely larger than the Brits who were paying! So the 6,000 population of Ashthorpe Magna became fully embroiled in political arguments in Europe.

The Town Council was a post-war institution, a fact constantly mentioned by the Bailiff from the shield of his 700-year-old post, and although theoretically ruled by an elected body was in actuality governed by the Town Clerk. This most unprepossessing little man had ruled the roost for over 20 years despite a terrible stammer which caused him to salivate from the corner of his lips when speaking. Such was his undoubted political skill and pomposity that when the Council in the 1980s decided the Mayor should have a robe so as not to appear inferior to the Bailiff of the Court Leet, he managed to get the Council agreement that the Town Clerk should also have one. But his in a rather imperial deep blue! He did not realise that with his slight build and short stature the robe actually looked more like the dressing gowns provided by Hilton Hotels than a gown of office to be respected. This same truth probably applied also to the Mayor, John Sleight, and whilst the Bailiff's description was due more to the rivalry and animosity between the two bodies it was probably true! Weasel features and ferret faced could not bring too much disagreement.

The Mayor, however, had the greater asset of being the most learned of the Council. He had for many years been the head of Classical Studies at a major public school in the West Country. He must certainly have developed an immunity of attack on his physical attributes on that most cruel and unforgiving of battlegrounds – the classrooms of an English Public School. Over the years his work had driven from him the rather attractive West Country burr into which he was born and brought up, to be replaced by the far less attractive squeaky whine of those trying to affect an upper class accent. Other than the retired Colonel on the Council, who oft referred to the Mayor as "that common little man", none of the other members would have noticed. Certainly not the Town Clerk who had been the son of a Bristol dockworker, won a scholarship to a Grammar School, subsequently becoming an Accountant with a practice in the North of

England. The rumours abounded as to why he left; nobody knew why. Was it misuse of funds, the most popular contender, was it some personal misdemeanour, or was it just incompetence? Whatever the cause he had run the Council's affairs for many years and it was certainly he who picked up most quickly on the benefits on offer from the Tourist Board.

Although the Mayor tried constantly to move away during the Tourist Board's presentations to avoid the shower emanating from the lips, the Clerk spoke in a hushed whisper throughout the talks. At the mention of Farmers' Market they both looked at each other knowing that this was the stand upon which to hang their coats. The Mayor, supported by his Clerk and those of the Council able to understand what was going on, summed up by thanking the Board for their presentation and committing to an immediate feasibility study for a Farmers' Market. Already in his own mind he had chosen the site – immediately in front of the Town Hall. The headquarters and domain of the Court Leet.

The Mayor's main dislike of the Court was, he claimed, that it was an unelected body. Actually this was untrue as once a year ALL townsfolk were invited to the Town Hall to "take the frankpledge" as they had since 1274. Whilst in this day and age a one pound coin is considered a frank, it is, as with all the 18 Courts Leet in England and Wales, open to all residents and ratepayers resident within the town boundary, to pay the frankpledge, become jurymen, and vote for the 17 officers. Furthermore although the Town Council is in theory a democratically elected body, on many, many occasions since its formation it has not found residents willing to stand for election so certain of their numbers were co-opted members; usually cronies of the Mayor.

The Bailiff's main dislike of the Mayor was living proof that the class system in rural England was not dead! The Bailiff had been to Harrow School, served without much distinction in the Army, made a great deal of money in property and lived in the Manor House. He did not rate the

Mayor or his Clerk highly. Certainly the Bailiff had, rather like King Henry VIII, the right figure for the Tudor style robes and whatever peoples' opinions of him he would be clapped when leading a procession down the High Street of Ashthorpe Magna.

Andy Gross, the Bailiff and a direct descendent of the 17th-century lexicographer, Francis Gross, had one driving ambition. It was not the well-being of the town, nor increasing tourism or trade, but almost entirely concentrated on the rolls of honour painted in gold upon ash boards in the Bailiff's Hall. Here are listed virtually all the Bailiffs going back to the thirteen hundreds. Yes, there are some blanks, but during meetings Major Gross could not take his eyes off the panel for the late 17th and early 18th Centuries where an R.P.W. Baldwin had served 4 terms in the office. The current Bailiff's dream, was that he, at the start of the 21st Century, could at least equal this record, perhaps even beat it.

His Reeve would normally take on the higher role at the end of a one-year tenure, but Cliff Breakshaft did not seem perturbed that he was now nearing the end of his second year. He was an ordinary working man, a delivery driver, and he held Andy Gross in great awe. Like the Scots, those with Birmingham antecedents never seem to lose the accent and expressions, and Cliff was no exception. Bailiff, Major Andrew Gross visibly cringed every time the Reeve greeted him in the manner so well know in Brummie territories: "Allroight then". The Bailiff's normal response in his Harrovian accent was normally something along the lines of:

"My dear boy, how lovely to see you!"

Cliff Breakshaft never quite learned how to deal with this, but having said that, he was well known and well liked by the citizens of Ashthorpe Magna. They had long forgiven the antics of him and his two brothers, 20 years earlier, when the lads were in their early twenties – forgiven but not forgotten! Some were almost written into the folklore of the area, and nobody around at the time forgot that, when after a drunken evening in The Firkin on the High Street, the boys and a friend had taken the then vicar's Morris Minor Traveller and lifted it bodily onto a fishing platform at the end of a narrow jetty on the river Dart (the Gloucestershire Dart rather than the Devonian Dart). Although everybody knew the culprits, including PC Corner, nobody would step forward officially to report them to the authorities. After days of pondering, a team of workers from the council resolved the situation at a cost of £200 to the Parochial Church Council. PC Mike Corner had a rather less than quiet word with Breakshaft's father who in the past had been well known to the police in Birmingham, the cause of his retreat to the hills, but to no avail. All of this said, Cliff tried his very best to support the Bailiff in his duties but he could still not get to grips with reading lessons at Christmas services in the old folks homes, chairing meetings or even such duties as presenting prizes at events such as the school galas. In short, a good support worker with a colourful past who could not in seriousness be regarded as a future Bailiff. Where most of the officers and their wives enjoyed visiting the four other courts in the South Midlands, to the current Reeve and his wife these were events viewed with a great fear; a fear almost as great as the occasions where he and Betty were obliged to go to Seagram Hall, the family seat of the Lord of the Manor, to be greeted by the 14th Earl of Ludcolmbe known to all by his name Mickey Carruthers.

None of these weaknesses were driving Cliff to seek election to his rightful post of Bailiff, and he was certainly happy to play second fiddle to the Major. Indeed it was this certainty that had caused the Bailiff to propose Cliff as Reeve at his own election nearly two years before. If the Reeve made it clear that he was worried and unhappy to become Bailiff the possibility of a 4, or even 5-year term became a distinct probability.

The Mayor asked the Town Clerk, appropriately named Keith Stammers, to organise a site meeting for the Farmers'

Market. The shrewd politician in the Clerk had caused him to warn the Mayor that it would be wise to look at every possible site in Ashthorpe Magna rather than announce a plan based solely on the Town Hall precinct. They both were fully aware that the Court Leet would see this as yet another way for the supposedly publicly elected body to take away their power – in reality little – and influence which was often greater than their modern constitution suggested. The Bailiff was enjoying his role as the first citizen of the town and he would fight tooth and nail to protect his position.

So it was that on a bright Tuesday evening at the end of June a group met in the front bar of the Old Bull to kick off the momentous decision which was to involve the whole of Ashthorpe Magna. Over a pint of Shires served by the ample landlady, Rosie den Bosch, they pondered over the town map. Ferret-faced Mayor, stammering Town Clerk who had advised that the group should be kept small for political reasons, Chairman of the Chamber of Trade, the Chairman of the South West Midland Farmers' Market Group and a rather pretty girl who handled grants at the District Council, decided that they should walk around six potential sites. The Mayor knew the answer, but joined in the commenting as they visited the town car park (if the market was there, then there would not be enough space for the cars and no electricity supply for the stalls who required this), at the side of the Post Office (bad access and no loos), behind the Firkin (miserable landlord would probably not agree), in front of the council offices (wrong side of the river), alongside Verdi's Ristorante on the Lechlade Road (too far from the town centre) and of course the Town Hall. The Hall could be opened to provide toilet facilities and an electricity supply, and true to form the Town Clerk produced documents showing that there had been a market there since Saxon times when the 17th-century current building had been an open wooden building, right until the coming of the, now defunct, railway line had allowed the farmers to take their produce to the more lucrative markets in Bristol.

The decision was unanimously agreed upon, and the clerk instructed to draw up the plans and costs. The redoubtable Chairman of the Chamber of Trade agreed to find and appoint a Chairman of the Farmers' Market; he suggested the formidable French widow, Lauren le Noir, and, as most of the town lived in fear of this long term resident, it was a choice which met with full agreement of the group. Melvyn Hughes, the Chairman of the Chamber had other motives. He had himself become a widower ten years previously, but even during the happy years of his marriage there were few unattached ladies in the area who had not succumbed to his undoubted charms. And, if rumours were true, then more than a few attached ladies!

For three years he had tried, and why not? Both were free, Melvyn for ten years, and the widow? Nobody knew, or had met her late husband. All that was known was that she had arrived some twenty years previous, as a very beautiful 30-year-old widow, and moved into an elegant Georgian house overlooking the River Dart, not that Melvyn had ever been invited into the house other than the occasion when Lauren had allowed her home to be used for a garden party in aid of Save the Children Fund. Not that she appeared totally disinterested. Twice he had taken her for dinner at the excellent Italian restaurant, Verdi's, and once to Gold Cup Day at Cheltenham. Whenever they met she kissed him, true Gallic style, on both cheeks and this was repeated whenever they parted, but whatever tactic he employed he seemed unable to take the matter further. Indeed in his official position as Chairman of the Chamber, Melvyn, naturally agreed the benefits the Farmers' Market would bring to Ashthorpe, but he was looking far more to the opportunities offered by such close proximity to Madame le Noir. The Mayor and Clerk, who both knew Lauren well, completely agreed with the decision, as they rightly felt she was the one person who could face and override the objections anticipated from the Court Leet and certain residents in the locality of the Town Hall. The tall, slender lady with hair colouring probably originally naturally blonde, had such a bearing that the lesser residents of the area called her "La Contessa", and many, when passing her in the street or meeting her in a shop, felt the impulse to bow slightly from the waist when greeting her. Her figure, for a woman of 50, was quite stunning, her pert breasts were clothed in the most elegant raiment Paris can provide and would appear to be thrust forward in a defiant manner as she walked, or rather glided along the High Street most mornings. Her thighs and bottom moved in perfect harmony that was the envy of any English women seeing her, and delight of every man.

It was no small wonder that Melvyn's attentions had been (almost) exclusively upon her, but others too had these same feelings, most notably Bailiff Major Andrew Gross. Andy himself was reputedly still married although he had shipped his wife to their villa in Marbella some years before, and whilst in the early years he would visit her on a regular basis in Spain, since he had become Reeve and then Bailiff it was some five years since they had met.

The Bailiff could certainly see how La Contessa could fit neatly into his life. Into a role as the First Lady, into the Manor House and most importantly into his specially-made huge double bed. Lauren was one of the few residents of Ashthorpe who was regularly invited to Seagram Hall at a purely social level, and whilst Lord Mickey Carruthers had an undoubted affection for her his intentions appeared to be totally honourable. If a bond with her could cause the Bailiff to be included in the social list by the 14th Earl, then indeed his status in life would be greatly enhanced. He could not have believed that his arch-rivals, the Mayor and his cohorts, the Clerk and the Chairman of the Chamber were successfully offering the Chairmanship of the Farmers' Market to Lauren. She accepted, to Melvyn's great joy, on the proviso that the post was called by its correct English title rather than the fashionable and rather stupid politically correct version of "Chair". PC had certainly not arrived in Ashthorpe Magna and Lauren le Noir most decidedly did not wish to be called after a piece of furniture upon which one rested one's bottom!

It was probably an exaggeration in the mind of Andy Gross that the post of Bailiff of the Manor of Ashthorpe carried such esteem, but it did go back a long way. After the carve-up of England by the Norman Barons, the country was ruled on behalf of the monarchs by the aristocracy in the small administrative areas of Hundreds.

Amongst many duties performed by the Courts in ancient times were those now handled by local authorities; law enforcement, river clearance, boundary dispute, weights and measures, food hygiene and quality control of bread and ale! On the Courts it is perhaps no surprise that the most popular modern posts are the Ale Tasters. Those 18 Courts remaining in England and Wales were legally ratified by the Administration of Justice Act of 1977, but whilst all the Courts maintain broadly the same posts, the ceremonies and duties are all slightly different. Ashthorpe Magna is one of only a few where the Lord of the Manor is still a member of the ruling aristocracy by whom the Courts were formed back in the 13th Century. Other Lords of the Manor have purchased their honorary title and include property developers, businessmen, and in one rather special case in Warwickshire the delightful American daughter of a US multi millionaire DIY chain owner. Despite the unprecedented acquisition of the Lord of the Manor title by a lady, she proved to be both active and generous to the Court. Sadly for Ashthorpe Magna the 14th Earl, undoubtedly generous with his time and his home, has little spare cash to undertake similar good works in the town. The Court of his Manor is today largely a ceremonial body, adding colour to the town whilst at the same time raising reasonable sums of money for local charitable work.

Only the retired Colonel was a member of the modern Town Council as well as being the holder of a medieval office on the Court Leet, that of Brooklooker. This fact appeared to have escaped the notice of the Mayor who referred to David Prentergast as Colonel Blimp, but the crafty Town Clerk regularly fed misinformation to the Colonel knowing that it would be fed back to the Bailiff. Indeed there was a bond between Andy Gross and David Prentergast as both had been to the same public school and both had been serving officers in the Army.

The Town Clerk called a special meeting of the Council to present his feasibility study and costings for the proposed Farmers' Market, and it came as no surprise to anybody when he reported that the area in front of the Town Hall had been selected as the only reasonable site for the market. The motion that these proposals should be placed before the District Council with a request for a grant was unanimously accepted, with only the Colonel abstaining, although it was suspected that he may have been asleep at the time.

The following day, Keith Stammers appeared on the doorstep of local District Councillor, John "Sleepy" Honey. Although on the council for many years, John had a reputation for doing nothing of any consequence for Ashthorpe Magna, especially if it required effort. The Clerk well knew of this tendency, so every document he handed to the Councillor was absolutely complete and clearly labelled with the name of the functionary who would actually give approval; in this fashion "Sleepy" had nothing to do other than act as postman which suited him well. Keith was somewhat surprised to be invited inside John Honey's house for coffee, and even more surprised when the District Councillor fired a barrage of questions. In minutes the wily Clerk realised why this totally unprecedented interest in such a matter had stirred the Councillor into action.

John Honey had first been elected to the council 15 years ago when there was a huge Liberal revival in the West Country, and whilst he had been re-elected on three occasions, at each election his majority was reduced by the Conservative candidate until the last occasion three and a half years ago when his lead was cut to a mere 150 votes. Whilst District Councils are unpaid, "Sleepy" had learned to use the expense system to its maximum and had grown dependant upon these funds to buy some meagre luxuries in his rather drab life. His questions to the Town Clerk demonstrated that, for the first time in years, the councillor was worried about the possible loss of his seat, and on several occasions he asked Keith whether the population wanted a Farmers' Market. He wanted to know how the residents of Upper Church Road would react at the loss of parking for one night a month – the market could only be held on the first Friday of each month – and what would be the town reaction to the inevitable criticisms from the Court Leet to the organisation of something by the Town Council in the precincts of what they felt to be THEIR Town Hall. For a change, the Town Clerk, himself a paid-up Conservative, was brutally honest. Yes, the residents of Upper Church Street would raise objections to the market, as they objected to everything else even the church bells and Christmas lights! They were, however, in any case mostly Conservatives and he felt the District Councillor would not be too concerned at upsetting them.

As far as the Court Leet was concerned the Clerk pointed out, probably incorrectly, that they were not especially popular in Town and called, mostly by the residents of the New Town area, the Court Elite. The Clerk truly believed that the majority of the population would be in favour of the market and it would be a good opportunity for the Councillor to be seen doing something in public well before the elections if he supported the application and also attended the opening ceremony. His instincts were correct, and after pondering the matter over a second cup of coffee Councillor John Honey announced that he would not only deliver the various documents produced by the Clerk, but also would speak with the grants people and table a motion at the next full Council meeting in chambers in only two weeks. This way would avoid the proposals being taken first to committee, thus creating an average delay of six months for the committee stage.

True to his word, but not to his nickname of Sleepy, the matter was pushed through Council with almost indecent haste. The state of the Council was "hung" with 18 Conservative and 18 Liberal members, the balance being held by a few Independents and a solitary and rather lonely Labour member. With elections looming nobody wanted to be seen as objecting to what should prove to be such a popular event.

The following morning Madame le Noir answered her telephone.

"Madame le Noir?"

"Yes."

"Councillor Honey. I am delighted to report that your grant application has been accepted and the Farmers' Market can go ahead. Please keep me informed especially on plans for the opening ceremony."

Within minutes she had called the Chairman of Chamber of Trade (to his considerable delight), the Mayor, the Town Clerk and the Farmers' Group Chairman. She had already called the Old Bull to book the snug for the following Monday evening to hold her first Committee Meeting, and all those she called agreed to be there. By that evening she had printed and circulated the agenda.

Ashthorpe Magna Farmers' Market Committee
Monday 9th July – The Old Bull – 19.30

AGENDA

1. Welcome
2. Date of first market and opening ceremony
3. Press Release
4. Out of town posters
5. Parking arrangements
6. Promotional flyers
7. Residents of Upper Church Road
8. Positioning of stalls
9. A.O.B.
10. Date of next meeting

Lauren le Noir – Chairman

By 7.00 pm the four men had arrived, and twenty-five minutes later were ordering their second pint of Shires in the main bar when Lauren arrived. As if by some magnetic force, her appearance stopped all conversation and every head turned to observe her entry. The only sound to be heard, other than the muted music emanating from a garish CD player behind the bar, was that of pint mugs being placed on the bar and tables so as not to interrupt the views of Lauren and perhaps the rather less than honourable thoughts going on in the minds of the drinkers.

In response to Melvyn's question, the Chairman ordered a large dry white wine and swept into the snug followed by her committee. The chatter in the pub returned, and even the three grumpy old men who occupied the corner of the bar next to the exit were reduced to a series of grunts varying from "Cor" to rather cruder expletives.

A brief welcome was followed by a lengthy discussion on when the first market should take place, and despite the Mayor wishing to start in January of the following year, the farmers' representative pointed out that his group insisted on an earlier start to ensure the market was well established prior to the lucrative pre-Christmas market. He also made the group aware that the January markets were traditionally those with the smallest attendance due to the lack of many fresh fruits and vegetables and the fact that most of the poultry producers sold out prior to the festive season and started rearing for the Easter rush. He also had to explain that whilst he understood the preference for a Saturday market, the farmers' group already attended long established events in two major towns on each Saturday of the year. Thus the first Friday of each month was agreed and the opening of the market would be on Friday 4th September, a mere two months ahead.

With little debate it was agreed that the opening party would include the committee, the 14th Earl of Ludcolmbe, and of course the District Councillor. When Lauren enquired about the Court Leet, the Mayor expressed the view that as the market was a commercial event rather than traditional, their inclusion was inappropriate. Nobody questioned this rather dubious view. They agreed that there should be a procession from the bottom of the High Street to the Town Hall led by a bagpiper and followed by the Mayor and Town Clerk in their robes, and once the 14th Earl had performed the opening ceremony the local group of Morris Men would put on a display.

The budget allocated by the District Council allowed for the production of signs to be placed on all the approach roads to Ashthorpe Magna, a banner for the High Street, 1,000 flyers to be distributed in the outlying villages and advertisements in the two local "freebie" newspapers. The

Chairman was asked to contact the local press, radio and TV to try and ensure the maximum publicity for the market, and the ever opportunistic Melvyn Hughes volunteered to let La Contessa have the list of media contacts which was constantly updated by the Chamber and used by many organisations in the town. To his absolute delight, and quite unexpectedly, Lauren asked him if he would mind dropping it in the next morning. As he rarely opened his haberdashery shop before 11.00 am they agreed a time of 10.30, but in truth he would have willingly shut at any time to take advantage of this first opportunity to get closer to the French beauty. As the last of the committee to be in the bar, he finished his pint through lips formed into the largest grin imaginable. Despite the four pints during the evening, and a couple of glasses of locally produced Merlot before retiring for the night, Melvyn did not sleep well for reasons that are somewhat obvious! Indeed he was up early to have a lingering shower, wash his thinning hair and trim his greying beard. He wished that he had been to the barber the previous week as he had promised himself, but after he donned his new sports jacket and cords he examined himself in the mirror – not too bad for a fifty-five year-old.

Armed with the Chamber document showing all the contact points for the media, he stood in front of the elegant deep blue Georgian door and struck the polished brass knocker fashioned as a dolphin. It seems a hackneyed expression, but he truly believed his heart raced when Lauren le Noir opened the door wearing a modest, but flimsy housecoat. On such a hot summer's morning he should not have been surprised that there appeared to be nothing under the coat, and the top button was undone, revealing the beautiful curvature of Lauren's milky coloured breasts. The next hour was a complete blur to him. Despite numerous telephone calls to the media, he was having huge difficulty in averting his gaze away from the lady's cleavage or her lovely legs, which she seemed to cross every few minutes revealing tantalising flashes of thigh. He hoped that he managed not to give the impression of drooling – which he certainly was!

The Ashthorpe Magna Chamber of Trade and Commerce Chairman, Melvyn Hughes, was by now totally enamoured by the newly appointed Farmers' Market Committee Chairman, Lauren le Noir.

The first paper to be published was the *Ashthorpe Gazette*, printed that very afternoon for delivery to all houses and businesses in the area. Although it claimed its origins in the mid 19th Century as a truly local paper with its offices on the High Street, by the time the 21st Century arrived it was merely an Ashthorpe Magna edition of a weekly "freebie" produced in the far larger town of Cirencester, some 12 miles to the west. At best, the front page and one or two inside pages were devoted to what news there was from Ashthorpe and the surrounding villages, and one cub reporter was given two days a week to gather in, or some said invent, local news. Having said that, the *Gazette* was better than the alternative "rag" which sometimes carried no local news whatsoever, and the local pages were certainly read by most residents.

Thus it was that at 7.30 on a warm July morning, the *Ashthorpe Gazette* thumped onto the hall floor of Ashthorpe Magna Manor, the home of Bailiff Andy Gross. The headlines on the front paper read "Date fixed for Farmers' Market in Ashthorpe Magna". The pretty little cub reporter, Claire, had done her job well and even managed to obtain a photograph of the Town Hall from the *Gazette's* records. She had succeeded in eliciting quotes from the Mayor congratulating the Chamber on its part in promoting the market, from the Chamber thanking the Mayor and District Council and even from the Rector of St Osmund's Church in the town centre thanking everybody for being so public-spirited.

Although the Manor House is set back some 200 yards from the High Street, reports that morning claimed that a roar

17

was heard up and down the street. Although Colonel Blimp had forewarned him, Andy was firmly of the belief that neither funding nor organisation would be available for a Farmers' Market. His huge bulk, draped in a tartan dressing gown, waddled towards the front door and with some difficulty bent over to pick up the paper lying on the polished wooden floor. Back into the kitchen for the daily ceremony of morning tea making, and the paper was opened.

For the first of many, many times the roar went out:
"FARMERS' BLOODY MARKET!"

George's Corner

In the corner of the bar in the Old Bull, usually occupied by the three grumpy old men, is attached a small brass plaque with the inscription "This corner of the bar belongs to George Higgins". From that area emanates the most amazing level of humour and one-line quips. Visitors usually try and sit within hearing distance, and will often spend an hour or more listening, and laughing.

"Wow! What a nice blouse the young lady over there is almost wearing."

"Yes, but the difference between her and the Grand Old Duke of York is that he only had 10,000 men!"

"I have to feel sorry for poor old Harry. He has a heart problem caused by booze, and his father died because of alcohol. He was run over on the way to the off-licence!"

"FARMERS' BLOODY MARKET!"

Chapter 2

Nobody knew where or whence the name Ashthorpe Magna had originated, and, as with many such rural communities throughout England the first proven reference was in William I *Doomsday Book*. Ash appears to come from Anglo-Saxon Old-English *Asc* meaning simply an ash tree, and *Thorpe* meaning a farmstead, thus a farm surrounded by Ash trees. This is simple enough until it is considered that Bronze-Age artefacts appear in the fields during ditching, ploughing or draining, on a regular basis. The most famous of these were uncovered in the 1930s by an amateur archaeologist, the then local GP Dr Merrick, searching without the benefit of a metal detector in the land 2 miles to the east of the town now used as part of the 200 acre vineyard, and they consisted of some unremarkable coinage along with a pair of gold drinking or ceremonial goblets. One of the latter was rather badly squashed, but the second was in perfect condition and decorated with exquisite carving suggesting that the so-called Dark Ages were not as uncivilised as teachers would have us believe. Since the war these two significant and important finds have been housed at the British Museum.

Later excavation of a Roman building site near the River Dart, and many finds of Saxon relics made both locally and in Northern Europe suggest a continuous occupation and industry over a period of more than 2,000 years. But none of this explains the name; Ashthorpe as shown above being Saxon, and Magna being the Latin term for Large. If so, where was, or indeed, was there an Ashthorpe Parva? Archaeologists and historians have mused over this for years, and the most logical argument is that if the larger Magna were undoubtedly tiny the smaller Parva would be smaller still. In all probability it could have been the home of a local Anglo-Saxon "aristocrat" based in or around the area in which the golden goblets were unearthed, but as Ashthorpe Court was built there in the 15th Century with many alterations and additions over the next two hundred years all traces of the earlier settlement would have long since disappeared. It has also been suggested that although the Roman occupation and administration finished in the 5th Century it is not unrealistic to suppose that the Anglo Saxons may have continued to use the terminology of their earlier masters.

The town is sited on the southern edge of the Cotswolds, with its near neighbours of Cirencester and Lechlade themselves enjoying an equally long and illustrious history. The former lies some 12 miles to the east, with Lechlade being 9 miles to the south and the Borough of Swindon and its 200,000 population being another 11 miles from Lechlade. Burford, known as the "Gateway to the Cotswolds" is some 8 miles to the east of Ashthorpe Magna, but the residents of Ashthorpe rarely visited Burford unless travelling to Oxford. Whilst Burford is undoubtedly a most attractive stone-built town, and hosts the nearby site of the popular Cotswold Wildlife Park, it is almost exclusively given over to the eateries, coffee shops, art galleries and antique shops so desired by the tourist industry. For major shopping trips the good citizens would go either to Cheltenham, or visit one of the many out-of-town supermarkets around the old railway town of Swindon, but the remainder of their requirements would have to be supplied by the mini-supermarket and the limited shops in town.

The town itself is formed around the River Dart which feeds the great trunk route of the Thames near its starting point in Lechlade-on-Thames, and Ashthorpe Magna is strictly divided into two at the bridge across the river on the Burford Road known as the Toll Bridge. It was in fact one of the later operating toll bridges in England only ceasing to collect fees just prior to the declaration of hostilities in 1939, and many artefacts from the long-since demolished Toll House are displayed on the walls of the ground floor in the Town Hall. Not only is the town separated geographically by the bridge and the river, but it defines the social split of the area with the Old Town to the south of the Toll Bridge, and New Town to the north. All the older buildings are to the south with the Church, the Manor House, two ancient pubs and many shops, cottages and houses going as far back at the 14th Century and up to the present time with many built of the beautiful honey-yellow Cotswold stone. With one exception of the old wool exchange demolished during the architectural madness of the 1960s, restoration and limited new building had taken place with great sympathy. New, Executive Estates had popped up over a period of 20 years on the outskirts of Ashthorpe on all three main entry roads from Cirencester, Burford and Lechlade.

Not so the other side! What used to be council estate now mostly privately owned, row after row of 3-bedroom privately owned but identical semis, the ugly council offices, the police station, two new pubs and an industrial estate now marred the medieval landscape. True it houses more people than the Old Town, but it is also the area where most social troubles in the area are said to emanate. Most of the area was built between the mid 1960s and mid 1970s, and whilst most of the "incomers" arrived as overspill from Bristol, a certain number came from Birmingham. Stories abound of the difficulties they had in mixing with the older residents – and vice-versa. The first of the roads to be occupied was New Town Drive and one can but imagine their delight at leaving the cities and moving to such a lovely area, but no! Within one year of arrival they presented a petition to the now defunct Rural District Council, signed by all but two of the residents, complaining about the noise and smell created by the sheep and cattle in the fields on the other bank of the river. It was felt by some locals to be a shame that the livestock could not petition against the reputed antics of the new occupiers which can best be described as "swinging sixties"!

Like so many other small Cotswold towns such as Chipping Campden and Moreton-in-Marsh, the wealth and importance of Ashthorpe Magna was built in medieval times by the powerful woollen industry. Although the few weavers who remained in the area survived well, their existence probably owes more to the musical and smoking rites of Woodstock, USA, than to medieval craftsmen. The previous existence of the industry was recorded by the little ancient lanes running from the High Street, Weavers Lane, Dyers Road, Spinners Road and even Sheep Street and Sheep Market. The Council was also planning a Weaving Museum in a little used area of the Council offices, and were awaiting news of their request for matched funding from the Heritage Lottery Fund to add to the already promised sums from District and County Councils.

The Dart Valley winding from North West to South East was bordered on both sides by beautiful, gently rolling slopes and a little over 200 acres 2 miles east was occupied by the Ashthorpe Vineyard claimed to be the third largest in England after Denbies in Surrey and Three Choirs on the borders of Gloucestershire and Herefordshire. The vineyard was part of the 1,000 acre estate belonging to Ashthorpe Court through the current owner, Nick Darling, a tall rangy character of around 60 years of age with dank greasy hair and, despite twelve years in Gloucestershire, still speaking with the strong accent of the East End of London. He had once, when in his cups, admitted that he had done time at Her Majesty's pleasure having been convicted of causing grievous bodily harm to be committed on one of his competitors, a fellow massage parlour and porn magazine owner, but it seemed that the grape-vine of rural England predated his admission and the information was already known by the locals. For pure curiosity the local solicitor,

Cliff Vintner, had searched the records and found that Darling had indeed spent 5 of an 8-year sentence in a south London jail but the court had been unable to reclaim much of his ill-gotten gain under the regulations in place in 1988.

At the time of his purchase, after his release, the Gothic style mansion which was Ashthorpe Court was in pretty bad shape, having been requisitioned for housing difficult conscientious objectors during the war, belonged to a Scottish family who occupied only part of the building until running out of funds, and finally to an East Anglian Estate Agents group who planned on turning it into an hotel, spent a million pounds to little effect and finally sold again. The Court with a hundred acres and the adjoining farmland were put up for auction, failed to reach the reserve for either and Nick Darling successfully made a private purchase for an undisclosed sum of money. During the first three years of restoration the farmland, other than the south-facing slope 200+ acres, was leased out to two local tenant sheep and wheat farmers, the first vines were planted and a heritage restoration company worked constantly on the building.

Needless to say Nick and his entourage of builders, vineyard workers and a regular supply of tarty-looking girls with London accents, were not accepted by the residents especially by the 14th Earl, the Rector and Major Andy Gross. Then an amazing occurrence took place. A gentle, somewhat school-ma'amly, lady walked into the butcher's shop with a huge order for meats, similarly to the green-grocer's and several other trades people and to each she asked if they could deliver to Ashthorpe Court and open an account. She gave her name as Mrs Nick Darling. Although all the traders had refused credit to her husband they readily complied with her request. It was quite clear that she was to become the power behind the throne.

Nothing further was seen of the young mini-skirted females to the Court and a number of unemployed farm labourers were employed by Mrs Darling to complete the work on the vineyard. Whilst the young, and inexpensive, oenologist employed by Nick had suggested that the only grapes which could be grown were of the Muller-Thurgau and Rhine Riesling varieties, the Australian expert with whom Mary had replaced him immediately started the more marketable Pinot Noir, Chardonnay, Merlot and Shiraz vine stock. After several visits to both English and French vineyards, Mary Darling employed an architectural group to design the visitor facilities of the venture, and a small cottage was restored to house the project manager for the three-year duration of his very lucrative contract to establish Ashthorpe Vineyard, not only as a producer of excellent quality wines, but a major tourist attraction.

Even Nick seemed to change. The East End accent moderated, probably due to the loss of the girls, but his normal apparel of rather shiny material suits worn with dark shirts and light silk ties was gradually replaced with what the French know as "style Anglais", Harris Tweed jackets, cord trousers, brogue shoes and knitted ties! Whilst the part did not fit the man, the man gradually altered to fit the part.

Nick Darling had never bothered to use the local hostelries, in fact in his early occupation he correctly picked up from the atmosphere that he was not welcome. His wife, however, being an excellent manager of people soon established a routine when they, their managers and key staff joined them for the excellent dinners at the Old Bull. The landlady, the voluptuous Rosie den Bosch, was of course delighted as often these Friday night groups would include visitors and be anything up to ten or twelve people. The trades folk were equally pleased as Mary made a point on the first Friday of each month of ensuring that the previous monthly account was settled in full; in the case of the off licence this could run into many hundreds of pounds. She made a point of joining the Ashthorpe Chamber of Trade and Commerce paying double the requested annual fee. They gave generously to local charities, especially Court Leet, and

25

even allowed a number of organisations, including the Town Council, to host events in their home. So the London crook was successfully, with the help of his wife, becoming a pillar of the community.

Major Andy Gross was less than sure and regularly aired his personal opinions in the various establishments around town, but Lord Mickey Carruthers showed no uncertainty:

"The man is a f...... little crook and should be drummed out of town" this from a man who, any on meeting would describe as both charming and gentle and indeed it was the first time anybody had heard him swear.

The final quest for acceptance during this period came when Mary Darling employed at her own expense the County Archaeological Department to search the area around the Court for any further evidence of Bronze Age occupation. All but the 14th Earl were thrilled that this aspect of the town's ancient history was at last being properly examined for the first time since Dr Merrick in the 1930s. The cynics had said that her motives were more a desire to find treasure trove, or, perhaps the more likely to entice more visitors to her ever-expanding visitor centre. To be fair to Mary Darling, whatever the motives for the archaeological excavations, the vineyard, known for the benefit of tourists from America and Australia as a winery, was by now fully operational. The wine had won international prizes for its quality, including the previous year the coveted *Medaille d'Or* at the famous and important Bordeaux Wine Festival for the Ashthorpe Merlot, but perhaps the greatest accolade came recently when the ageing President of France had complimented the quality when drinking it in the Mansion House in London. Mary had also in the past twelve months come to an arrangement with a major tourist bus operating company to offer a one-day visit to the "winery" to some of the 6 million visitors to Oxford and 3 million visitors to Stratford-upon-Avon.

Certainly the Ashthorpe Experience was ready now to accept the anticipated flood of tourists; the visitors enjoyed a ride on a miniature steam railway around the planted area of 201 acres to look at the estimated 240,000 vines, terminating at the main visitor centre. The latter was built in a style that combined the attractiveness of a giant Cotswold barn with the utilitarian benefits of Chelmsford Tesco and the inevitable clock tower at the centre. Built around a courtyard, one side was occupied by presses, an array of 1,000 and 5,000 litre stainless steel fermentation tanks, for the highly specialist wines there was a section where the production process was undertaken in beautifully hand-crafted Italian oak casks, and finally in the production area the bottling, corking and labelling lines handling some 320,000 bottles a year. The other three sides of the quadrangle housed the money-making sales outlets with an upmarket restaurant seating 120 people, a café which appeared to be full all day, a wine bar selling their own products along with continental snacks and the Winery Shop selling what can best be described as interesting, but tatty wine-related gifts including little carriers containing three different wines. All built without the need for a single government grant, but few enquired about the origin of the huge sums utilised.

There is no doubt that Mary Darling had brought to the area a fantastic and viable tourist attraction which could benefit the whole town for years to come. She had asked the 14th Earl to conduct the official opening ceremony, and was genuinely surprised and thrilled when, against his better judgement, Mickey Carruthers had actually agreed. In common with most small communities in England, and probably through most of the world, Ashthorpe Magna survived on tittle-tattle and gossip, but no version of the reasons for the Earl agreeing to visit the lions' den to conduct the ceremony agreed with any other. One version was that he was shorter of money than usual and was receiving payment, another that he was so envious he wanted to replicate the success at Seagram Hall, another that because there would be an inscribed plaque and he could not bear the fact of another neighbouring aristocrat having their name in perpetuity, but in probability it could just have been curiosity. Whenever he was asked, as he was frequently by many especially the Bailiff, Andy Gross, he would merely reply:

"Noblesse Oblige"!

Mary worked hard on the PR. First to invite the great and the good from the area, the land-owners, major business-men, Chairman of the Regional Tourist Board, their rarely seen MP and even more rarely seen MEP, Chairmen of the District and County Councils and the town dignitaries, the Mayor, Deputy Mayor and Town Clerk, the Bailiff, Reeve and Marshall from the Court Leet, the Rector, Catholic Priest, Methodist Minister and Baptist Pastor, Chairman of Chamber and the newly appointed Chairman of the Farmers' Market, the luscious Lauren le Noir.

In all 120 invitations went out and, with the exception of 4 people on holiday, 116 replied in the affirmative. It may have been the attraction of excellent food and wine, the guaranteed presence of TV and radio, or maybe like the 14th Earl, curiosity, but Mary Darling was surprised and delighted by the response. She was not surprised at the Priest and the Rector, who was far more Roman than his opposite number from the Roman Church, accepting as both were known to be more than a little fond of the produce of the grape, but the Methodists and Baptists? Mary was of the belief that they preached against the evils of alcohol and had only invited them out of courtesy with little hope of success. Whatever the reason for such a success it was to be the largest party in the area since the father of Lord Mickey Carruthers, Henry, the 12th Earl, had hosted a victory party in 1947! The big difference is that the wife of the infamous Nick Darling paid for everything whereas the children of the trades folk used by the 12th Earl moaned even 20 years after the event that their parents were never paid for their goods.

As the day loomed preparations moved efficiently and swiftly onwards at the vineyard, whilst the speakers,

Chairman of the Tourist Board, Bailiff and Lord Mickey were working on their presentations which were to be kept strictly within a 10-minute span. On the very day before, Andy Gross was unable to walk. His gout, which had bedevilled him for years due to his excessive weight and a possible over-consumption of liquid refreshment, had returned in the most violent attack he had ever known. His left foot was so swollen that he could barely stand when trying to leave his reinforced bed to make the ritual cup of tea, and certainly there was no chance of even putting on his bedroom slippers. Andy knew from experience that even taking the, now banned, PBZ tablets he had kept from years past, there would be no possibility of even leaving the Manor House for at least 4 days ahead.

He phoned the Marshall, Ray Spicer, and asked him to call round with great urgency. Ray lectured in IT at the local College of Further Education on a part-time basis and also appeared to run some sort of a consultancy business from home. He certainly appeared to be acquiring the trappings of success and was even looking to change his 3 bed-roomed semi for a 4 bed-roomed detached in Ashthorpe. He was certainly the youngest member of the Court Leet and whilst somewhat difficult to pin down was probably in his early forties. He was not a tall man, but his thickset muscular body and spiky hair certainly added many inches to the perception of his stature. The Marshall gave the impression of cleverness, and clearly from the Court documents he produced he was brilliant in his field, but it was difficult to engage him in any other form of communication outside a football pitch. He quickly realised what the Bailiff was saying when he suggested that Cliff, the Reeve, was unable to represent the Court Leet with a speech at such an important event, and Ray, seeing the possibilities offered by standing before virtually everybody of importance from the County, readily agreed. This mischance of the timing of the

Bailiff's gout was to have long-term implications to both his own future and that of the Reeve.

News of the event spread as rapidly as Asian flu around Ashthorpe. Speculation abounded amongst the peasants as to the cost of the feast, and as usual whilst the rumour started as tens of thousands of pounds, by the time it reached the landlady of the Old Bull, Rosie den Bosch, it had had risen to the million mark. Even the three grumpy old men who had their regular places at the corner of the back bar leading onto the entrance corridor with a door out to the garden to their backs showed a passing interest. Not that they ever used the garden. It was either too hot, too cold or:

"Too many noisy bloody children."

Their main object of attention was normally centred on the more than ample bosoms of the landlady, but now the speculation as to whom had been invited to the opening of Ashthorpe Vineyard had temporarily changed their focus. Some of their ideas were pretty crackpot and, knowing of the rumours of Nick Darling's past, the names of long-departed gangsters such as the Kray twins, Ronnie Biggs and Buster Edwards were all suggested as possible visitors, but this was after at least four pints of Old Spot! Although they were known as the three grumpy old men of Ashthorpe, and indeed to look at them one would be forgiven for thinking this, they all had a delightful sense of humour. And they were not all that old. Certainly Peter Epsom was actually in his early eighties, but whilst being rather overweight (five pints of Shires a night?) he was as fit as a fiddle; Old George, although looking rather more, was in fact only 64; whilst Angus Theakestone the comedian of the trio was a mere 58. They provided great entertainment for other patrons of the back bar and any visitor on their own, stranger or no, even if feeling somewhat depressed and determined to drown their sorrows, would soon be drawn into the banter and certainly leave a much happier person. Most people realised that the grumpy old men added to the charm of the pub, and even in a

Sunday Telegraph article the previous year the incognito reporter had mentioned the trio as adding local character to the Old Bull. It received a five-star rating!

Rosie had once been married to a Dutch Merchant Marine Captain, hence the name den Bosch, but shortly after his death some ten years previously she had sold her home near Rotterdam, moved back to England and purchased with a great deal of assistance from friends and family a large, rambling and run-down pub in Ashthorpe Magna, the Old Bull. For three months the pub was closed and a huge number of family and friends moved in with saws, screwdrivers, paintbrushes and every variety of garden implement. Rosie herself worked from seven in the morning until seven at night supervising the installation of the preparation and cooking areas of the kitchen, and cajoling the workers from the suppliers of the equipment to work far longer and harder than they ever recalled doing. She achieved this by a constant exploitation of her extensive feminine charms and the provision of free ale towards the end of their working day.

Rosie, by reason of her copious bosoms, looked far taller than she really was and this was accentuated by her preference for mini skirts that barely concealed her ample thighs. Perhaps a little unwise for a lady approaching her fiftieth year, but it certainly had the desired effect upon her workmen, both volunteers and paid! Her current boyfriend, Rollo Firtle, known affectionately by some, and unkindly by others, as Mr Blobby due to his size and shape, took on the job of completely clearing the overrun garden and building a new one from the start. He threw himself completely into the task set and within a very few weeks it took shape.

The pub was opened quietly and without ceremony as it probably took a week to fully stock the bar with four guest real ales, two regulars from the local Gloucestershire Uley Brewery, and the usual variety of bottled soft drinks, mixers and wines. The best staff were poached from other local establishments and the chef was given a further week to prepare menus and stock for the opening of the restaurant. A mixture of town dignitaries and local businessmen from the industrial estate were invited to a buffet lunch in the function room, newly decorated by Rollo Firtle and friends, to promote the food side of the business. It proved a great success and, to the amazement of the many cynics, within weeks the Old Bush was the success story of the region with the bars and three restaurant areas full most lunchtimes and evenings, and bookings taken on the function room from many of the town organisations who moved their regular dinner meetings from other hostelries. All this involved Rosie and Firtle in working from seven or eight in the morning until well past midnight, and cracks were already beginning to show in their personal relationship. Clearly Rosie needed the strength and hard work of her boyfriend, but he was no match for her intellectually and found it difficult at times working for a boss whose bed he had just left. Even when she was clearly exhausted she was wonderful with customers, but displayed her tiredness by sniping at Firtle who didn't really understand why.

Their success did not really damage the business at the other town centre pub, The Firkin. It was so different in its nature, best described as an ale house, that its more "down to earth" clientele preferred the cold, sombre atmosphere and even enjoyed the rudeness of the ageing landlord, Jamie Rivers, whose catchphrase whenever anyone had the temerity to order more than one drink at a time was:

"Are you sure?"

Despite that the beer was, and still is superb at the Firkin and it regularly receives awards from CAMRA for the quality. Old misery was more than a match in the cellars, with his forty years experience, for the newcomer to the art, Rollo Firtle.

The Court Leet used the now well-established front restaurant at the Old Bull on Mondays for their regular meetings. The kitchens were closed on Mondays so Rosie was happy to provide the room free of charge to bring in on average 15 people on a night traditionally the quietest in the licensed trade. On hearing the news that the Farmers' Market was to become a reality Andy Gross, the Bailiff, had called an emergency meeting and on that occasion had a one hundred per cent turnout. Unbeknownst to any of his officers the Bailiff had visited the occupants of the 20 or so cottages and houses who had no parking at their homes and who parked on the area in front of the Town Hall as of right. Or so they seemed to believe – there was no right, but as the land did not belong to either the Town Hall or any council, neither were there any parking regulations. A number of the residents were known as regular complainants in Ashthorpe Magna and the editor of the *Ashthorpe Gazette* was inundated by letters from them on a routine basis. A few years previously they had joined together and petitioned against the bells of St Osmund's Church, and had even written to the Bishop to complain about the rather lovely lights which the church put on its spire over the Christmas period. The response Andy had received from these people was sufficient to convince him that a so-called majority of residents would be against the Farmers' Market.

For a good 40 minutes the Bailiff railed against the market from every conceivable angle. Parking problems, damage to local traders, other than a few, the good people of Ashthorpe could not afford the prices of high-quality fresh produce, the trouble caused by traffic would be a danger and on and on. Nobody had the courage to interrupt the Bailiff but it should have been obvious by the expressions on many faces that there was a large level of disbelief, and probably a goodly proportion of the officers were actually in favour of the market. The brighter attendees were only too aware that Andy's tirade was nothing whatsoever to do with the objections he was raising, but all about his dislike of the Mayor the Town Clerk and the Town Council in general. Not that this was mentioned, and it was of no surprise when unanimous agreement was given to the proposition that the Court Leet should raise an objection to the Farmers' Market and their solicitor, Cliff Vintner, would be asked to write to the District Council stating their objection. Cliff Breakshaft, the Reeve, looked perplexed throughout, but the Bailiff should have wondered at the obvious display of pleasure on the face of the Marshall, Ray Spicer, throughout the meeting.

By eleven o'clock the next morning the majority of the residents of Ashthorpe Magna knew the contents of the Court Leet meeting, and even those with little interest in politics struggled to understand the reasons behind the Bailiff's outpouring. The article announcing the success achieved by the Farmers' Market Committee had gone into some detail as to the benefits to the town in bringing in more shoppers from the outlying areas, to promoting tourism and even to having produce available which had not been flown half way around the world. The normally well-hidden feelings towards the bombastic Bailiff rose to the surface and people were openly discussing his anachronistic role in the 21st Century.

The Chairman of the Farmers' Market Committee, Lauren le Noir, to the delight once more of Melvyn Hughes, called an extra meeting that Friday evening to work out their response to the astonishing news. She had on this occasion decided to invite the Mayor and the Rector of St Osmund's Church to come to the meeting.

The Mayor was so honoured because of his help in raising the necessary funding, and the Rector because of both his local influence and the proximity of the Church and the Rectory to the proposed market. St Osmund's Church was one of the few, spired churches in the area, and the earlier parts of the existing church had been built between 1490 and 1510, but no remains could be seen of the earlier church, St Mary's, which had been traced back to the 9th Century. It was reputed that the Bishop of Salisbury was a regular visitor during his occupation of the see between 1078 and 1099 when he died.

The Bishop had arrived in England with the Conquest in 1066 and was the son of Count Henry of Seez and Isabella, one of the many half sisters of William of Normandy. He enjoyed an illustrious career prior to taking on the Bishop's mantle; he worked on the *Doomsday Book*, created the Earl of Dorset, was Lord Chancellor between 1070 and 1078 after which he became the Bishop of Salisbury. After his death many miraculous happenings were attributed to him, and he was beatified in 1457 as St Osmund so it was no surprise that the new church in Ashthorpe Magna was named after him when it was consecrated a little over 30 years later.

So the battle lines were drawn up, and clearly the team assembled by Lauren le Noir was the outright favourite even boasting a saint, or rather, his representative, on her team.

George's Corner

"Old Ghostbuster is in again tonight, I call him that because every time he comes round to my house all the spirits disappear."

"I call him Titus Ulike, and you can see he is out of breath – he had to run to catch the last 30 seconds of Happy Hour."

Chapter 3

Mickey Carruthers was more than pleased to learn of the Farmers' Market. To give him his full, and noble name he was actually Right Honourable Michael Edward Botreaux Hervey-Carruthers, 14th Earl of Ludcolmbe, and like so many aristocratic families, their surnames revealed much of interest to those who study heraldry and genealogy. In this case it shows that Mickey held one of the earliest Earldoms in England, when the Barony that had been created by Edward III in 1372, and was upgraded by Charles I to the higher title of Earl in 1633. The oldest of the family titles was that of Botreaux, also granted by Edward III in 1368 for services to the crown.

As with most old families, the services provided included the raising of armies for whatever campaign on foreign soil the monarch of the time was embarking upon, including at that time Scotland. Edward III was the son of Edward II and Queen Isabella of France and having spent the previous decade invading Scotland, with varying degrees of success in support of the ill-fated Edward Balliol, in 1340 he declared himself King of France, heralding the start of the 100 Years War. This would require a constant and long-term supply of knights and foot soldiers, and was also to provide many noble families with titles, bounty and extra lands. The campaign was very popular in the country, and Edward battled through until his death in 1377. The Earls of Ludcolmbe increased their holdings from the small area around Ashthorpe Magna to a massive estimated 15,000 acres in Gloucestershire, Wiltshire and as far away as North Devon. To add further to their power, their children were married into the great families of the land, including the

Nevilles (Warwick), Percys (Northumberland) and Howards (Norfolk) thus increasing their influence both through the length and breadth of England, and especially important in those times, at the Royal Court.

Although their position in society had escalated, a series of bad political judgements, or, perhaps a heightened sense of duty and loyalty, caused much of that which had been gained to go into decline. During the Wars of the Roses they had supported their Plantaganet cousin, Richard III, to the day he died at the Battle of Bosworth Field (1485), later misreported by the Elizabethan spin-doctor, William Shakespeare, surely the Tudor equivalent of Max Clifford? Like so many of the great landowners, the Yorkist Ludcolmbe family retreated quietly to the country with their depleted army of farm workers and peasants.

During the reign of Henry VIII (1509–1547) they suffered more for their refusal to accept the Protestant faith and the fact that the monarch was the head of the Church. One member of the family was amongst the 81 Catholics who refused to recant, and were executed for the cause. Respite came in the form of Mary Tudor who brought back Catholicism as an acceptable practice during her reign until 1588 when their fortunes took another downturn during the rule of Elizabeth I, and later James I of England.

For the third time in 200 years they backed the wrong side!

The family were firmly Royalist during the Civil Wars and were forced, upon the execution of the King in 1649, to hand over their estates to a cousin for safe-keeping, and took exile with a few remaining assets in Normandy where they were in constant contact with the many expatriate Stuart supporters. During the time of the Commonwealth there were continual plots for the Restoration of the Monarchy and most of these emanated from the exiles, supported with considerable largesse by the French Catholic Aristocracy from whom most were descended, and who still upheld many rites and traditions of the Knights Templar (banned by the Vatican 200 years earlier) and the Freemasons (not banned by the Vatican until 150 years later). Within these groups were many of the Scottish Earls (Jarls) and Knights whose membership of the various Templar groups went back to the "Black Friday" of 1308 when a Templar fleet of 6 ships set sail from La Rochelle in France, and a week later landed in Musselburgh, the port 5 miles to the East of Edinburgh; a camaraderie evolved whereby the English and the Scots were of one mind.

By 1659 when the House of Stuart was restored to the monarchy of England and Scotland, the Ludcolmbe estates through all the events, especially the Dissolution of the Monasteries, were reduced from 15,000 acres to a little under half, and that only in Gloucestershire. Despite this loss, the family fared well during the quarter-century reign of Charles II, and indeed it was a second cousin, Father John Huddleston, who received the King into the Catholic Church on his deathbed. The family lived quietly thereafter on the Seagram Hall Estate at Ashthorpe Magna for the next three centuries, providing Judges, Cabinet Ministers, and officers of both the army and navy. The Catholic Church, for whom they had paid so dearly in both blood and money, fell away from the family.

Mickey's father, Henry the 13th Earl, was born in 1920 and inherited the title from his father at the age of 6, but his uncle, himself a competent estate manager, took on the running of the estate for the next 20 years living in the elegant Dower House to the right of the mile-long drive leading up to the Hall. Henry served with great distinction in the Royal Artillery during the Second World War, earning a Military Cross at El Alamein, and a Bar to the MC at Anzio in Italy, and returned in 1946 to take over the estate from his ageing uncle, although the latter busied himself around the farms until his death three years later. The return from the wars was, amazingly, his first time in England since his

٭

marriage to Isabella whilst on leave in late 1942, and was indeed the first time he had met his beloved son, Mickey, who was born after Henry's return to North Africa in 1943. Although having been brought up as a nominal member of the Church of England, but having no real interest in religion, Henry had, during the last two years of the war, prayed to a god, any god, every single day that his life be saved to allow him to see his son.

The main Hall was a shambles; it had been commandeered as a military hospital for officers during the war, and little or nothing had been done to maintain or repair the fabric since 1941. Isabella, daughter of a GP and a teacher, was impecunious but extremely active. Begging and borrowing materials from friends and family, by the time her husband returned she had restored the kitchens, the main sitting room and their own bedroom to a state which at least made them habitable. Henry's uncle had been a remarkable help, and despite his age had installed a second-hand central heating system to the liveable areas. It had also taken him a year to repair the damage to the drive with the help of a reparation grant from the War Office. In 1946 Henry returned, without fanfare, to the home he had so missed, his uncle who had played such a part in his life, the wife he little knew and to his son and heir, Mickey.

When Mickey was old enough to go to school his father sent him to the local Infant and Primary School, St Osmund's. The reason given by Henry to the Headmistress was that he had spent too much time away from his son, and had no intention of sending him to a boarding Prep School, the normal route into Public Schools. The locals, without malice, all suspected that Lord Henry had completely run out of money and could not afford the fees, especially after the fiasco that was the post war celebration at the Hall. None complained as, in fact, they were rather proud of their local gentleman and his military achievements, although the tradesmen did remember the lack of payment of their bills.

Mickey at the age of 13, passed the entrance examination to his father's old school in Devon and also a scholarship which paid the fees, and here it was family who believed that the school had taken pity on the Ludcolmbes and had used one of the many dowries the school received to cover these costs. Although Mickey was certainly not academic, he was charming and gregarious, good-looking and good at any sport to which he turned his hand. Even at the age of 10 he was brave on the hunting field and tackled fences others more experienced, and supposedly more skilled, turned down.

So it was, that, once at Public School, he was soon engaged in rowing, rugby, sailing and cricket with a far lesser emphasis on class lessons. One, possibly inherited, talent was for languages and the only subjects in which he was above average were Latin, French and German, and having scraped through the mandatory 5 subjects at "O" Level GCE, he managed to gain a pass in Latin, French and, miraculously, Mathematics at "A" Level. Not normally enough to get into Oxford, but the heir to a senior Earldom managed to get a place on a PPE (Politics, Philosophy and Economics) course at the excellent Peterhouse College. In true form he threw himself into student life with great gusto, embracing all the things not available at school, and in particular girls and real ale! Not for him the dubious attractions of Watney's Red Barrel!

Vacation periods were spent working on the estate and drinking at one of the two town-centre pubs in Ashthorpe Magna. He was well liked, especially for his excellent, and sometimes outrageous sense of humour. One incident, which was to go down in the annals of the town, was an occasion when Mickey was drinking at the Old Bull with a group of his friends and one of them found spare brewery signs that are normally used to clip on the front of the beer hand pumps. With great relish Mickey Carruthers tucked them into his pocket and subsequently took them home where he carefully removed the clips. The following night he, rather mysteriously, went into the Gentlemens' Toilets and looked at the five Victorian porcelain stalls. These were of the type, fashionable for many years, made by Ideal Standard which were designed to stop any splashing, and with side pieces to allow an element of privacy. He removed the brewery plaques from his pocket, minus their clips, and also a tube of super glue, and proceeded to attach one to the top of each stall. From left to right each urinal was labelled Hobsen's Bitter, Black Sheep, Guinness, Carlsberg Lager and Everard's Mild.

The English, being English, the clientele obeyed the new instruction, and people used the stall labelled with the particular drink they were tippling in the bar. To the great amusement of the small group "in the know" they observed at regular intervals queues forming behind the stalls labelled with the two most popular beers, Hobsen's and Black Sheep, whilst the other urinals remained unused. Rollo Firtle was furious when he found out, but nobody owned up to the dastardly deed, and whilst he may have been suspicious, due to the number of visits to the toilet by Mickey and his chums, he was unable to publicly make any accusations. He was even less pleased when he spent most of the following morning removing the signs.

The day arrived for the official opening of Ashthorpe Vineyard, and the great and good all arrived early. The owners, the MP and the two speakers, the 14th Earl and the Marshall, standing in for Andy Gross, were placed on a rostrum in front of the Visitor Centre. TV cameras from both the BBC and ITV channels rolled, and a throng of photographers from local, regional and national press as well as wine and spirit trade press were given a roped-off area in front of the platform. The position was planned so that any shots taken would include the Visitor Centre as a backdrop.

Ray Spicer had worked hard on his speech and made no mention of the absence of the Bailiff and Reeve, merely introducing himself as the representative of the Ancient Court Leet of Ashthorpe Magna. He thanked all those attending, most of whom had no idea as to who he was, and introduced the 14th Earl of Ludcolmbe in a manner many thought to be a little too familiar. Overall the speech was well crafted, but his flat voice and accent revealing his working origins, left the audience wishing he would stop earlier than his allocated ten minutes. End it did, right on time, and a quiet ripple of polite applause permeated the warm summer's air.

At the opposite end of speech-making skills, Mickey Carruthers enthralled, amused and flattered his audience. They even cheered when he opened a bottle of champagne-style Ashthorpe Celebration fizzy white wine and sprayed it, Formula 1 style, over some of the dignitaries. Considering he was known to have very severe doubts and reservations about the retired porn baron, he even offered the olive branch by inviting Nick and Mary Darling to Seagram Hall for dinner on some unspecified future occasion on the understanding that they brought the excellent local wines! He also pointed out that although he *was* proud and delighted to open a "new" vineyard; it was probably the site which would have been chosen by the Romans who were known to have grown vines some 2,000 years earlier. He received tumultuous applause when he declared Ashthorpe Vineyard and Winery Visitor Centre open. Although now in his sixties, Mickey Carruthers was still an attractive man, and it was quite clear that every female in the audience pushed forward to be photographed with him.

The visitors were loaded onto the miniature steam train, which transported them through the acres of vines, already heavily laden with grapes, and then back to the Centre to sample the wines and eat the voluminous amounts of food provided. It was late afternoon when the first of the invited audience departed, well fed and watered, but many stayed until the waitresses took away the wine and glasses. Both TV Channels featured the ceremony on their early-evening local news programmes, and the Darlings were later to find out that even national trade papers, such as the *Publican*, carried features of the opening. In all, an out-and-out success.

Many of the town visitors adjourned to the Old Bull in various states of intoxication, and by eight that evening the Ashthorpe Magna tom-toms had done their part in broadcasting the news of the events at Ashthorpe Court. Only the Bailiff reacted badly when, first ITV and then BBC on their early-evening regional news programmes, took the ceremony into his sitting room at the Manor, complete with his Marshall looking somewhat smug on the platform. The already black mood, brought on by the pain of gout, deepened, and despite knowing that alcohol and gout do not go well together, he resorted to his favourite Grouse Whisky.

Lord Ludcolmbe had invited Lauren le Noir back to Seagram Hall to help sample the bottles from the dozen provided by Nick Darling, or rather, Mary, and the Gallic beauty accepted with alacrity as she thoroughly enjoyed the company of the aristocrat. He was happy to talk in French, and she equally happy with English, so their long conversations were conducted in a mixture of both languages. She often wondered why he had never tried to make more of their relationship and assumed that this was normal behaviour from the English ruling classes.

Poor Melvyn Hughes, complete with recently cut hair and trimmed beard, had asked her after the ceremony to join him for dinner in the Old Bull, and displayed his sorrow, perhaps too obviously, when she told him that she would love to, but had already accepted the Earl's invitation. She even felt a momentary twinge of guilt when, complete with the peck on either cheek, she bade him farewell, and in an attempt to assuage his misery she suggested she would love to take up his offer the following week. Melvyn decided he was too miserable for the lively banter at the Old Bull, and sat on his own at the bar of the Firkin knowing full well that the visage of landlord, Jamie Rivers, would reflect his own downcast mood. Nor was there any risk of striking up a conversation. Having had more than his fair share of wine at the vineyard, it did not take many pints to well and truly drown his sorrows.

Cliff Breakshaft, the Reeve, completed his delivery run the following day in his large, somewhat battered, white van. As usual he had terrorised other drivers on the roads, who he swore were determined to slow his progress, thus lengthening his already long working days. Especially he hated the mothers driving their offspring to and from school in huge 4 wheel drive vehicles usually containing just mother and one child. Cliff was terrified of being caught on speed cameras which were popping up everywhere, and especially in neighbouring Warwickshire where he had already been caught twice, and was awarded six penalty points on his licence. Although he was barely able to undertake the public duties, which were the norm for previous Reeves to the Court Leet, he was helpful in many practical matters.

The Bailiff had asked for volunteers to paint the upper windows on the outside of the Town Hall, and as usual it was only Cliff and the diminutive Ale Taster, Barry Green, who had raised their hands. The latter, barely 5 feet in height, was a simple soul who would volunteer for almost everything that came along, but despite 20 years on the Court, had achieved the highest office he was likely to reach. The day after the opening of the vineyard, to which neither had been invited, the two agreed to meet at the Old Bull and later complete the painting of the final two windows on the Town Hall opposite.

Perhaps the fact that the rendezvous was in the front bar of the pub had something to do with the accident, or perhaps that Cliff's old wooden ladder had seen better days, but nobody ever knew. The outcome was that Barry dashed into the pub, shouted for an ambulance to be called and subsequently accompanied Cliff to the A & E Department at Cirencester Hospital. The X-ray revealed that Cliff had broken his leg in three places and was to be kept overnight until an orthopaedic surgeon could see him and set the complicated fractures. In the event he was kept in hospital for ten days and two operations, and was told that he would be unable to walk for at least a further week, and probably not able to work for a month or more after that. Cliff was self-employed so it was perhaps opportune that his bouncy, little round wife had recently accepted a full-time position in a shop in Lechlade.

The bus service to Ashthorpe Magna was virtually non-existent, and what little there was had become notoriously unreliable and expensive, however the townsfolk were generous in driving others to the larger outlying conurbations. Although Cliff's wife, Sharon, had to take some time off work, she had been able to juggle her hours and scrounge lifts both to see her husband in hospital, and keep some income coming in from the job. The lack of a good transport system proved difficult for those too old or too poor to own a car, but the social implications on the youth were even greater. In the past there had been a bus going through the town which left Cirencester at about 11.00 pm, but this had been cancelled about a year before, it was claimed due to disorderly behaviour and threats to bus drivers. Many of Ashthorpe's teenagers had used the late service to enable them to have a night out doing whatever it is that youth do! Since the withdrawal of the service, groups of disgruntled youngsters would stand around the town, creating litter, and worse, intimidating old folk by the use of disgusting language, spitting and even urinating in public.

The more timid old folk no longer felt able to go out after dark, something that would have seemed impossible only a few years before.

The Council tried to tackle the problem by the provision of a small Youth Club, but constant vandalism had added to the costs dramatically, causing it to be closed after only a few months. One or two of the young adults did indeed have cars, usually old Fiestas or Metros, which they painted up, added flashing lights and large, noisy exhaust pipes. In the year following the withdrawal of public transport services, two of the "boy racers" had fatal accidents, one under the influence of alcohol, and the other drugs. The calming measures taken by the County Council, provision of speed humps and narrowing of some straight roads in places, seemed to have an opposite effect and appeared to have provided chicanes for the roaring little vehicles with youthful drivers showing off their limited skills.

Andy Gross, on hearing the news of the Reeve's incapacity, rather reluctantly summoned the Marshall.

Having been let into the Manor House by the red-haired Sonia, the Major's cleaning lady, Ray Spicer was shown into the small sitting room which doubled as Andy's study. It was difficult for him not to burst into laughter at the sight of the huge bulk, clothed in a silk, padded robe, seated upon a leather armchair, his gouty foot placed, still without a slipper, on a Victorian gout stool the Bailiff's wife had purchased for him years ago when they were still speaking. Ray could not resist the thought that it was a sight more akin to a Conan Doyle play than Ashthorpe in the early 21st Century.

"Ray, you will have to take over my duties for the next month."

Ray had been quite delighted when he realised that, with both the Bailiff and the Reeve out of action, he would effectively control the Court Leet for at least a month. He, still at that stage secretly, actually supported the Farmers' Market, but he nodded in agreement when Andy Gross issued his instructions:

"Firstly, Ray, I want you to search the County Records Office to see if there is any ancient Act we can invoke stating that a market cannot be held, and then I want you to instigate a "whispering campaign" suggesting that the Farmers' Market is merely a way to increase the precept paid by the Town Council."

The crafty Marshall had done his homework well, and already had the information. This he did not share with the Bailiff, but records had revealed that not only was there nothing stopping a market, but one had existed for many centuries on the very spot, and it was suggested that it even was extant in Saxon times. As far as a whispering campaign, Ray totally understood its efficacy, but had no intentions of using it against the Farmers' Market.

Ashthorpe Magna boasted many talented and artistic people amongst its population – writers, musicians, sculptors, and artists of many styles. There were two art galleries, one combined with a high quality gift shop, and the other in a recently opened coffee shop, and the town was host to two painting clubs, which were always well attended. Two of the artists were well known outside the area, indeed one of them, Petr Theodorov, had already exhibited in the US with two more exhibitions planned there for the following year. Petr was a gentle giant of a man with a huge shock of greying hair and it amazed all who knew him that such large hands could produce such delicate work. He had, over the years, specialised in different subjects as diverse as portraiture and landscape, but much of his success was based on his hobby of fine wines and the walls of the café/gallery had a wide variety of still life prints which were virtually a world tour of great wines; Chateau Latour, Chateau Lafitte, Chateau Margaux and even New World ones from the Napa Valley in California and Hunter Valley in New South Wales. As all were painted with a half-full bottle, and a nearly empty glass, one can imagine the pleasure Petr gained from his subjects, more even, he claimed, from the pleasures Toulouse Lautrec gained from his ladies-of-the night or Leonardo from the Mona Lisa.

As the originals of these works were selling for several thousands of pounds, he was only able to offer artists' proofs through the Ashthorpe Gallery, but sell they did. Unlike those of his long-term friendly rival, Johnnie Castle. The problem was that Johnnie had been working for many years in Ashthorpe Magna and virtually everybody already had at least one of his original works. There was no doubt of his talent, but his anarchistic temperament and refusal to join any organisation often brought Mr Castle into conflict with many authorities. He once, when being told off by the feisty coffee shop owner, Carole Rhodes, for stealing brown sugar lumps from the table, which had, she pointed out cost her one penny each, told the story of a female relative of his wife's which caused the two to cease talking 20 years previously. Johnnie and his wife were visiting the lady concerned and accepted a coffee.

"How many lumps of sugar, Johnnie?" the lady enquired.

"Six please," came back the reply.

"Shall I just pour the coffee into the sugar bowl?" came the terse response.

"If you wish," snapped back Johnnie.

The lady then proceeded to fill the elegant silver bowl with coffee and slammed it on the table in front of the irate artist. He drank it almost immediately.

"That was lovely, any chance of another?" All future communications between the two ceased.

Johnnie and Petr met at least twice a week in Carole's coffee emporium, and the banter generally lasted for more than an hour, often with locals and visitors alike either joining in, or at the worst sitting quietly enjoying the entertainment. The owner would occasionally intervene, especially when she felt they were using up her lighting and heating without drinking enough coffee! As she was doing rather well selling art they allowed her to indulge in this little bit of tight-fistedness! Carole did, however, get rid of the brown sugar lumps to save costs.

Ray called an emergency Court Leet meeting at the Old Bull, the first under his jurisdiction, and he asked that no minutes be taken. His first question was that of finding out what the Officers really thought of the Farmers' Market. To his amazement, whilst one or two admitted they thought it was a good idea, the majority displayed an abject apathy. It was only Colonel Blimp who expressed the view, probably already thought by most, that the whole row was nothing to do with the market, and all about the relationship between the Mayor and the Bailiff. They all agreed that, despite Andy's instructions, they would have nothing to do with any form of protest, or of influencing any resident to react against the market.

As always, the Mayor learned very quickly that the level of opposition from the Court Leet had fallen well below the levels he had been led to believe, and both he and the Town Clerk believed that they could gain overwhelming support from the population. Melvyn, from the Chamber of Trade, had sounded out all the trades-folk, and even the local butcher, Glynn, and the excellent vegetable shop owner, the rather camp, but definitely heterosexual, Claude Evadne, while not being overly enthusiastic, definitely raised no objections. In fact the only objector, for some inexplicable reason, was Tony, the owner of a rather down-market card and balloon shop. Farmers do not sell cards and balloons so the Chamber of Trade thought that he would be much in favour of an event it was hoped would bring more visitors into Ashthorpe Magna. Tony had lost much local trade due to his constant swearing to customers, and generally coarse and suggestive behaviour, so perhaps his objection came as no surprise; in any case it did not worry either Melvyn, or the Farmers' Market Chairman, Lauren le Noir.

John Sleight, the Mayor, on the advice of Keith Stammers, the Clerk, telephoned Lauren and asked if it would be possible to call a meeting asking all interested parties to a public meeting to be held in the Council Chambers, this being less contentious than the Town Hall. She agreed to do this as soon as possible to ensure that neither the Bailiff nor the Reeve would be able to attend, and a letter signed by Lauren was sent to every household as an insert with the next copy of the *Ashthorpe Gazette*.

Most of the residents, the complainers, of Upper Church Street, were middle-aged, retired and middle class. This did not apply to the occupant of the charming little cottage, number 22, opposite the Old Bull and the Town Hall, who was a man in his thirties with three small children and definitely not retired. Nobody quite knew what he did, but he regularly used up three parking spaces on the planned area, one for his English sports car, one for the family car, a large French estate car and one for a large, rather smart white van he used for work. Perhaps it was laziness but he, more than many of the older residents, was the most vociferous in his objection, and whenever the subject was mentioned Dave Lounds said that he would refuse to move his vehicles unless instructed by the police. As had been ascertained, the land was not Council owned, nor was owned by the Town Hall, so the police were unable to issue a Road Closure Notice and said making the space for up to 20 stalls would be totally at the discretion and goodwill of the residents.

The night arrived for the meeting, and the top table was arranged for the Farmers' Market Chairman, the Mayor, the Clerk, Melvyn Hughes and, amazingly for the Marshall, Ray Spicer who, whilst he did not contribute to the meeting, demonstrated a gesture of support by his very presence. Despite the efforts of the top table, the meeting was best described as dull. The ladies of Upper Church Street, who by now had been nicknamed "the Witches of Church Street" had not turned up for the meeting leaving the aforementioned Dave Lounds as the only one speaking out against the market. It became quite clear, during his diatribe that his motivation was purely selfish, and displayed little or no interest in the well-being of the town. At one point, Colonel Blimp, one of only a dozen or so residents who had turned up, was heard to mutter in a loud stage whisper;

"Silly young ass," (pronounced arse) "why doesn't he sit down?"

A vote was taken, recorded by Keith Stammers, as 15 in favour, 1 against (Dave Lounds) and 1 abstention (Ray Spicer). Lauren asked the Clerk to write to the press informing them that a public meeting had taken place, and an overwhelming majority were in favour of the Farmers' Market.

With such small numbers of attendees, the meeting finished much earlier than anticipated, and Lauren reminded Melvyn about dinner at the Old Bull, which he instantly agreed was a great idea. Twenty minutes later they were in a very quiet corner of the dining room, and Melvyn asked for a bottle of *Muscadet sur Lie* from *Sevres et Maine* to be delivered while they studied the menu. It was pure chance, but the choice excited Lauren who explained that, when she was in her teens, her whole family moved out of the elegant 5 bed-roomed apartment they rented in the 16th *Arrondisement* in Paris, to the farmhouse on the borders of Normandy and Brittany which had been in her family for five generations. On the basis of his choice of wine, Lauren asked Melvyn to choose from the menu, and having read somewhere that seafood was the way to a lady's heart, although in this case it was perhaps not the heart about which he was thinking, proceeded to order *moules marinière* to start, and langoustine with home made garlic mayonnaise as a main course.

Lauren was enthralled with his choice, as was Melvyn. There is something inherently sensuous about a beautiful woman picking up a shellfish, putting it into her mouth, and wiping the corners of her lips with a starched white napkin to remove the inevitable drizzle of sauce from the corners. Also the time taken to eat in this manner is considerably longer than more normal restaurant dishes such as prawn cocktails, steaks or chops, and this allows more wine to be imbibed, especially when so good, and soon a second bottle was being ordered. It was Lauren who suggested that, as her coffee was probably better than that at the Old Bull, they should go to her house for coffee and Armagnac. Melvyn paid the bill, which was most reasonable for such excellent quality, and he readily agreed to drive.

On arrival she gave him the key to unlock the door, and he allowed her to enter first to turn on the main lights and turn off the burglar alarm. When they were both safely inside Lauren gave what was still a double kiss on the cheeks, but this time in a non-Gallic style. The norm for our French cousins is to stand some distance apart and bend forward to make the lip to cheek contact, without any bodily contact. On this occasion Lauren moved closely into Melvyn to allow the maximum pressure on the body. He was somewhat disappointed when she suggested they move to the kitchen for coffee and the digestif, but they both consumed these with an almost indecent haste.

Anybody out and about in Ashthorpe Magna at 6.30 am would have seen a rather dishevelled Madame le Noir, being escorted from his car to her own by the Chairman of Chamber and Trade.

Unbeknownst to either of them Dave Lounds was loading up his white van and spotted them from the corner of his eye.

George's Corner

"Poor old Maurice, his back goes out these days more than he does."

"Did you know, George keeps an empty milk bottle in his fridge in case anybody wants black coffee. Going a bit potty, but I've been worried since he told me Doris Day was a public holiday."

Libby was well educated, but disguised the fact well by her language and dress. She came over to George's Corner and said,

"I've just been to the Firkin. Jamie Rivers was his usual rude self, so I asked him why I should stand there and be insulted. He peered over the top of his glasses and replied 'If you prefer you can go home, and I can ring you there!' Bloody cheek!"

Chapter 4

Miss Baines did not appear to be that old, but she had lived for ten tears or so in a rather charming sheltered housing scheme, which had been developed from Victorian weavers' cottages on Weavers Lane, opposite the Council Offices. She was in fact 72 years old, but was always sprightly and immaculately turned out. The development, sponsored by County and District Councils and the Gloucestershire Housing Association, contained 15 single bed-room cottages and 9 two bed-roomed. The development had a small community hall, housed in what had originally been a Quaker Meeting Room, and most valuably to the residents, a laundry centre with excellent washing and drying machines. Miss Baines occupied one of the one bed-roomed residences, and would often tell anybody prepared to listen how happy she was there. She had obviously led a lonely existence, without any family as far as anybody knew, and the Weavers Lane set-up provided her with constant companionship along with the security of a 24-hour panic button in the event of any unforeseen emergency.

For the first couple of years, Miss Baines rarely left the development and seemed nervous to meet new people, but this, due to the friendliness of the Ashthorpe residents, had gradually changed. Her needs were very simple and she gradually adjusted her meagre income to a newfound lifestyle. Once a month she would treat herself to Sunday luncheon at the Old Bull where, quietly, the good-hearted Rosie would only charge her £5 for the standard two-course "roast of the day" and pudding menu, rather than the normal £7.95, and a glass of house wine was always placed in front of her for which no charge was ever made. Other than that she would meet friends from Weavers Lane on Tuesday and Friday mornings for two glasses of sherry at the Firkin, and on Thursdays and Saturdays would go into Carole's coffee shop making a glass of hot chocolate last for nearly an hour, giving her the opportunity to read the papers available for customers. By the standards to which Miss Baines had been previously accustomed, her life had become a social whirl.

Despite the appearance of sprightliness and smartness, the ravages of age had not totally passed Miss Baines by. One particular Thursday she went, as per normal, to Carole's shop, ordered her hot chocolate, a bar of Kit Kat, and started reading the *Daily Mail*. The other tables were occupied, and she glanced up to see a smartly dressed man, in his late forties or early fifties, standing next to her.

"Do you mind if I sit at your table, there's no other space?" said the stranger.

"Please sit down," was her response as she buried her head into the *Mail*.

The stranger, probably a Company Representative biding time prior to an appointment, received his Americano Coffee concurrently with Miss Baines' hot chocolate with miniature marshmallows floating on top. Using her long-handled spoon, she proceeded to devour the marshmallows, opened the Kit Kat removing one of the two sticks of chocolate biscuit, and with relish ate that. To her utmost amazement the stranger took the other stick, broke it in half and put the piece into his mouth. She hastily grabbed the other half, and finished the chocolate treat. The stranger stood up, moved to another table, which had become vacant, and asked Carole for a blueberry muffin into which he bit. Miss Baines, totally perplexed by this time, finished her drink, paid up and flounced out with all the dignity she could muster. For, probably, the first time in her life, she then acted totally out of character.

The stranger was seated at the table by the door, and some impulse made Miss Baines pick up the partly devoured muffin, take a healthy bite, slammed it back on the table and left the shop saying,

"There!"

To his eternal credit, the stranger, after a couple of minutes of bemused silence, burst out laughing. Carole, who had, in her normal manner, observed everything that had happened, sat down by the stranger. Atypically, for the shop owner, she apologised for Miss Baines, and told him his coffee and snacks were "on the house".

"Absolutely not necessary. I can dine out on this story for weeks! In fact can I leave an extra £1 towards her next snack?"

Miss Baines completed the five-minute walk to her cottage and sat down for a rest. She opened her handbag to take out the hairpins she had bought earlier, and there it was. An unopened bar of Kit Kat.

The earliest of the executive estates, built on the Cirencester Road about 1 mile from the town centre, was a development of 20 four and five bed-roomed houses, with large gardens and in a style generally known as "Dorking Tudor". Whilst the original development was now nearly 30 years old, they still looked like a modern development, although with the many trees and shrubs planted at the time, Roman Way certainly gave the impression of being well established. Each time a new planning application was granted, the District Council warned against over-development and stated that this was the last! But, after a 20-year period, the original planning consent for 20 residences had risen to a massive 200 houses each with smaller gardens and higher price tags.

There were certainly no objections from the traders in town, who could envisage a new, wealthier clientele, nor from the Town Council who gleefully thought of the increases in their precepts. Over the past ten years two other similar developments had taken place, one on the Burford Road, and the most expensive of all being some 50 houses backing onto the River Dart off the Lechlade Road with current values of in excess of half a million pounds.

The population had risen during this period by nearly 2,000 people, but it was not without major problems, nor did it bring any great benefit to the town as had been so eagerly anticipated. St Osmund's School, which had boasted one of the smallest class sizes in the County, was now decidedly overcrowded for a rural school. In fact, the school hall had become so inadequate for the total number of pupils, that the age old tradition of the whole school meeting at nine o'clock each morning for the Morning Assembly had to be abandoned in favour of the younger children having an assembly on Tuesday and Thursday, with the older ones having theirs on Wednesday and Friday. One could be forgiven for thinking that it did not really matter, but all the teachers and some parents observed a certain change of attitude from many pupils.

The typical "incomers" were husband, wife and two or three children, with at least two cars, until older children became of an age where they too could drive, and more cars were added. Whilst some houses were unoccupied for much of the time, as they belonged to Londoners who used them as weekend and holiday homes, in most cases the husbands commuted, some to London, but most to Gloucester, Bristol or Oxford. The majority did not arrive home until after seven in the evening, and they were rarely seen out and about in Ashthorpe Magna. Shopping was done at weekends, generally in Cirencester, or even further away, and the local shops were used only for emergency top-ups to the weekly basket. Very few of the incomers involved themselves with any local community activities, although the Ashthorpe Masonic Craft Lodge did see a gradual increase in members, and to the obvious pleasure of the Rector of St Osmund's his depleted attendances started to move upwards.

The only real financial beneficiary was the owner of Verdi's Ristorante which, with its excellent, but expensive food, and idyllic setting overlooking the river, appealed to the incomers, especially as it was within walking distance for many. The main loser was probably the ageing, and overweight policeman, PC Corner, whose workload increased dramatically, with a large number of break-ins on the new estates that had become a prime target for villains from major conurbations in the South Midlands. Mike Corner had the last remaining Police House in his Force, but the Chief Constable had decided to leave him there, with the "Police Station" in the front room, as Mike had only a year to complete before his retirement after 35 years. He had always been regarded as a good Community Policeman, his bulky figure seen every day ponderously cycling around Ashthorpe on a "sit up and beg" 1960's Raleigh bicycle which he had owned from new, always wearing his helmet. Not for Mike the comforts of a patrol car and flat cap! Whilst he was able to control the unruly, and bored youth of the area, (he had generally known their parents since their youth), Mike was definitely no match for the professional gangs of housebreakers visiting the estates.

The big problem, sociologically, was that while two distinct groups had previously existed in the town, the residents of the old council estate, and lower-priced private developments in the New Town area, and the established residents of the Old Town, now a third group of the 2,000 or so occupants of the executive estates were a new, and different group. Worst of all was the fact that few, if any, young people could afford to live in the town in which they had been brought up.

The Bailiff, Major Andrew Gross, having recovered enough from his gout to be able to walk again with the aid of a walking stick, and one foot shod in a bedroom slipper, could feel instinctively that something was wrong for the Court Leet. He called a meeting, this time at his home for security reasons, of what he considered to be the inner circle, or elite of the Court. The Marshall, the Constable, the Town Crier, the Ale Tasters and the Searcher and Sealer of Leather all went round to the Manor House, and were greeted in an unusually friendly manner by Andy, who even provided them with a tasty glass of Bordeaux wine.

"None of that over-priced local rubbish," he murmured.

Since the opening of the vineyard, which he had been unable to attend, the Bailiff had refused to support the enterprise.

"With the Town Council and their allies supporting this Farmers' Bloody Market, the Court must be seen to do something of real importance, and quickly!"

Debate raged, and ideas flew around. Andy, generously refilled the glasses, and they talked for two hours. It was the Marshall, Ray Spicer, who eventually came up with a suggestion to which all agreed.

"We are all aware of the problems we see every night with groups of 16–20 year-old yobs intimidating passers by. Something must be done to try and stop this, and our PC Plod certainly can't. Equally we all know that the main cause is boredom. Could we not put on a monthly Rock music night at the Town Hall, to at least demonstrate that we acknowledge the problem, and are trying to do something about it?" he suggested.

"The press would love us for that; they're always complaining about our youth problems," responded the Bailiff.

They agreed on the first Friday of each month; Saturdays were impossible as the Town Hall was regularly booked for wedding receptions. Although this gave them a little over two weeks before the first event, they all felt this was a possibility, and the various tasks were allocated. They felt it would be unwise to serve alcohol, and they could be severely criticised if they did this, but the bar would be opened for the sale of soft drinks.

"Better stock up on Colas" came the sensible suggestion of the senior Ale Taster, who was also responsible for the bar when it was required for functions.

The Town Crier, himself a published author, agreed to do a press release to hit the papers both ten days and three days before, and the second Ale Taster, who had himself been something of a musician in his youth, agreed to book a live group and a small disco to play when the band were on a break. He felt that he could do this without attracting charges as not only did his son have a disco set-up, which he and his wife hated, but also he was very friendly with John "Notorious" who had a well-liked local Rock Group. The Bailiff was to book the hall, and, as he was the person responsible for collecting fees for the Town Hall, there would be no charge on this first occasion. They agreed, that with effectively no costs, and an income from the sale of soft drinks, they would only charge £1 for entry, which, it was felt, would attract a maximum number of entrants. The most they could have was 150, which was the figure set by the Health and Safety inspection some years before, but even with that number they should certainly raise at least £300 which could then be used for future events.

The Town Crier, Angus McDuff, a tall, slim Scotsman, who had maintained his accent despite living in Ashthorpe for a quarter of a century, was true to his word and spoke at length to the young *Gazette* reporter allocated to the town, and she made copious notes. The senior Ale Taster phoned the suppliers and ordered extra supplies of the more popular soft drinks, and his deputy phoned, and arranged to meet, John "Notorious" in the Old Bull that evening. The Marshall visited the local printer and talked him into producing 500 fliers for nothing, and the Bailiff sat at home with his sore foot propped up on his gout stool. He was feeling pleased with himself, and confident that the Rock evening would restore some of the prestige of the Court, which the Mayor had sought to undermine.

John "Notorious", (nobody actually knew his real name), was a strange character of around 55 years of age. Little and round, he usually dressed in a style best described as shabby, but when he met with the Ale Taster he actually looked quite smart. It appeared that he supplemented his income with private tuition on the guitar, and he had come straight from such a job. He ordered his customary pint of lager, and rolled a cigarette paper around tobacco, or at least that is what he claimed it to be! He had worked in the music industry for many years, and had apparently played in a number of well-known groups in the Sixties. His group normally played at two or three "gigs" a week, but he confirmed that the Friday in question was free, and he was willing, subject to the approval of his colleagues, to forego any fees on this one occasion.

The headlines of the *Ashthorpe Gazette* that week read:

BAILIFF OF ASHTHORPE MAGNA WOOS THE YOUTH MARKET

The article, as anticipated, praised the Bailiff and his Court for taking positive action on the difficult youth problem of small country towns. The feature concluded with the journalist wishing the event every success, and with the hope that many other towns would follow the example set by Bailiff Major Gross.

Tickets were printed and distributed to three shops that had agreed to sell them, and Court Leet Officers distributed the newly printed leaflets around the New Town estates in one evening. All was in place.

At the weekend, just six days before the event, Ray Spicer visited the shops concerned and was both surprised, and delighted, to find that within two days all 150 tickets had been sold. Success was virtually guaranteed.

The Reeve, still in heavy plaster, had, perhaps unwisely, agreed to sit at the entrance door collecting tickets telling the visitors that if they wished to go out at any time he would issue a pass-out. The doors had opened at 7.30 pm and by eight o'clock the upper floor was packed to overflowing. Cliff Breakshaft had not noticed that many of the youngsters were either carrying large, heavy-looking handbags, or had rather suspicious lumps under their jackets. The bar downstairs was doing a roaring trade with soft drinks, predominately tonic waters and Colas, and the noise level emanating from the disco – it could not be described as music – was so loud that residents, hundreds of yards away, came to their front doors to see what was happening.

The noise did not abate when John "Notorious" and his group came on. If anything the level of decibels increased. To the three Court Leet members, who had agreed to help on the evening, the upper hall in which the music and "dancing" took place had become a "no go" area, partly because of the crowd and partly because of the cacophonous sounds erupting from the makeshift stage. This was probably the reason that nobody had spotted the fact that, under most of the chairs around the hall were bottles of Vodka, Gin and White Rum.

As the evening wore on the behaviour deteriorated, and it was absolutely clear that somehow well over 150 youngsters were gathered either in, or around the Town Hall. Scuffles were breaking out, already two young men could be seen throwing up next to the church wall and several young couples were writhing in drunken ecstasy on the trimly mown grass in front of the church. In the hall the dancing had lost any pretence of form, and had the appearance of a bacchanalian orgy with the breasts of many young girls exposed and fondled by spotty youths, hands on, and in, minute thongs barely hidden by pieces of material purporting to be skirts, youngsters of both sexes falling over, and even inside the hall a girl being sick in the corner. At one end a fight had broken out between two lads who appeared intent upon beating each other senseless with broken chairs.

Several local residents had telephoned PC Corner who quickly arrived outside the Town Hall, assessed the situation, and used his radio to summon back-up from Cirencester, and to be safe he also requested an ambulance. Although it was a little after 10.30 pm by this time, the back-up arrived in less that ten minutes in the form of two patrol cars, and shortly afterwards a police van and an ambulance.

Mike Corner led the way up to the main hall, switched on all the lights and bellowed,

"Stop Immediately!"

The sight was something the police had never seen; the stench was unimaginable and the hall looked as though it had been the subject of a terrorist attack. Drunken youngsters were shepherded to one end by three policemen who were barraged with both verbal, and physical abuse, and even, by now empty, spirit bottles were thrown at them, in one case cutting the face of one of the force members. Four immediate arrests were made, and one by one the revellers, sobering up rather quickly, were led to the lower hall to give statements to the sergeant who had arrived to take charge and had set up his desk in a position where none could sneak past.

Each of the young persons was obliged to give their name and address, with PC Corner on hand to identify as many as possible, and each was searched to see if they were carrying illegal substances. The area outside was now thronged with interested residents, and many youths had the presence of mind to beat a hasty retreat, but a group of policemen were trying to control those remaining by herding them into a corner.

The injured policeman was being patched up by the paramedics, now supported by a second ambulance, and several of the party-goers were already in the first ambulance which soon sped off, fully loaded, heading for the A & E Unit. It was nearly four in the morning when the constabulary felt they had all the information they required, and a total of nine arrests had been made with charges varying from possession of illegal substances, attacking policemen, and disorderly behaviour to the accusation of urinating in public. A further eight people had been taken to hospital where several policemen and women had been sent to ensure there was no further trouble. A later consequence was that of two under-age pregnancies resulting from the night.

The Bailiff who had been summoned, as the licence holder, had managed to hobble up the road with the assistance of his walking stick. The old soldier had assessed the situation at a glance, and immediately started calling the Court Officers on his mobile to seek their assistance in cleaning up the hall and surrounding area before daylight, in a form of damage limitation. He need not have bothered. Two ambulances and three police vehicles, all with flashing lights and bells, had woken virtually the whole population of the Old Town, and by the time they left, in the region of 200 spectators had seen the full extent of the results of the night's activities.

The Bailiff, only too aware of the potential press coverage, called an emergency meeting of the Court, which he scheduled for Sunday morning. Although it was again held at the Manor, on this occasion there was no wine!

"Once the press get onto this, which is bound to happen with all the crowds, we will be pilloried. What the bloody hell went wrong?" asked Major Gross.

The Marshall, with a gentle snipe at the Bailiff said:

"If only you did not have gout, and had been present, you would certainly have seen the problem and stopped it happening. It was not a good idea leaving the Reeve in charge due to his leg problems." What he really meant was that Cliff Breakshaft was not up to the task.

"If you had been there, Marshall, the same would be true," stated the Bailiff, to which the Marshall replied:

"Unfortunately I was at a hotel in West Sussex for my niece's wedding yesterday."

So the argument continued, each Officer blaming others, and none accepting any responsibility. Nor could they agree what to do about the press, some feeling it was best to let "sleeping dogs lie" and others believing that they should pre-empt any article by issuing a statement in advance.

During the meeting the telephone rang which Andy answered.

"Good morning, BBC Radio Gloucester here, am I speaking to Major Gross the Bailiff of Ashthorpe Magna?"

"You are indeed."

"Major Gross, we are on air. Have you any comment to make about the riots we heard about last night in Ashthorpe Magna?"

"I would hardly describe the incident as a riot!"

"How would you describe it then?"

"We are currently having an emergency Court Leet meeting, and if you will leave me your name and number you will be called back."

"So the incident is significant enough that you have a meeting on Sunday morning?"

"No comment. I will call you back."

This made the decision for the Bailiff – no press release and no talking to the media.

Minutes later the same caller was speaking to John Sleight, the Mayor.

"Mr Mayor, we are on air. Have you any comment to make about the riots we heard about in Ashthorpe last night?"

"It was an absolute disgrace. I understand that, although the Town Hall is only licensed for 150 people, there were around double that number present. I also understand that there was no responsible person supervising in the upper floor where the music and dancing were taking place. The Court Leet must be held responsible for the events, responsible for the drinking, responsible for the drugs and responsible for the riotous behaviour."

"What caused the incident?"

"Total lack of understanding, by the Court Leet, of young people. They were well out of their depth in organising an event like this."

"Wasn't the Bailiff praised for trying to do something for youngsters of the town?"

"He may have been, but I perceive it to be a callous way of making money from those least able to afford it. As I understand it they made nearly £500."

The next 24 hours saw a flood of reporters, with their photographers many of whom had never before heard of Ashthorpe Magna, interviewing as many people as they could find, including those Court Leet Officers willing to ignore the Bailiff's instructions.

Monday saw the arrival of TV Crews from the BBC, ITV and Channel 4 News, and this time, unlike the opening of Ashthorpe Vineyard, the town was on the main news broadcasts, rather than regional news, spurred on by many newspaper articles in Monday morning's editions.

The Sun summed it all up in its headline:

SEX, DRUGS AND ROCK'N'ROLL IN QUIET COTSWOLD VILLAGE.

Even *The Times*, on an inside page, carried the news which it developed into a more learned discussion on youth problems generally.

The weasel-faced Mayor, and his equally unattractive Clerk, were interviewed constantly and certainly achieved their 15 minutes of fame. The only sign of the Bailiff was behind the windows of the Manor House, looking out as cameras rolled and flashed, and reporters protested that the man responsible would not come out of his "fortress". Never before had Ashthorpe Magna received so much publicity, albeit of the wrong type.

With one exception, those who had been arrested were found guilty and fined by the Magistrates' Court, and PC Corner had a list of some thirty parents to whom he would pay a visit and "Read the Riot Act", and for the first time in his long career, this oft-misused expression was very near to the truth.

After a few days it all quietened down, and Ashthorpe returned to normal. The only difference was that the perception of the Court Leet had deteriorated, and the Bailiff had become the butt of many jokes.

Miss Baines was amazed, and somewhat embarrassed, when Carole informed her that last week's stranger had left some money to buy a chocolate biscuit for her, explaining that, far from being annoyed, the stranger was highly amused with the whole situation. He had told Carole at the time that her feisty behaviour, especially the final departing bite from his muffin, reminded him of his mother, who would have been about the same age as Miss Baines, and who had died only two years before. On learning this, Miss Baines accepted the offer and ordered her Hot Chocolate.

To her surprise, the stranger walked in, and said:

"May I join you?"

"Please do," came the swift response from Miss Baines.

"My name is John Brookes."

"Miss Baines."

John gave her his card showing that he was indeed the Area Manager for a well-known office supply and stationery company based in Bristol. They talked, seemingly for an age, ordered second drinks, and talked some more. John Brookes spoke about his children, who he only saw on alternate weekends since his divorce a year before, and he often spoke of his mother of whom he had clearly been very fond. Miss Baines, too, opened up and spoke of her own background for the first time in decades. She told him about her engagement, in 1954, at the age of 20, to a young man who had accepted an RAF Short-Service Commission for 3 years rather than do National Service.

They spent his last 7-day leave before the planned wedding together, and used the time to book the church and the reception at her hometown of Epsom in Surrey. For the remaining five days they headed to North Devon in her fiancé's battered old, open-topped, MG TC. The spring days were unusually warm, and she was overwhelmed with the love she felt. For the first night they stayed in a B & B at Ashthorpe Magna walking by the river, hand-in-hand, and loved the area so much that they vowed one day to return and live there together as man and wife. They booked the last night of his leave at the same accommodation, and set off to tour North Devon for a few days.

This was in an age when it was not normal for couples to sleep together before marriage, even when engaged. However, the depth of both their feelings for each other was so strong that, on their last night together in Ashthorpe Magna, Sheila, for that was her name, crept into her fiancé's room and they made rather fumbling, but none the less significant, love together. As the future would show, this was the only time in Sheila's life that she was to sleep with a man.

She was totally devastated when the Air Ministry called her parents' home. Her fiancé, had completed his primary training in a Chipmunk, his advanced in a Balliol, basic jet training on what today is known as a flight simulator, but was then called a Link Trainer, and finally, was flying solo in a twin-seated Meteor training aircraft. He had been on a night flying training exercise over the North Sea, and the control tower had suddenly lost contact with the young pilot. The jet had plunged into the sea and obviously the pilot, for whatever reason, had been unable to bale out. The aircraft was located in shallow water, and the subsequent Court of Enquiry showed that the port side Rolls Royce engine had been subject to "flare-out". Clearly the pilot had been trying to head for the base, but had been forced to ditch, with tragic results.

John Brookes, at first discomforted at being the recipient of such a moving story, gradually came to realise that, for some inexplicable reason, he was acting as a cathartic presence, enabling Sheila to engage in an outpouring of feelings in which she had never previously indulged. Unbeknownst to himself, Sheila had become pregnant after the one night of indulgence at Ashthorpe Magna, but the subsequent tragedy, with the loss of her fiancé's life, caused the loss of the unborn child. The doctors had told her that the foetus was that of a male. The year was 1954, the year in which John Brookes had said he was born.

Many people talk of their lives being ruined, but in the case of Miss Baines it was undoubtedly true. At the time of the disaster she was working for a large accountancy practice in the City, already studying for her first set of examinations, but she gave all this up. She had spent a few years in the Tax Office, never rising above Tax Officer Higher Grade, but due to her remoteness by then, and her inability to get close to any of her colleagues, she left and spent the rest of her working life in more menial jobs such as check-out girl in supermarkets, and shop assistant in a variety of establishments. At least the years at the Tax Office were pensionable, at this provided a few pounds each week to allow her little luxuries such as Sky Television and her monthly luncheon at the Old Bull.

On those rare nights when she was able to sleep properly, and dreamt of pleasant things, the place was always a B & B in Ashthorpe Magna, and her subconscious mind reminded her of the last night with her fiancé along with the creation of their boy child. A year before her due retirement age of 62, she visited the town, and it seemed quite natural that she put her name on the list for Weavers Lane.

Whatever the reasons, she enjoyed meeting John, and he not only arranged his programme to have coffee with her each Thursday, but also took to coming across to Ashthorpe Magna once a month, when it was not his turn with the children, to take Sheila Baines to luncheon in one of the outlying villages. On one occasion he brought his children, by then in their mid-teens, to Ashthorpe and they had coffee at Carole's, visited the Ashthorpe Vineyard, and had lunch at the Old Bull. The children, having only lost their grandmother three years before, instantly adored the elderly lady, and she them.

A few weeks after this visit Miss Baines received a note (she did not bother with a telephone), from John in a rather shaky hand:

I am sorry to say that I have been admitted to hospital. I am sure it is nothing too serious, and I look forward to my next visit to Ashthorpe. Love, John

Three days later:

Dear Miss Baines
I am sorry to be the bearer of bad news, but I have to tell you that John died yesterday in Bristol Royal Infirmary having been admitted at the weekend with a brain haemorrhage. I know that John had become very fond of you, as were our children after only one meeting, and would want you to be at his funeral if at all possible. The details of the time and place followed, and the note finished *Both I, and the children, would be very pleased if you feel able to attend. With my best wishes. Liz Brookes.*

Miss Baines was driven to the sombre occasion by a volunteer from the local Help the Aged Branch. She felt a moment of panic when she entered the crowded church, and sat at the back until 14 year-old Emily Brookes tugged her arm, pulled her to the front, and introduced her to Liz Brookes:

"Mummy, this is Granny Sheila."

The children, and to her credit, their mother, did keep in contact with Sheila Baines for many years, and they even, one Christmas, purchased a mobile phone for her:

"At least we will not worry that you cannot contact us in an emergency."

After training, she also felt at peace with this item of new technology.

Miss Baines lived for many more years in her cottage, only occasionally mentioned John Brookes or his children, and then only to Carole, but seemed perfectly content, and even happy, that at least a short part of her adult life had been, by her standards, blissfully content.

George's Corner

"Dear old PC Corner is well past his sell-by date – his definition of sex and violence is being hit over the head with a vibrator!"

"Very funny, but we do live in an age when a Pizza can get to your door before the Police."

Chapter 5

After graduating from Oxford, Mickey Carruthers drove down the *Autoroute du Soleil* to stay with an old school chum whose parents had a magnificent villa on the hillside overlooking the *Vielle Port* at Antibes, perhaps the most glamorous old town on the Côte d'Azur. He went with the intention of staying for a month, and stayed for a year. Due to his status as *"Un Lord Anglais"*, the French hotel owner was happy to employ him as Guest Relations Manager at a reasonable wage. Fellow house-guest, Penelope, worked there also. He and Penelope, known by close friends as PJ, were equally happy as, by then, their relationship was very close.

It was not purely a physical attraction, for indeed they were both attractive young people, but her own father was a Scottish Earl who lived in a large castle in the Highlands, but had also had problems with Inheritance Tax, or Death Duties, as is was still known, and had sold 200,000 acres of the land to an Arabian Oil Sheik, leaving a mere 200 acres around the castle. After paying off all his debts and tax, the Earl was spending money on the castle itself to convert it into a very, very upmarket "boarding house". Hence PJ had been sent to a College in Edinburgh to take a 1 year Diploma in Hotel and Catering Management, and was now doing work experience for 12 months in France.

It was perhaps the happiest time in Mickey Carruthers's life. He had an enjoyable job, was living in splendour in one of the most beautiful places on earth, and had a warm and lovely girl friend with common interests. He realised that he could not do this forever, but could not decide what to do instead. As an Earl-to-be he could not, like so many of his

Oxford friends, consider becoming a politician, and in reality was not actually bright enough to become an economist. It was his father who, during the visit Mickey had paid to England to introduce PJ to his father, made a suggestion which was acceptable to the young man. A Short Service Commission, which, if he enjoyed it, could be converted to a full-time career in the Army.

The Regimental Sergeant Major at the Mons Officer Training School, hated the young aristocrat under his guardianship. Rather than call him "My Lord", he would only address him as "Sir" stated with the emphasis and vehemence that would indicate the spelling as "Cur"!

"Am I hurting you, SIR?" growled the RSM from behind the lanky officer.

"No, Sergeant Major."

"I thought I might have been standing on your bloody hair, SIR. Get it cut, SIR."

And only days later,

"If you don't hold your f-ing rifle straight, SIR, I'll wrap it round your f-ing neck. SIR."

Mickey was more than thrilled when his training was completed and both his father, the 13th Earl, and PJ who had flown over for the occasion, attended the Passing Out Ceremony. To Mickey's utmost surprise, and his old-soldier father's obvious pleasure, he was awarded the Sword of Honour. The RSM's boot slammed the gravel on the parade ground, and he saluted the Earl.

"You can be proud of your son, sir. It has been an honour and pleasure working with him."

To Mickey,

"Good Luck, Sir," this time spelt "Sir".

Mickey and PJ promised to visit Henry, Mickey's father, on their way back from the Highlands to see her father. The Scottish Earl had, like so many fathers with an only daughter, hated the succession of, often spotty, young men his daughter had taken to visit the family pile. This one was different, and to PJ's obvious annoyance, the two men talked long into the night, spurred on by the bottle and a half of Glenfiddich Single Malt Whisky, which they consumed between them. Next morning the two youngsters were shown around every detail of the wonderful restoration work nearing completion.

Mickey was unusually quiet, nothing to do with the hangover, and at the end of the two-hour tour could only say,

"I wish to god we could do something like this with Seagram Hall."

The assumptive "we" in Penelope's response took him by surprise,

"Perhaps we can!"

This one word was to completely alter their relationship. They both assumed that the course of the rest of their lives was to be together. It was less than a year later, having spent all Mickey's periods of leave together either at Ashthorpe Magna, or at the Scottish castle, that the *Times* announced their engagement. Although the more interested press tried to contact them, they were unable to do so. Mickey had been based in Nurnberg with his regiment when PJ finished her work experience at Antibes, and they decided to spend his local leave together while exploring Heidelberg. They visited some long-lost distant relatives in this beautiful city, Mickey's great-grandmother had been a German Baroness, and soon they made some very good friends. All too soon the leave was over, Mickey returned to his regiment and PJ to work with her father in Scotland.

Cliff Breakshaft, the Reeve, still had part of his leg in plaster, but at least was able to drive and do light delivery and collection work. He had received a commission from an art gallery in Cirencester to go to a gallery just off the M20 in

Kent and collect 10 paintings, which the two galleries felt may sell better in the Cotswolds.

He left very early in the morning to try and avoid some of the hold-ups for which the M25 had become so infamous, but on the day in question luck was with him. He reached the gallery by shortly after nine thirty, and eagerly accepted the owner's offer of a coffee and croissant. Although the pain in his leg was considerably improved, he was feeling tired and almost fell asleep on the settee on which he had been seated. The gallery owner was sympathetic with his situation, and said,

"The pictures are already wrapped in bubble-wrap, so you just finish your breakfast quietly whilst I load them into the van for you."

True to her word, when an hour later he emerged feeling much better, not only were the paintings in the van but the owner had secured them with straps to the bars along the inside of the compartment to stop any rattling. They shook hands, and Cliff hopped back into his trusty white steed. Again he was in luck, and the journey around the M25 and onto the M4 was only subject to one short delay caused by the breakdown of an old car, which had to be pushed by the police patrol onto the hard shoulder. There were short delays around Swindon due, he supposed, to a lunchtime build-up of traffic, but by midday he was heading west towards Cirencester.

Shortly after he was on a country road, and only just glimpsed a cat running under the front of the van. The thump as it hit left him in no doubt that serious damage had been done, and despite the pain in his leg, Cliff braked as hard as he could. The battered white van drew to a halt, and he reversed back a hundred or so yards to where he guessed the collision had taken place. There on the grass verge lay a rather mangy looking tabby cat, still twitching. Cliff pondered for a while as he was, despite the rough exterior, something of a cat lover. The cat was still twitching and he concluded that the only thing he could do was to take the shovel he always carried in the van, and put the poor creature out of its misery. He wanted to close his eyes, but for the sake of the creature, he could not. The shovel was accurately aimed, and the blow was hard. Cliff swore that in the last seconds of its life, the old tabby opened its eyes for a split second, and gave him a look of gratitude.

He bent over and felt it to make sure it was dead, and after a few seconds threw the body into the ditch behind the grass verge. Cliff, with tears in his eyes, climbed back into the van and drove slowly away. A few miles later, just the other side of Lechlade, on the Cirencester road, and close to the turning for his home-town, he heard a police siren, and saw a blue, flashing light in his rear view mirror. He pulled over to let the police car overtake, and was most surprised when the car slowed in front of him and signalled him to stop.

"Hello, sir, did you see a cat a few miles back?"

"Yes, I did officer."

He then told the policeman the whole story, including the last part when he felt that the only course of action was to hit the animal on the head.

"That's odd sir. An elderly lady phoned us with your vehicle description and number, and said she saw you deliberately stop, get out of the vehicle and kill her pet cat."

"That certainly isn't true, we'll probably see marks on the front of the van to show where it hit."

They walked round to the front of the vehicle, and certainly there was a dent on the radiator grill.

"I can see fur there," said the police constable.

"Can you open the bonnet, please?" he asked of Cliff.

Cliff went to the driver's door, leaned in and pulled the lever, which released the bonnet catch.

"Oh shit," came from the policeman as he held open the bonnet. There inside, lodged between the radiator and the grill, was one very dead cat.

Cliff was mortified when he realised that not only had his van killed one cat but he had, after all, killed an old lady's pet as it lay sleeping on the grassy verge.

The policeman could see how distressed Cliff was, and said as gently as he could,

"I'm really sorry, sir, but I am going to have to put in a report on this. I will certainly write down the whole story, and I definitely believe everything you have told me."

Some weeks later, Cliff who was never really the same after the incident, received a letter from the County Constabulary saying that they were not going to take the matter any further. Rather foolishly Cliff had told a couple of his drinking mates in the Firkin the story of the cats, and had become the subject of many wisecracks and jokes around Ashthorpe Magna. This added to his great guilt complex in this matter, and it was some weeks before he resumed his custom of dropping into the pub for a couple of pints on the way home.

Mickey's time as a 2nd Lieutenant with the Oxfordshire Light Infantry, sped by, and he and PJ made plans for the wedding in late June of 1969 about a month after his Army career ended. The service was to be held in the Scottish Episcopalian Church in the little village 3 miles from the castle, and PJ planned the reception in the castle itself. Despite their position in society, the young couple were only too aware of the Scottish Earl's financial situation, and kept the guest list down to about 50 close relatives and friends. If they had left the wedding for another year the situation would have been very different, as once the castle opened its doors to paying guests the shooting parties booked all the rooms for the whole of the season. As these were predominately wealthy Arabs, along with groups of Japanese Bankers, they were ready to pay the highly inflated prices to stay with a real Scottish Earl – the business became an outrageous success.

After their honeymoon back at the villa in Antibes, the newly weds spent 3 months in the Scottish castle, and then moved down to Ashthorpe Magna to help with the lengthy, and often tedious task of restoration of Seagram Hall. They both realised that they should, at this particular stage, be doing rather more with their lives as PJ's father now had his son, Lord Mauchline, back at the castle running the successful Scottish business with him, and despite the fact that the 13th Earl of Ludcolmbe was on his own with the ageing uncle at Seagram Hall, he certainly encouraged the couple to look elsewhere.

At this point, Mickey received a call from James d'Albini, an old friend from both Oxford and school days, asking him, and his new wife, to come up to London for a few days as he had a proposition to put to him. However hard he tried, Mickey could not extract any more information on the mysterious proposal.

"Mickey, it's lovely to see you, and to meet your beautiful wife for the first time."

They sat in the large, beautiful drawing room of the four bed-roomed apartment, drinking an excellent white Burgundy and admiring the many oil paintings adorning the walls. The building was on Flood Street, a much sought after address, running between Kings Road in Chelsea, and the Chelsea Embankment, and the flat itself would today have a price tag running well into the millions.

"Come on, James, what is this all about?" asked the young aristocrat.

"Well, you know that I took over the family Estate Agency when my Dad died two years ago?"

"Yes."

"It has done extraordinarily well, and last month I signed a deal with a New York Realtor to purchase that business as from next January. It has cost a great deal of money, and the only way I can protect this is to spend the first three years in the States," said James.

"So where do I fit in, James?"

"There are two things I would like you, and of course PJ, to consider. Firstly there is this apartment. After Dad died, my sister Charlotte and I shared out his considerable collection of art, and I am terrified to leave these unguarded. Equally I have seen so many horrors of properties that have been rented out that I dare not risk that option. Secondly, whilst I have every confidence that Charlotte can, as she does now, run the administration side of d'Albini & Son very efficiently, I will need somebody whom I can trust to take over my main role as Senior Negotiator at the business. In short I need you to start immediately to learn the job, and for the three years during which I plan to be away, to live here in Flood Street."

"I am very honoured and flattered, James, but I do need a little time in which to discuss it with PJ, and to find out a little more about the work. I would hate to let you down," responded Mickey.

"OK. I understand, so let us go down to the offices in the morning, allow PJ to meet Charlotte, and I will go into more detail."

They had an excellent Italian meal that evening at the Meridiana restaurant, a short walk away.

It was clear that PJ loved being at the centre of things in the smart area of London, and later that night she made it quite clear to her husband that, although the decision would be his, she would certainly be very pleased to accept the offer. The following morning they all went to the offices of d'Albini & Son near the underground station in South Kensington. The premises were in a block containing several other Real Estate Agencies, but Albies, as it was affectionately known, stood out with its elegant sign painted in glossy black, with lettering and border in gold leaf paint and the d'Albini family crest to one end.

The interior was equally as striking, with antique furnishings and even the racks holding the details of properties on offer were of polished mahogany. Charlotte and PJ got along famously, and James explained the intricacies of estate agency to Mickey. In that area of London the most important part of the job was getting sole agency rights for as many suitable properties as possible. Inevitably, this was largely done by a mixture of reputation and personal contact.

At luncheon at Maroush, the famous Lebanese restaurant on Beauchamp Place, Mickey, who had insisted on paying on this occasion, asked the waiter for a bottle of Champagne. It was duly delivered, opened, and glasses filled without a drop spilled. Mickey stood up and offered his outstretched hand to James,

"James, I accept your kind offer. Thank you for your trust, and I look forward to working with you."

Dave Lounds, Ashthorpe Magna's most vociferous opponent of the Farmers' Market, pondered long and hard about the information that he had gained early one morning. Like so many who protested on seemingly any subject, Dave did nothing for the town. He had never joined any organisation, however worthy, and was reputed to regularly cross over the High Street to avoid the collecting tins for Red Cross, Macmillan Nurses, RNLI or even the Royal British Legion selling poppies. It was reputedly his wife, of whom he was terrified, who objected most to the loss of her car parking space on one occasion a month to make room for the Farmers' Market. Firstly she did not wish to walk 500 yards to her car for the school delivery run, and secondly she did not wish to buy fresh local produce and was perfectly happy to drive the 20-mile round trip to buy her food in plastic packaging from Tesco. No persuasion would convince her that she was contributing to the hard times experienced by local Farmers, to the loss of thousands of small businesses in rural towns or even the global effects of buying tasteless, uniform shaped and coloured vegetables imported from the other side of the world.

The result of Dave's pondering was that he decided to consult the Bailiff who he knew to be against the market for his own different reasons.

"Major Gross, are you aware that the Chairman of the Ashthorpe Magna Chamber of Trade and Commerce is having an affair with the Chairman of the Farmers' Market, Madame le Noir?"

"WHAT?!" roared the Bailiff.

Dave explained the circumstances, and described exactly what he saw at 6.30 in the morning. Andy Gross agreed that there could only be one explanation as to why Melvyn Hughes had taken Lauren back to her car. Whilst he was furious that somebody else, rather than himself, had obviously bedded the lovely French woman, he was also exhilarated by the prospect of having some ammunition to use against the Farmers' Market Committee.

"Here's what we'll do, Dave..."

Dave Lounds nodded and listened intently.

"We need to discredit the pair of them, and by doing that we will discredit the whole concept of the Farmers' Market, and by doing that, in turn we discredit that weasel-faced pair, the Mayor and his Clerk! Where do you drink, Dave?" asked Major Gross.

"Normally the Firkin, but occasionally the New Inn on New Town Road."

"OK, you deal with them, and I will handle the other organisations and individuals. What people will need to realise is that this clearly shows that the main motivation for the bloody Farmers' Market was the sexual gratification of the Chairman of the Chamber and NOT for the benefit of Ashthorpe Magna."

Sonia, the Bailiff's cleaning lady worked for him, doing whatever cleaning ladies do, for three days a week, and on other days and at the weekend she cleaned for a number of others, including Melvyn Hughes, and also did occasional bar work at the Old Bull. It was a few months previously that Sonia had been talking to Melvyn at the pub, in between pulling pints, and she asked him if he had any cleaning work at his shop or in the spacious flat above.

"Yes, I could do with somebody to sort out the flat for a couple of hours a week."

Melvyn soon came to realise that not only did Sonia need the additional cash, but also she hated being on her own and craved company. She was a short, nearly dumpy girl in her early thirties, but had gorgeous red hair, which cascaded over her shoulders emphasising the ample cleavage, which she regularly displayed. She chatted constantly in a soft Gloucestershire brogue, and was not slow to describe, in perhaps too great a detail, a series of failed relationships over the past five years.

On the night of the Vineyard opening, Melvyn was rolling home from the Firkin and literally bumped into Sonia. Never one to miss an opportunity, he invited her into the flat for a glass of wine.

"Yes, I'd love to." Her face lit up with a broad smile.

Their love-making was not very special on that first occasion, in truth Melvyn was too drunk to perform properly, but he more than made up for this failure the following morning. She seemed to have no objection to a number of repeat performances both on her cleaning day, but also occasionally when she had finished her bar work at the Old Bull. There was no talk of love, or any long-term commitment, so the arrangement seemed to suit both of them.

On the day that Dave Lounds had visited the Bailiff, Sonia had been to the doctor for a check-up. She was absolutely horrified when the Practice Nurse, with little feeling, told her that in fact she was pregnant. There had only been one relationship in the past year, that with the Chairman of Chamber, Melvyn Hughes.

The Major and Dave Lounds instigated the whispering campaign with great alacrity, and soon the news of the affair between Melvyn and Lauren was well and truly in the public domain. It was only a couple of days later that Sonia confided her predicament to a friend whom she had sworn to confidence. In Ashthorpe Magna!!!

Suddenly the news of both situations was the talk of the town. Sonia found out that everybody knew she was pregnant from Rosie at the Old Bull, Lauren was told of both affairs by the window cleaner, and Melvyn had a constant stream of visitors to his shop eager to get his views. Lauren phoned Melvyn with a one-word comment,

"BASTARD." She was obviously in tears as she shouted out the word.

Sonia dropped in a note one evening saying that she would no longer be Melvyn's "cleaner".

The Mayor called his Town Clerk, and they met up.

"I don't see how any of this will affect the Farmers' Market Committee," the Mayor commented.

"Will Lauren be prepared to carry on as the Chairman?" asked the Town Clerk.

"I will call her and tactfully find out," came the response.

Melvyn did not know what to do. His one marriage had failed to produce any children, but now the situation had arisen where a girl he barely knew, and was twenty years his junior, was carrying his child. The sexual relationship with her had started before he and Lauren had come together, and he was sure in his own mind that Lauren would have become a permanent fixture. He had even contemplated marriage to her at some future point.

Despite his sexual dalliances throughout his adult life, Melvyn was not a bad person, and he did want to do the right thing by Sonia. But what was that? He hoped she would not contemplate abortion, but if that were her decision he would stand by her and pay all the costs, but if she decided to keep the child then Melvyn accepted the fact that he would accept financial responsibility.

He was not sure what to expect as he knocked at the door of the studio apartment Sonia shared with a girl friend. Would she see him? Would she fly into a rage?

"What do you want, Melvyn?" began Sonia.

"We need to talk, Sonia."

They went into the room and she beckoned him to sit on the settee.

"So, what do you want to talk about?"

"About us. About the baby."

"I decided of my own free will to screw you. I knew I wasn't on the pill, and I also knew that you weren't using a condom. It is my responsibility, not yours, so you don't have to feel bad on my account!"

"But, it is my child so I must help."

"Even if you offered marriage, I would turn you down. I am lousy at long-term relationships with men. When I became aware of this the one thing that really made me sad was the fact that I would never have a child. In fact I am thrilled this has happened. I have already spoken with Social Services and they have already agreed to look for a two bed-roomed place for me, so I'll be better off than I am now. If you want to do anything, just accept that you are the father so that at least the child will grow up knowing who both of his, or her, parents are."

"Of course I will."

As Melvyn got up to leave he was amazed that Sonia came over, kissed him on the cheek and actually thanked him. They were to remain friends, nothing more, for twenty years.

During 1970 and onwards Mickey and PJ settled into the routine of Kensington and Chelsea, and when James moved to New York, Mickey quickly adapted to the life of an up-market London estate agent. More than that, he excelled. A number of his friends from Oxford were living in London and working for the numerous Japanese and Arabian Banks who at that time were setting up in London; d'Albinis became the agent of choice for most of these, house prices rocketed and Mickey was making huge fees from his half a per cent commission on each and every deal. A year or so later, PJ became pregnant and they became parents to the future Earl of Ludcolmbe, and the little lad was joined eighteen months later by a second son. Sadly it was a very difficult birth, and although the baby was fit and healthy, the Consultant broke the news to PJ and Mickey that they would not be able to have any more children.

PJ and the boys were spending more time at Ashthorpe Magna as they all agreed that the country was a healthier place for children to be raised, and Mickey took to spending most weekends and his holidays at Seagram Hall. Most of the considerable earnings from the agency were spent on the restoration of many rooms within the hall, although the replacement roof was still beyond reach, but overall the Ludcolmbes were more comfortable than they had been for many years. Fortunately for Mickey, his friend James was much enjoying the lifestyle in the Big Apple. He was also enjoying the extra profits Mickey was bringing into his company, and on one of his quarterly visits for board meetings he said that, unless it would create problems, he would like to stay in New York on a more or less permanent basis. Naturally, there was no objection, and as a result Mickey Carruthers joined the Board of Directors.

The 13th Earl had, very wisely, used his army pension to purchase Education Insurance Policies for his grandchildren, and as each of the boys reached the age of 7 they were bundled off to Prep School. As the uncle had died some time previously, this left only the old Earl and PJ living in the vast mansion, and as Mickey's work load increased, his visits became less frequent. There were no rows or arguments, but the couple, now into their thirties, were almost imperceptibly growing apart. PJ was spending more time both with her family in Scotland, and paid regular visits to d'Albini & Son in Park Lane, New York. James, who had quickly married and divorced, was pleased to have the company.

The great shock came in 1984 when Henry Ludcolmbe telephoned both his son in London, and his daughter-in-law in Scotland, to tell them that he had been diagnosed with lung cancer. It became obvious to the couple, when they arrived at Seagram Hall the following day, that Henry was indeed very ill, and certainly in no fit state to manage the estate for very long. James flew in from New York a couple of days later, and with great regret had to accept the fact that Mickey had to return to Ashthorpe Magna, and could only spare a couple of days a week to look after a few special clients. As a result of this James, who was regularly chased by larger International Estate Agents, decided to close the London Branch and sell out.

During his first year back at the family seat Mickey devoted much of his time negotiating with both the National Trust and English Heritage to try and persuade them to take the Hall under their wings. The economic boom of the previous decade had not continued, agricultural rents had decreased in real terms, and even these, normally wealthy bodies were having to cut back on investments and concentrate on maximising income from their existing properties. Mickey's efforts failed. As did his attempts to interest an English Country House Hotel Group, a prestigious

French Hotel Company and a Saudi Arabian investor he knew from London.

In 1986 the 13th Earl died. It was much to the relief of his family and friends as, during the last year of his life, he had needed 24-hour nursing, and certainly did not have any quality of life. The little family chapel, on an island in the ornamental lake, was quickly cleaned up and Henry was buried under a slab in the main aisle. The Inheritance Tax bill was estimated by the Government as £1.5 million and the last high quality painting in the hall, a Munnings, was sold at Christies for a little over £3 million leaving just enough to undertake the much needed repair and replacement work on the roof.

A note, from Lauren le Noir, was received by all the members of the Farmers' Market Committee summoning them to a meeting at the Old Bull.

George's Corner

"I don't trust the new chef. They say he uses the smoke detector as a meat timer!"

"Well, he's better than the other guy whose definition of a seven-course meal was a hot dog and a six-pack."

91

Chapter 6

The Rector of St Osmund's was the first to arrive in the Old Bull for the Farmers' Market Committee meeting. He had held the post at Ashthorpe Magna for nearly 20 years, and whilst not universally popular, was probably the most well liked incumbent since the Second World War. The number of complaints received by the Parochial Parish Council were almost equal from the older, traditionalist parishioners who accused him of being too "happy clappy", and from the younger evangelical Christians, many of whom had joined Alpha, a charismatic Christian group, who hated the traditional choir, services and organ. They would have preferred guitars and drums! The Rev Mike Shaw himself saw the need to appeal to both sides, but in truth, leaned definitely towards the High Anglican Church and even Rome. He much enjoyed including what he described as the "smoking handbag", the thurible or incense burner, in occasional services; was known to listen to Gregorian Chant in Latin, and had even been on a retreat in a Benedictine Monastery. Mike argued regularly with his boss, the Bishop, about the role of women priests, gay vicars of either sex, and more recently the possibility of women Bishops. The reality was that Fr Mike, his preferred title, was, after 35 years in the priesthood, fed up with much about the Anglican Church in the 21st Century. None of which detracted from his enjoyment of his first pint of real ale for the evening.

The, normally, jovial atmosphere of the Old Bull seemed to have disappeared on this occasion. Rosie den Bosch, the epitome of a jolly, welcoming landlady, was red-eyed and sullen, barely acknowledging anybody present. Even the three, grumpy, old men in their usual corner, were treated with politeness, which always suggested something adrift. Also noticeable was the absence of the faithful Firtle, who by this time of day would normally have been stacking shelves, changing barrels as required and generally intimidating the bar and restaurant staff.

Never to be awed by a situation, grumpy old George, who looked like a benevolent version of Joe Stalin, came straight out with it:

"Where's Firtle then, Rosie?"

The response took them all by surprise,

"Mind your own fucking business, George!"

At which point Rosie burst into tears and stomped out, followed by grumpy old Peter, who despite his public face was one of the warmest men on earth, and who knew Rosie better than the others.

"Darling, what is the matter?" asked the kindly octogenarian.

"You know that skinny young waitress who started last week?" the landlady spluttered through her tears,

"Yes, Eileen something-or-other," replied Peter.

"I walked into the Restaurant last night when they were clearing up, and there he was snogging her!"

"It may have been quite innocent," came the typical response from Peter.

"What! With one hand up her skirt and into her knickers, and the other fondling the pathetic apologies for breasts," Rosie snarled, "I fired her on the spot, and as soon as she had left the room I grabbed the willow-pattern platter from the Welsh Dresser, and smashed it over Firtle's bloody head!"

She almost smiled through the tears at this recollection, and with Peter's arm around her shoulders, went on,

"I went upstairs, and Firtle first cleared away the shattered antique and then went in to help finish off in the bars – he knew I would not permit any after-hours drinking last night!"

She carried on, "It was nearly midnight when I came down, and Firtle was just letting the last barmaid out of the front door, which he firmly locked behind her. I went behind the bar and poured myself a large Gin and Tonic, and then we started!!"

It appeared that they settled into an increasingly drunken, verbal brawl, and, by 3 am, Rosie was bolting the pub door behind her now erstwhile boyfriend, Rollo Firtle. He was gripping his overnight bag with one hand, and mobile phone with the other, drunkenly trying to find somebody awake to accommodate him for the night.

Rosie, having dried her eyes, and done whatever it is ladies do in these matters to try and disguise the fact they have been crying, moved back into the bar and accepted Peter's offer of a Gin and Tonic.

True to her form as a real professional, within minutes Rosie had recovered and was circulating in the bars greeting her customers with the customary kiss on the cheek, and introducing herself to any newcomers on the premises. And then, silence fell with a crashing nothingness. All chatter ceased, pints were placed on the counter, Rosie stopped in her tracks and all eyes turned to the new arrival; Melvyn Hughes the Chairman of the Ashthorpe Chamber of Trade and Commerce.

With a jaunty air he greeted all and sundry:

"Evenin' all!"

Silence remained.

"Evening all!" Melvyn repeated in a louder voice.

A few grunts of response started coming in, except for the Rector,

"Hello, Melvyn, glad you could make it."

It was the first time since the call from Lauren, and the visit from Sonia, that Melvyn had ventured out into the public domain. He had been a little concerned, but as a long-term resident of Ashthorpe Magna he knew the only way to deal with such a matter was to brazen it out. Fr Mike was, as anticipated, totally oblivious of any problems, and carried on chatting with Melvyn until the arrival of the two weasely officials, the Mayor and the Town Clerk, who joined them.

The arrival of the final committee member to attend that evening caused eyes to turn. Lauren le Noir's entry, as always, did this, but on this occasion it was her reaction to Melvyn that was the subject of interest rather than her natural grace and beauty.

The melodic, Gallic, sexy, simply stunning voice halted every man in his tracks;

"Good evening, jentlemen!"

With nothing said, Melvyn produced a glass of dry white wine, and they all followed Lauren into the snug.

After the death of the 13th Earl of Ludcolmbe in 1986, when Mickey was forced to sell off the Munnings to pay Death Duties and replace the roof of Seagram Hall, PJ was spending less-and-less time at Ashthorpe Magna with her husband. Those periods they were together were frenetically busy trying to hold the house and estate together, and, of course being there either to look after the boys during holiday times or to visit their school for various sporting events. Not that anyone from the outside would notice any sort of a rift between the couple. They were always friendly and polite, but their relationship was missing the warm tactility that had previously existed between them.

Their conversations centred around the practicalities of the estate, the children or PJ's travels. Mickey did not understand what was happening, or, indeed, why. Life changed little until 1990 when the eldest son, Damien, Lord Botreaux, completed his schooling and the proud parents and younger brother attended the end-of-year prize giving. To the delight of all, they learned that Damien had achieved 4 Grade A Passes at GCSE A Level, along with an offer of a place at his father's old college at Oxford. PJ warmly congratulated her son, kissed him affectionately and departed for New York leaving her husband, once more, to sort out the details.

Damien was less than thrilled;

"Dad, I am not accepting the offer," came the bombshell from Damien.

"Why the hell not? You worked your balls off, and you deserve it!" Mickey's reply indicated, for the first time, an irritation with his son.

"We have an ancient building and estate. Henry VIII is reputed to have stayed here. We have acres of prime English land, and are still desperate for liquid capital. You've got to face it, Dad, the estate has been mismanaged throughout both my and your living memory. We are no longer feudal landlords, and we must drag ourselves and our birthright into the 20th Century, let alone the 21st which is not so far away. If we don't, neither we nor Seagram Hall, will survive."

The rangy figure of the Earl seemed to sink back into the rather tatty winged chair, as if looking for a place of hiding.

"So, Son, what the blue blazes do you think you can do about it? What can you contribute without the highest possible education you can achieve?"

"Dad, the finest Agricultural College in the world is only 10 miles away from here, and they offer a degree course on Estate Management," Damien replied.

"You don't need a degree to milk a cow, lay a hedge or plough a field," the Earl tersely responded.

"That, Father, is a pathetic attitude. The course teaches way beyond that. It teaches what we need – how to develop land for the best possible income, be that from agriculture, agritourism or even the environment. If we just look at tenant farmers and occasional visitors, most of whom never pay, we cannot possibly survive."

Gradually Mickey came to realise that whilst his son had all of his own aristocratic charm, he had overtaken his father in the intellectual stakes. Damien pulled the final coup-de-grace:

"Dad, at least do this. Here is the prospectus for the Estate Management course, please will you go through it together with me?"

Although Damien was an occasional visitor to the local hostelries, and had on several occasions at boarding school been reprimanded with his friends for sneaking down to the village pub, Mickey had, like so many parents, not really been aware that his son was now a young adult.

Hands clasped behind his back, Mickey walked around and eventually, saying nothing, headed for the wine cellar. Damien waited in silence, not really knowing what to expect, and his Father returned clutching two wine glasses, and a bottle of his favourite "*Gris de Gris*". Mickey felt a pang of nostalgia as he opened the bottle. It was from the last crate that he and PJ had brought back from a trip to the mystical area of the *Camargue* where the River Rhone flows into the Mediterranean over the flat, sandy, marshy lands inhabited by wild white horses and black bulls. The wine itself was described as a *Vin de Pays de Sable*, or Wine of the Sand Country.

Bottle opened, the first of many glasses poured, and Mickey eventually said,

"OK, Son, let's look at the brochure!"

Every possible, and many impossible, objections the Earl could think of, were answered by the beautifully presented prospectus. After several hours, and a second bottle (or was it a third?) Mickey put his arm around Damien;

"I wish I had done this. You have my complete support. I know your Mother would have preferred you to be a Merchant Banker or something equally useless and boring, but I am totally proud of your decision. I apologise for my doubting your decision. Only one condition, you tell Mum!!"

Superficially, Lauren showed no sign of embarrassment. She was about to start the meeting when the last attendee arrived; to her delight it was the 23-year-old Damien Lord Botreaux, whom she had known for most of his life. He plonked his, opened, bottle of wine and glass on the table, and languidly draped himself over a chair at the bottom of the table.

"Apologies, Madam Chairman, I had trouble in getting the old car started."

"No problem, Damien, I was about to start," came the reply from the head of the table. Lauren carried on:

"First item on the agenda. The procession. I suggest we assemble at the Post Office, parade around the corner, up the High Street and to the Town Hall Place."

"Sounds reasonable," said the Town Clerk.

"OK, but who is going to parade, and in what order?" enquired the Mayor.

"As we are hoping to get local press and TV coverage, we must make it as spectacular as possible," she replied.

"My Father is doing the official opening, so I suggest he and I wait by the front of the Town Hall for the procession to arrive," Damien suggested.

"Yes, agreed, but who is processing?" the Mayor repeated.

An unusually subdued Melvyn decided it was time to join in, if only to impress Lauren with his loyalty and support:

"May I suggest, Madam Chairman, that the parade is led by Angus, with his bagpipes, followed by yourself and the Mayor."

"No, Melvyn, I feel the first two should be the Rector and the Mayor, led by the piper, and followed by you and I, then the Town Clerk and other members of this committee." They were all somewhat surprised, not only by the idea that she would parade with Melvyn, but especially by a certain warmth in her voice.

They all agreed on this, and also agreed that certain other local dignitaries, Chairmen of local groups and charities, council members, Gloucestershire Farmers' Market Chairman and other Church officials should also be invited. They finally agreed that the procession should be brought up at the rear by the Ashthorpe Magna Morris Men to add a final bit of colour!

The Rector asked the question all had been avoiding:

"What about the Court Leet?"

The debate on this item continued for nearly an hour. Lauren, the Chairman, was wise enough to call for a break in the middle to enable the committee to replenish their drinks, and she accepted the offer of a shared bottle with Damien, the young aristocrat.

In the end it was Damien who came up with a proposal:

"We know that the Bailiff is opposed to the market, and that Cliff will do whatever his master orders!" No dissension there. "We also know that the Marshall is sharpening his knife against the two leading Officers of the Court, and probably for that reason alone would like to be involved." Damien displayed a, hitherto unseen, political skill, and went on:

"May I suggest that we invite the Court to join in the procession, unrobed, with the general group of dignitaries? That way we cannot be accused of ignoring them, and we know that very few will accept the invitation."

This was considered by all present to be the ideal solution, and both Lauren and Melvyn congratulated Damien for his suggestion. They finally agreed upon who should do the routine tasks such as applying to the Police for a Road Closure Order, deal with the press, and even clearing-up duties after the market.

It was typical of Ashthorpe Magna that, by the time the whole committee retired to the bar, the centre of attention for the local gossips had moved away from Melvyn, Lauren and Sonia, and was firmly placed in the court of Rosie and Firtle. In fact, after the Mayor and his Clerk had taken their leave, the remaining group occupied a table in what was known as Firtle's garden, and settled in for a most convivial evening. The only change from the previous meeting was that Melvyn's offer of a lift to the Chairman was declined, but she accepted the one offered by the son of her friend, Mickey Carruthers.

Despite a slight hangover, Lauren printed out the invitations the next morning, and within 24 hours they had all, including those to the Court Leet Officers, been delivered. The only difference to the Court Leet invitees, was that at the top of each card was inscribed, in black ink, the words "No Robes".

The Rector, Fr Mike, had enjoyed his evening, and settled down to watch the late night news and have a final whisky before retiring for the night. He decided to read some of the archives that Chris, the Senior Church Warden, was cataloguing and had left for his perusal. The one that caught his eye, and demanded his attention, was a story in the Parish Magazine written in the late 1950s, long after the retirement of the incumbent Rector, Major the Revd David Shore, who had nursed several parishes at the end of the Second World War. Fr Mike mused on the differences both in the Church, and in England in general, even in his own lifetime. He felt that, even though it was a little article, written in a tiny part of the country, the document was part of social history.

St Osmund's Parish News
June 1959

The Vicar's Shorts. A "Short" Story by John Aulton

John, the author, was still alive, and living in a lovely little cottage in Ashthorpe Magna where he was actually born some 75 years previously. Despite his considerable bulk, and 52" waistline, he was still quite fit and cycled several miles each day. A true local character whose main hobby since retirement, in addition to travel and wine, was writing, and over the years he had been a regular contributor to local publications. His story about Major the Revd David Shore is reproduced verbatim:

My tale begins in the late 1940s, Ashthorpe, or the country for that matter, had not recovered from years of grinding war, but slowly things were getting back to normal.

As usual the middle-classes led the way and the working class tagged along behind, cap in hand, 'twas ever thus.

The vicar was a large, red-faced, jovial man not so much loved by his flock as respected. He didn't talk about it, but everyone knew that when it mattered he was in the thick of it at Dunkerque and much later in Normandy where he was wounded but didn't tell anyone until he fainted due to loss of blood. War enables a man to put a stamp on life and the vicar had not shirked his responsibilities.

However, when it was learned that he and his wife were to take a short seaside holiday this news had a mixed reception. Working class people rarely went on holiday in those days, often a week's holiday from a factory job presented an opportunity to supplement the meagre wages by working on the land. Even the middle classes were not renowned for gadding off abroad, after all appearances had to be kept up at home, that's what the middle-classes are for.

Unfortunately for the vicar the grumbling was not the end of the matter.

As he strolled along the front at Bognor one brisk yet sunny morning, a full English breakfast inside him, the Manchester Guardian tucked under his arm and with a fresh breeze ruffling his sandy hair he was suddenly confronted by one of his parishioners, in fact he was confronted by the whole family, mother, father, children and in-laws. No words can describe the looks of horror and fascination that registered on their faces for you see NOT ONLY WAS THE VICAR NOT WEARING HIS BADGE OF RANK, HIS DOG COLLAR, THE VICAR WAS WEARING... SHORTS!!!!

Beneath his generous midriff his ex-Army shorts flapped in the breeze like the sails of a tea-clipper at anchor. From beneath the shorts protruded a pair of very large, very red and very hairy legs. Embarrassed greetings were exchanged and off the vicar went, swiftly forgetting the incident amongst the excitement of adding to his collection of seaweed and having to pay proper attention to his delightful wife.

By Monday the cauldron of gossip was being stirred and the taverns and tearooms of Ashthorpe were soon alive with the tales of the Vicar's shorts. Like any good story it was much improved by repetition and innuendo, one version was that he was stripped to the waist, another that he had a tattoo of a lady on his chest and the name underneath was NOT that of his wife. As the ale flowed we learned that he had a good-looking young man with him or was it a young woman? Better still TWO young women with whom he was arm-in-arm.

The working men of the town, some of whom had stopped wearing shorts when they left school, put it down to the fact that ALL vicars were a bit limp-wristed, but the ladies gave him the benefit of the doubt as it was known that the seaside sun was much stronger than Ashthorpe sun and after all, he was not wearing a knotted handkerchief on his head, although in some stories he was wearing a jaunty lilac beret.

The vicar enjoyed his few days on the Coast and returned to St Osmund's in good spirits and refreshed.

However, those spirits sank at Sunday Matins when only a handful of people turned up and despite a little up-turn, attendance was very poor the next Sunday and the Sunday after that.

Of course, being the Church of England everyone was far too polite to tell him what the problem was and it was only whilst drinking a well-earned warmer with the gravedigger after a particularly chilly funeral that the truth was revealed. In

*common with most men in his profession the gravedigger was
an atheist and after another glass of punch he revealed to the
vicar the cause of his much depleted congregation.*

*The vicar never went on holiday again and a few months
later a pair of large, baggy khaki shorts changed hands at a
church bazaar for the princely sum of one shilling and six
pence.*

THE END

"Literature. No," mused Fr Mike. "Social history. Yes." He
was pleased the little tale had been preserved.

During Damien's last two years at Cirencester he had
undertaken three periods of one month on work experience.
The first, and probably the most fascinating, was on the
estate of Sir Thomas Louis Bt of Perse Devitt in Dorset. The
majority of the farming land, which the family had owned for
six generations, had been sold off to pay off a succession of
swingeing death duty payments throughout the 20th Century.
Other than the 300 acre Home Farm, the remainder had been
let out to long-term tenant Farmers.

Damien's main fascination came from the efforts they
were making to get the ancient Palladian hulk of a building,
Perse Hall, to pay for itself. Two things had happened in the
immediate past which were to affect, not only the Louis
family, but also subsequently the Ludcolmbe estates. The
first was that the government had decided that buildings
other than churches and registry offices, were to be allowed
to apply for licences for weddings to take place on their
premises, and this had opened a flood gate to Hotels, Stately
Homes and various other types of buildings wanting to get on
the bandwagon. In a mere 12 months since the announcement
of the relaxation of the regulations, some 350 places had

applied for inclusion, and of those nearly 300 were waiting for a licence once the bill had been finalised in Parliament.

The second factor, which was to benefit both families, was the success of the National Lottery, and the subsequent setting up of a Lottery Heritage Fund that distributed millions of pounds to preserve British Heritage, and clearly Perse Hall fitted this description. So it was that Sir Thomas, who had taken an instant liking to Damien, explained in minute detail the machinations of applying for grants.

"Damien, the main thing is to apply in the language they want to hear," the Baronet explained.

"But how do I know?" asked Damien.

"Read the instructions carefully, and underline every word that either looks out of place, or a word you would not use yourself in normal communication, or a word which seems to have some weight for them. Look at this!"

Thomas took out a copy of the latest Lottery Heritage Application Guidance Notes, and they went through it together.

"Here they are. Diversity. Sustainability. Ecological Principles. Employment. Tourism." And so they went on, and on, and...

"So, Damien, even in this one booklet we have underlined 25 words and phrases which are the ones on which they will base their decision. If you do decide this is a route for Seagram Hall, when you write the application, throw all these words back at them, several times over!" The old Baronet looked almost smug as he imparted his wisdom.

Unlike Seagram Hall, Perse Hall did not have a chapel of any sort, either in the Hall, or in the grounds. One of the most imposing parts of the house was the Long Gallery, over 100 metres in length, one side completely covered with a series of huge windows stretching from floor to ceiling, and the other side dominated by a huge Louis XV fireplace reputed to have been imported from Versailles itself. Either side of the fireplace was covered, probably for a distance of 40 metres, by beautiful Honduran mahogany shelving, housing the considerable collection of books owned by the family. Each section was protected by raffia screens to avoid damage to the books from sunlight, which streamed into the Long Gallery throughout the year. This was the designated area registered for marriages with a maximum of 90 guests permitted, although the Registrars often turned a blind eye to a few extras who occasionally crept in!

Throughout his stay on work experience, Damien was converting everything he learned to the potential needs of Seagram Hall.

His other two visits, one to a purely farming estate in North Yorkshire, and the second to a racehorse stud in Berkshire, proved extremely interesting and enjoyable, but of perhaps less value to the Ludcolmbe family.

Major Andy Gross had recovered from his gout – for that occasion. He was still not happy; the news of Firtle and Rosie had superseded the Melvyn, Lauren and Sonia scenario for the town gossips, which had defeated his efforts to undermine the Farmers' Market Committee. He did not yet know about the invitations!

He had faced the cool exterior of the landlord of the Firkin earlier in the evening to enjoy the pleasure of a few ales with some of the locals, and settled down in front of the television with a plate of liver, bacon and onions that Sonia had prepared for him. Not an ideal diet for a gout sufferer, especially when accompanied by a bottle of Red Rioja made from the exquisite Tempranillo grape.

Andy's bed had, according to its label, first been manufactured in 1920, and still had the original chain-link mesh base that could be tightened every few years with the manufacturer's spanner, still kept in a slot under the head of the bed. The original frame itself was made of 2" x 4" solid pine, but as the Bailiff's weight had increased he had instructed a carpenter to put in two extra support pieces. Over the previous two years the comparatively new, (and very expensive) mattress had started to sag in the middle which meant that whatever position Andy chose for his sleep, the configuration caused him to be rolled into the middle of the bed.

Like many thousands of others, he had been attracted to a new form of high-tech foam mattress "designed by NASA", although the Major could not really work out why the Space Agency should be designing bedding! The glossy brochure, and the accompanying video, certainly convinced him, and the new device had been delivered that morning. Rather than waste the existing mattress he decided to ask the delivery men to place the new one on top of the extant interior sprung version. Sonia had made up the bed for him, and Andy, slightly the worse for wear after four pints of Hobsen's, and a bottle of Rioja, was looking forward to bed.

Then came the first problem. Andy stood by the side of his bed in his favourite cotton, summer nightshirt and realised that the already mammoth structure, with the added height of an additional mattress, placed the edge of the bed level with the most voluminous part of his corpulent stomach. The only way he could get onto the bed was to do a little roll which left him, much like a beached whale, straddled across the bed with the duck-down duvet pushed to the far side, and his hands and upper arms flapping over the edge of that side, and his feet over the side from which he had mounted the monolith! Eventually, in what would have been seen as a series of hilarious athletic moves, he wriggled himself into what could best be described as a fore-and-aft position, but the inevitable happened and the duvet fell resolutely onto the floor on the other side of the bed! Almost in tears of frustration, he grabbed the edge of the mattress on the side on which the duvet had fallen, and managed to lever and pull himself to the edge where he could lean over to retrieve the duvet. But this was not to be, and the Bailiff, Major Andrew Gross, found himself firmly dumped onto the floor on the far side of the bed.

In all it took the poor man nearly an hour from start to finish to get to bed, but when achieved he did get a good night's sleep!

The next morning saw him by the front door picking up the mail, when, not for the first time, came the by now familiar roar,

"FARMERS' BLOODY MARKET!"

"How can that French whore tell me when, or when not, to wear robes!"

If the Bailiff's whispering campaign had been scuppered by the Rosie and Firtle situation, the Machiavellian deviousness of Dave Lounds certainly had not. The previous Saturday morning Dave had been invited to the home of one of the Witches of Church Close for coffee, and was delighted to find that the main three objectors were all there. He knew that a procession and opening ceremony would be planned, and saw the Witches as his route to spoiling the event, and especially demonstrating to any media presence that not everybody wanted the market.

The Witches were all remarkably similar. They were all of a certain age, probably early to mid sixties, all with thinning hair accentuated by over back-combing and unwise use of dyestuffs, and all had sharp, unwelcoming features. In short, ideal for Dave's plan. Two of them, Dave thought unfairly, but did not mention this, volunteered to recruit the assistance of their daughters to conduct a protest during the procession, and Dave produced the mock-ups of the posters he proposed to make up for them;

SAY NO – PROTECT LOCAL SHOPS
SAY NO –WHERE CAN THEY PARK
SAY NO – SUPPORT ASHTHORPE

They all agreed to carry these, and when he later delivered them, the placards were appropriately mounted on broom handles. Even, the normally humourless, Dave Lounds, could not help smiling at the thought of providing them with broomsticks!

So the scene was set. The procession was planned, the opening ceremony organised and to be conducted by the 14th Earl, the guests invited and the protest arranged to gain maximum impact.

George's Corner

"Dear Old Ellie is in again. She knows exactly where her husband is every night because she is a widow."

"Yes, but she still enjoys a man's company – when he owns it!"

"Excuse me – 20 minutes up. Time to rotate George to prevent bar sores!"

"OK; it's worth it – do you remember when he went tea-total and claims it was the worst two hours of his life."

Chapter 7

In June 1994 Mickey Carruthers, and his wife PJ, joined hundreds of other proud parents to see their son, Damien, awarded a 2.1 Honours Degree in Estate Management. They hired the obligatory mortarboard and gown, and queued for the exorbitantly priced photograph of their son to be taken. Whilst the college was probably the most prestigious in the country, the parents were from all walks of life and the 14th Earl was seated between a Labour Party Life Peer, and the far more interesting production line supervisor from MG Rover in Longbridge. There were, of course, a smattering of the "great and the good", but they were by no means the majority, and Mickey mused that there must be something of an equalising force in the preservation of English countryside. He wondered if the large number of Chinese students, collecting a major proportion of 1.1 and 2.1 degrees, had been affected by this.

The departure took seemingly hours as students, some of whom barely knew each other, made their fond farewells, exchanged addresses and vowed to stay in contact. It was good that Sir Thomas Louis Bt had made the journey to see the young man he considered his protégé collect the rewards of four years' labour. He readily accepted the invitation from Mickey and PJ to visit Ashthorpe Magna during the summer and stay at Seagram Hall.

That evening, Damien and his younger brother, Jocelyn, decided to celebrate in the Old Bush. Jocelyn had recently, for the second year running, failed his A Levels miserably, and ended up with just one Grade D in English – nothing else after three years of study. The school had tactfully suggested to his father that there was little point in Jocelyn carrying on any further, and there was no hope of any university place available to him.

"What the hell am I going to do, Damien?" the younger man enquired.

"OK, I'll tell you what my plans are, but you must promise not to tell Dad or Mum at this stage," Damien replied.

"Alright, you have my word," Jocelyn assured him.

"You remember meeting Sir Thomas Louis today?" enquired Damien.

"Yes, he seemed a delightful old boy."

Damien and Jocelyn moved into the corner of the snug, replenished their pints and settled down to private discussions.

"Thomas has completely turned around his home and estate. He applied for Heritage Lottery Grants and used those to restore great tracts of Perse Hall. He also applied for a Licence to allow marriage ceremonies to be held at the Hall, put in commercial catering facilities, and converted eight bedrooms to en-suite luxury accommodation. The old boy achieved this in less than three years, and he is now booked for months ahead," Damien explained. "All he has to wait for is the White Paper to go through Parliament to allow weddings to be solemnised."

"Are you planning the same?" asked Jocelyn.

"Yes, but there is more," came the response from Damien.

"You know this Darling fellow at Ashthorpe Court has planted a mega-sized vineyard," he continued.

"Yes, I actually went up there at Easter and had a good poke around!" replied Jocelyn. "It all looked pretty impressive."

"Well, I understand that the guy has a reasonably civilised wife, and she is starting work on developing the whole thing as a full-scale tourist centre, and there are already teams of designers, architects and planners crawling over the place," Damien replied.

"So, do you want a vineyard, Damien?"

"No, you ass. They started planting three years ago, and it will take at least another four years until it the vineyard itself is fully operational, let alone the setting up of the Visitor Centre and all the other things they seem to have planned."

"So, Big Brother, how does this affect us, and specifically, how does this affect my future?"

"Well it seems that Mary Darling is pretty switched on, and there is no doubt that over the next few years more and more tourists will be attracted to Ashthorpe Magna and its environs."

"So?" was the curt question from Jocelyn.

Damien looked at his brother with the sort of expression a teacher would adopt with a pupil who failed to grasp what was being said,

"Jocelyn, the one aspect of the estate you have always enjoyed more than the rest of us, has been the livestock. Even at the age of 12 you were the one out in the sheds at all times during the lambing season, you are the one who learned how to shear sheep, and you are the one who insisted on bringing in a few pigs."

"Yes, Damien, but none of these ventures ever made any money, in fact I don't think that we even broke even on them."

"But, Jocelyn, we are not attempting to make the main bulk of money from the actual farming aspect, but more from tourism."

"Shit, Damien, I don't understand."

"Look, Joe Public is fascinated with what they consider to be the original rural life, the rural idyll! Only 18 miles away we have the excellent Cotswold Farm Park, at Temple Guiting, which works with the Rare Breeds Survival Trust to ensure a future for the old, and sometimes threatened, breeds of English livestock. But, more importantly, it attracts many thousands of visitors each year."

"Mmmmm," Jocelyn looked as though he was beginning to understand what the older brother was getting at, and Damien carried on;

"Even at Honeybourne, near Evesham, is the Domestic Fowl Trust which has a superb collection of rare breed hens, and whilst it seems to make money from selling both stock and equipment, there are paying visitors looking round throughout the year, many of whom use the catering facilities on offer."

"OK, Damien, but what are we really looking at?"

"I suggest that before we mention anything to parents, you and I, with a bit of help from Thomas Louis, look at a few facilities in existence, and get together a business plan. It will be a three-pronged attack, firstly, opening up the chapel on the island and restoring it for use as a place for upmarket weddings, secondly applying for grants to allow the Great Hall to be used for functions and receptions with maybe a dozen luxury bedrooms, and thirdly to put in a Rare Breeds Farm to cash in on the visitors the Darlings will, undoubtedly, bring to the area. You could be responsible for the Rare Breeds."

The young men talked on way past closing time, and agreed a plan of action which would take them, during the next weeks, to some 6 similar tourist attractions, and also to see Sir Thomas.

Even after a cooling-off period for breakfast, Andy Gross was still fuming at the stylishly written "No Robes" on his invitation card to join the procession for the opening of the Farmers' Market. He managed, that morning, to contact twelve of the Court Leet Officers. To each he said the same:

"The decision must be yours, but I thought I would let you know that I shall not be going to the opening, and I would really rather that none of the other officers attended."

He received a mixed reception, most of which could have been anticipated. From Cliff, the Reeve:

"Of course Andy, I won't be available."

From the Marshall, Ray Spicer:

"I'm not sure, Bailiff, it may be an opportunity to pick up some new contacts for my business."

From Col Blimp:

"Don't be such an oaf, Major. I'll bloody well go if I want to."

Overall it seemed that maybe six would heed the plea for a boycott, but as many as six may actually turn up. A further five were unobtainable, thus their plans unknown. Andy Gross was not happy with the result and felt that the control of the Court Leet may be slipping from his grasp.

Ray Spicer had also done a "ring-around", and came up with much the same conclusion as the Bailiff, and he arranged for a group of them to meet for coffee the following morning.

The Marshall started the informal meeting with the first of many lies;

"Gentlemen, I don't want to undermine what the Bailiff has said," that being precisely what he did wish to do, "but, I think it is important to establish that there are many people and organisations in Ashthorpe Magna who do wish to see the Farmers' Market held here. All the produce will be grown within a 35 mile radius of here, and everything will be seasonally fresh. It is not going to affect Dave at the vegetable shop as he will be able to continue to sell the imported, non-seasonal products which make up the bulk of his business, and hopefully the additional visitors in the town could actually increase his takings."

"We all know that the Bailiff's motives are a personal vendetta with the Mayor and Town Clerk, and have nothing to do with the needs of Ashthorpe Magna. I think we will look stupid if the whole Court Leet boycotts what, after all, is a significant event in the town's year."

Eight Officers had turned up for coffee, rather surprising in Ashthorpe where meetings and beer were more oft associated, and all eight, including Col Blimp, gave their support to Ray Spicer. Although they had been asked not to wear robes, and indeed without permission of the Bailiff they could not do so, but the Brooklooker pointed out that they all had dark blazers, with the crest of Ashthorpe Magna stitched to the pockets, and to present a creditable group they should wear these with dark trousers, white shirt and the Ashthorpe tie. Robes, no, but uniform and parading in a coherent and identifiable group, yes.

Later that day, Col Blimp reported on the results of the gathering to the Mayor who was, understandably, delighted, and immediately phoned round the Farmers' Market Committee to inform them, and especially to thank Damien for his brilliant solution to the problem. Lauren, who had been quite concerned once the news of her probable affair with Melvyn had broken, was so thrilled that she phoned Melvyn and invited him to dinner that evening.

After about a week of absence, Firtle returned, somewhat sheepishly, to the Old Bull. Both the verbal, and non-verbal communication between he and Rosie den Bosch, indicated that his return did not signify a return to the previous relationship. The reality was that he was both hard working, and honest, two attributes rare in the licensed trade, and Rosie could not do without him. Digs had been arranged with one of the part-time bar staff who needed the extra cash, and the whole affair was soon forgotten.

Firtle immediately went to work on what he considered to be his garden. Even after a week's absence there was plenty to be done. The cellar had not been cleaned and restocked properly, so he did this, and within 24 hours everything was returned to the high standards that had been imposed for the many years Rosie had owned the establishment.

One area of concern for Firtle was the Gentlemen's Toilets, with its row of Victorian porcelain stalls – those very same which had been the subject of a, now legendary, practical joke many years before. They all had slow leaks, coming from the point at which the old water pipes from the uneven walls joined the back of the stalls, and whilst nothing was obvious, the floor was constantly awash with water, much to the annoyance of the customers, especially those wearing "flip-flops" in the garden during the long summer evenings.

A local plumber was in having a couple of beers, and Firtle asked him to take a look at the offending items. The diagnosis was not encouraging. Either all the stalls could be removed, restored, sealed and remounted, or the whole lot could be taken out and replaced with a stainless-steel trough at half the cost. Perhaps, under the earlier regime, Firtle would have made the decision himself, but he felt that with the current circumstances he should present the facts to Rosie, and allow her to decide.

Unfortunately, like all females of our species, Rosie was not aware of the niceties and etiquette of male urinals. She considered the cost, and also the fact that stainless-steel had a far cleaner and more hygienic image than 100-year-old pottery! She placed the order for the new trough, and rather than spend more money asked Firtle if he would be able to fit the new edifice – he agreed.

Cliff Breakshaft, the Reeve, had mentioned he needed to go to the Builders Merchant in Swindon the following morning, and kindly agreed to pick up the new urinal. Two other locals had agreed to help Firtle, and by seven in the morning they made a start by unscrewing the existing stalls, and transporting them behind a screen at the bottom of the garden where they could subsequently be smashed up and removed.

By ten o'clock the stalls had disappeared and they had given the walls a much-needed coat of paint. Cliff arrived back from his visit to Swindon, and they all helped unload the new urinal. In the catalogue it had looked quite compact and neat, but the reality was that in the narrow, corridor-like toilets the nine foot long hunk of steel was a nightmare to manoeuvre.

"Up your end!"

"Towards you"

"Too far…"

And on it went until Firtle was satisfied that he had marked the screw holes in the correct position so that the water pipe would fit neatly into the pre-drilled hole on the urinal. With maximum effect he produced a Black and Decker drill, fitted it with a masonry bit, drilled the holes and put in the appropriate plugs to take the screws. The point-of-no-return came when they spread the silicone sealant around the water inlet pipe, and around the flanges by which the device was to be attached to the wall, and the plastic screw device that would hold the water inlet to the urinal.

Not that it looked anything like a urinal. They all agreed that it was probably a sheep trough designed for a high-tech intensive farm unit. The final attachment came, one local at each end of the trough, and Firtle, screwdriver and screws poised, in the centre issuing instructions. Eventually the task was complete, and they all stood back to admire their handiwork:

"Are you sure it is level?" asked George.

"Of course it is. We measured it!" came the riposte from Firtle.

The instructions on the quick-curing silicone had stated that the material must be left to cure for two hours before re-connecting the water supply. The sign went up:

GENTLEMEN'S TOILETS TEMPORARILY CLOSED.
PLEASE USE FACILITIES IN RESTAURANT.

It seemed quite natural that they should retire to the bar and enjoy the free pints Rosie poured for them. Two hours later the sign was removed, and without ceremony the new urinal opened.

"The whole bloody thing is leaning forward, and unless you stand back about two feet the 'splash back' actually directs your pee straight back onto your trousers!" came the irate comment from the first customer to use the new facilities.

One by one, Firtle and his helpers went into the Gents to see for themselves. The man was right.

"Worse than that, Firtle, the sheep trough is running downhill, from left to right, so steeply that all the pee is building up at the left-hand end," said George.

"Is that a problem, George?"

"It may not be for you, Cliff, but it is for me. I take a Liver Pill which colours my urine blue, and the guy on the left nearly had a fit when he saw a wall of blue-coloured pee streaming down towards him!"

Rosie, with almost an air of acceptance, telephoned the real plumber and agreed a figure of £200 for him to come straight in and fix the problem. She had no alternative as 32 Masons were booked in for dinner, their "Festive Board", after the Lodge Meeting later that day in the Town Hall. Still allowing two hours for curing, the plumber assured her that it should be open for use again at six o'clock, and the Masons were not due in until 7.30 pm.

Duly, at the appointed hour, Rosie parted with her £200, glaring at her original helpers as she did, and the new Gents was again open for use.

At the end of the Lodge Meeting, the Masons poured into the bar, and not unnaturally many headed for the toilets; after all they had been sitting in on the meeting for nearly two hours. Rosie could not understand that virtually every person returning from the loo was wiping the top of his shoes against the back of his pinstripe, Masonic morning suit trousers.

As Firtle was down in the cellar, Rosie asked Melvyn, who had popped in for a drink, to go down to see if he could spot a problem. He arrived back, eyes watering and red-faced from the effort of stifling laughter. He spluttered:

"Rosie, that design will never work!"

"What do you mean, Melvyn?"

"Because the toilet is full, and there are at least 6 using the urinal, but there is absolutely no privacy. No Englishman wants to be seen looking at another chap's willy, so they are standing there in a long row and looking up at the ceiling in case they were thought to be looking at another's member. Inevitably, eyes are directed at the ceiling, the pee is going everywhere, especially over their own shoes." Melvyn could not help laughing at the embarrassed antics of the soggy-shoed Freemasons! Other customers gradually grasped what was happening, and never before had so many people walked down to the toilets for amusement!

Rosie was fed up with the whole subject by then, having wasted much of her day, poured six or more free beers to pay the original "workers", and then paid out a further £200 to the plumbers.

"Well, you'll bloody well have to get used either to looking at each other, or to timing your visits to only have two on each occasion!"

She stomped into the kitchen to help out there for the rest of the evening.

The two brothers threw themselves into learning about the potential of rare breeds within the agritourism business. There was no doubt that the elder, Damien, was correct in assuming that his younger, less academic brother would be the perfect partner in such an enterprise. His personal knowledge, gained whilst taking his degree in Estate Management, and from everything he had learned from Sir Thomas Louis, was the perfect foil for Jocelyn's love of livestock and interest in rare breeds.

It must have been something of a shock to the greying administrators of the Rare Breeds Survival Trust, when the two young enthusiasts arrived, by appointment, at their Headquarters at Stoneleigh Park, near Kenilworth in Warwickshire, known to many thousands of people as the Royal Show Ground. The young men were equally surprised to feel the huge level of support and enthusiasm accorded to them. Most of the day was spent being shown around the site, and seeing brochures and videos of the increasing numbers of RBST Approved Farm Parks.

The RBST currently had approaching 7,000 members and had the proud claim that, since its formation in 1973, not one British farm species had become extinct. The organisation worked closely with the Ministry of Agriculture, later to become DEFRA, and was involved in every end of the individual enterprise from setting up centres, buying rare breed stock, tourism and finally marketing meat products from rare breed animals. The theory, shown to be correct, was that if the public could be encouraged, through specialist butchers and Farmers' Markets, to pay a little more in return for better taste, healthier product and total traceability of livestock, then farmers would be encouraged to stock the vulnerable breeds thus preserving the breeding stocks. Damien and Jocelyn were provided with piles of brochures, and many back-copies of the *ARK*, the excellent magazine produced by the charity, which were to provide hours of reading. They left with a warm feeling, and full of optimism.

The amazing thing was that their father barely noticed that they were away during many of the weekdays. He was more bemused, and pleased that his wife, PJ, had not even mentioned returning to New York. Their relationship was, perhaps best described, as comfortable. Little signs of affection seemed to be creeping in over the summer days, and they had even been spotted holding hands whilst exploring the somewhat overgrown island on which the chapel stood. The gestures were returning, the hand on shoulder, arms almost unnoticeably interlinked, and the little cuddle of excitement when they spotted something special such as the Kingfisher silhouetted by the evening sunshine, or the flashes of colour from the many varieties of dragonfly hovering above the small lake.

Both failed to notice the coded, and somewhat stilted conversations, between their two sons at dinner table in the evenings.

"What have you two been up to today?" enquired Mickey.

"We've been to the Cotswold Farm Park to look at the rare breeds," replied Jocelyn.

"How exciting," exclaimed PJ, "I'd love to go up there some day. Can't we all pay a visit?"

"Yes, it's possible," replied Damien, "they are not open to the public on Mondays, but I am sure I can arrange something."

Mickey, who knew his children rather better than their Mother did, raised an eyebrow. Something was going on!

In fact, over the past two weeks, following their visit to Stoneleigh, Damien and Jocelyn had visited Rare Breed Farms in the Sherwood Forest in Nottinghamshire, Sandwell in the West Midlands, and in Buckinghamshire, and also had been to the Traditional Breeds Meat Marketing Company at Cirencester to understand the economics of specialist sales and production. Twice during the period they had visited Thomas Louis, who on one occasion had entertained them to lunch with his Merchant Banker as a guest. They had worked hard, and the draft business plan was nearing completion.

"Oh, Damien, can you fix something up – I really would love to see what they do," asked PJ.

"Sure, I'll call them tomorrow," responded Damien.

The following Monday saw something long since forgotten; father, mother and two sons, setting off for a day out together.

The short, but beautiful, drive took them through Bourton-on-the-Water, through the Slaughters, Upper and Lower, thence through Guiting Power to the Cotswold Farm Park. The National Chairman of the RBST, in view of the importance of the visitors, had driven over from Warwickshire and was waiting for them with the Park Managers.

"Damien, Jocelyn, how lovely to see you again," was the warm greeting from the Chairman, with similar warmth from the local management.

"Lord and Lady Ludcolmbe, it is an honour and pleasure to welcome you here. Your fantastic sons are well known to us, but it is a delight to meet their parents."

Mickey took an opportunity to whisper in his wife's ear, "What the blue blazes are the young buggers up to?!"

The 14th Earl got his answer over lunch when the National Chairman turned to him and said;

"We were just so thrilled when we learned that Seagram Hall was planning on becoming a Rare Breeds Farm. As, I am sure Damien and Jocelyn told you, we at the Trust will provide one hundred per cent support and advice to get the venture going."

Lord Ludcolmbe did not let his sons down and merely replied;

"We still have a long way to go with all the boring stuff like preparing business plans."

"Actually, Dad, we haven't had chance to tell you, but the draft business plan is actually being typed out by Libby today. We can all start going through it together tomorrow morning," interjected Damien.

Despite a slight sense of irritation that he knew nothing about all of this, Mickey's main feelings were of pride that his two sons had shown such great initiative, and he treated the whole table to a beaming smile, and replied,

"I am most impressed with everything you are doing up here, and whilst I am not as knowledgeable as the boys, I give the venture my full support – providing the business plan stacks up tomorrow."

The remainder of the visit was seeing the various visitor attractions, and even PJ reverted to her previous career skills learned in France and Scotland, and asked many pertinent questions about catering, conferences and hospitality generally.

It is true of the majority of communities in England, both rural and inner city "villages", that the lifespan of a scandal bears no relationship to its seriousness. In fact it may be proven, by a highly funded university research project, that the less serious the scandal, the longer it lingers in the public arena; maybe the next Tech College to receive University Status (Nether Wapping?) should apply for European Funding to establish PhD Courses on Gossip and Scandal.

Ashthorpe Magna could be considered archetypal. Drugs and alcohol at the Town Hall Disco, the affair between Lauren and Melvyn, Sonia's pregnancy, the Bailiff's vendetta with the Mayor, Rosie kicking out Firtle, but no – the erection of the stainless steel, sheep trough, urinal became the talk of the county!

The English believe that it is our neighbours, the French, who are obsessed with matters lavatorial, but is this really so? Are we so different? The argument in favour of a Gallic obsession would probably be based on a book, written by Gabriel Chevallier in the 1920s, called *Clochemerle*. It was later, in 1951, published by Penguin in England, and subsequently reprinted on many occasions, but its finest hour came with a highly acclaimed BBC television series based on the book. What was it about? A lavatory. A urinal. A pissoir.

It is probably best summed up by the introduction to the 1957 Penguin paperback version, published in association with Secker and Warburg;

"The story of Clochemerle has been the rage of France for many years, both as a novel and as a film. It is a candid, uninhibited comedy of the goings-on in a small provincial town, and of the fantastic feuds which developed from the decision to erect a public convenience near the parish church."

All except the unfortunate Freemasons, Rosie den Bosch, Firtle and poor grumpy old George who seemed to bear some of the responsibility merely for having helped, seemed fascinated by the new Gents! As the story spread other publicans found many different excuses to visit the Old Bull, and as they spread the story even wider complete strangers would arrive at the bar, order a drink, and retire to the toilet in almost indecent haste.

Rosie was becoming used to the question when she was out and about, even as far away as the Cash and Carry in Swindon.

"How's the new urinal, Rosie?!" She never answered.

Nobody knew when the reporter came to the Old Bull, complete with camera. For years the reporters, and even photographers, for the *Ashthorpe Gazette* had been young, and often attractive, ladies. The Editor of the paper, which was also the *Cirencester Gazette*, lived between Ashthorpe and Cirencester, and as was his wont, a few days after the installation of the sheep trough, he had called in at his local on the way home. The story of the urinal and the Freemasons' shoes was the number one topic of conversation. As always, the story became embellished with each retelling, and the latest version was that the Masons were actually wearing their aprons and regalia, which they never did after their Lodge Meeting in the Town Hall, and these valuable items of ceremonial dress were ruined by the trough.

This was such an unusual story that it could not be missed. The Editor, Tim Kinshin, was himself a fairly senior Mason, being an officer in several Masonic Orders, and he was all too aware of the somewhat ambivalent attitude of non-Masonic public to the men in dark suits, carrying black bags, who in late afternoons up and down the country, marched down the streets of cities, towns and villages to their lodge meetings. Some of these, in larger centres, are held in dedicated buildings, Masonic Halls, where the Inner Temples are a permanent fixture, but many thousands of Lodges meet in public places, such as Hotels, Restaurants, Town Halls and even disused back rooms of pubs, and unload the necessary furniture and regalia prior to each meeting. The one identical feature is that whenever a meeting has been opened, the outer door is locked and guarded by both an inner and outer guard to ensure that none but a Mason can enter.

The dark suits, and black bags, give the impression that they are a fairly humourless bunch, but this had never been the case. The members are ordinary members of the public, with the common objective of charity, fraternity and traditional ceremony, and it would certainly be unfair and untrue to describe them as humourless. Even Tim, a Grand Lodge Officer with many senior posts in various types of lodge, howled with laughter at the prospect of a row of Brethren lined up against the stainless steel urinal, gaze averted to the heavens (to the Great Architect in the Sky?), and peeing on their polished black shoes!

Tim was certain that the incident should be reported; with so much interest, for whatever reason, being shown in the urinal, it would be going against his journalistic instinct and duty not to do so! His paper had a new, young reporter, who only the month before had become the lowest rank of Craft Mason, an Entered Apprentice, as Tim wanted to be certain that any article, however amusing, should not actually mock the Masons, but merely show them as a group who could laugh at themselves, he called young David Norman into his office.

"Dave, do you know of this story of the loo at the Old Bull at Ashthorpe?" asked the charismatic Editor.

"Yes, Tim, and I'm sorry, but I thought it was bloody hilarious!" the new boy responded.

"Don't be sorry, so did I, so did I… but how best to make the story?"

"We'll need a photograph," said David.

"Yes, but we can't get or use one with half a dozen Masons lined up having a pee!"

"Listen, boss, next Sunday the Court Leet are having a parade, I think it's some sort of Town Criers' Competition, and they always finish the parade at the Old Bull," suggested the young reporter.

The Editor thought for a few moments, and replied,

"I'd rather make fun of that pompous idiot, the Bailiff, especially after the fiasco with the music evening at the Town Hall where we got egg on our faces by supporting him. OK, Dave, it's all yours. See what you can get."

As the Parade was due to finish at 12.30, ten minutes in advance David Norman was ensconced in the pub, looking as casual as possible and a tiny, but powerful, digital camera tucked away in his pocket. The parade ended, and true to form there was a rush for the toilets before the Court Leet Officers gathered in the bar. Just before, Dave had seen through the window that they were coming, and dashed down to the toilet and into the one WC cubicle. Seconds later the Officers arrived.

Giving them a couple of minutes, Dave came out of the cubicle and casually headed towards the washbasin, camera secreted in the palm of his hand.

The opportunity could not have been more perfect. As he came out, there were seven Officers lined up at the trough, robes raised to enable access to their zips and members, and all looking to the ceiling. Two clicks of the camera, and Dave returned to the bar. He had a surreptitious glance at the images – they were perfect. It was obvious what was happening, but nothing of a pornographic nature was revealed.

The headlines of the *Ashthorpe Gazette* next week read:

TOWN IN UPROAR OVER NEW URINAL

The Court Leet of Ashthorpe Magna put in a violent complaint to the landlady of the Old Bull about the design of the new stainless steel urinal in the Gents Toilets.

So the story continued, well written and thoroughly amusing. Tim was delighted with the work produced by his young staff member, who himself was relieved to have seen and photographed the incident without anybody recognising him.

Ashthorpe Magna, for years a backwater in national affairs, for the second time in a matter of weeks, attracted interest from far afield.

A National Tabloid, the one that had shown such interest in the Town Hall disco scandal, carried Dave's photograph of the Officers lined up, and the wonderful headline:

GETTING THEIR OWN BACK

Even the satirical, political French newspaper, *Le Canard*, carried the story, and the photograph. They never missed an opportunity to make fun of "*Les Rosbifs*" and on this occasion they went to town, even likening Ashthorpe Magna to *Clochemerle-en-Beaujolais*. The amazing thing was that in the months to come French visitors were, for the first time in the memory of most, seen looking around the Cotswold town. The power of the pissoir in the French mind!

George's Corner

"I cannot believe that when George was still married, he claimed that his wife had lost two stones when swimming. He was fed up because he thought that he had tied them on securely enough!"

"Look, that old scrooge, Titus, is back in and limping! Apparently he found a packet of corn plasters on the pavement, so went out deliberately to buy a small pair of shoes."

Chapter 8

Ashthorpe High Street, from the viewpoint of a window cleaner, is rather like the Forth Bridge. As soon as it is finished, it is time to start again. Although on occasions, modern, slick, quick and professional window cleaning companies from one of the larger towns had tried to muscle in on the Ashthorpe Magna business, in fact, only two window cleaners had maintained the round for over half a century.

Tommy Jones had been born in Ashthorpe shortly after the First World War, and had been brought up as best as possible by his impoverished mother in the building which, until as late as the 1930s, was the local workhouse, and was now old folks accommodation. He told tales of his upbringing, both funny and sad, which seem to be impossible in the 20th Century, and the wild young man was only too pleased to be called up for Army service in 1939. Tommy was not the brightest of candidates and ended up with the Army's builders, the Pioneer Corps, in which he served for nearly seven years.

His almost uncontrollable temper led him into regular scrapes, and he spent nearly as much time in the "glass house" as he did playing at being a soldier. Largely for this reason, he was never sent to the field of battle, and spent all of his war in England. After his de-mob he had a series of labouring jobs, including, for one short period, work on the forestry section at Seagram Hall, but inevitably he would row with his supervisor or foreman, end up in a scrap, and getting fired! It did not help matters that his evenings were spent drinking in a number of local establishments, and, during the walk home at night to his council studio, shouting at passers-by! Perhaps, even worse, his envy for what he imagined to be wealthy people, (probably by his standards they were), manifested itself in a hatred of motorcars. In his cups he would see vehicles as some sort of dragon sent to oppress the poor, and in his befuddled state he would attack the enemy with sticks, stones or whatever else he could get his hands on! Rather like his Army career, this meant that he spent much time in the Magistrates' Court, and many nights in police custody, which he enjoyed for the warmth and the cooked breakfast!

Despite his failings, when he was sober, Tommy was a popular local character and liked by most of the residents who would pass the time of day with him. He was little, scruffy and always looked somewhat grubby! It was the Rector, he of baggy shorts fame, who decided it was his duty to try and help Tommy:

"Tommy, you can't go on like this. We must find something for you to do." The priest almost pleaded.

"Yes but, Padre, what can I do? I can't really read and write, and I always end up with problems when I work for somebody else," replied Tommy.

"Surely then, the answer is to find something you can do for yourself so you are not answerable to a boss," said the kindly Rector of St Osmund's.

For several weeks they spoke together, and every suggestion was met with an excuse as to why it was not possible.

Then the Priest experienced an almost Damascene moment:

"WINDOW CLEANER!" he shouted with an air of triumph.

"WHAT?" said Tommy.

"A window cleaner; you could set up a window cleaning round."

"Yes, but I'd need a trolley of some sort, buckets, leathers and ladders! Do you know how much all that would cost?" he asked.

"Leave that to me, but would you do it, and promise to do it properly?" the Rector enquired.

Tommy thought long and hard, and eventually answered in the affirmative.

True to his word, the Rector visited the Social Security Department, to whom Tommy was a well-known case, and they discussed the idea in detail. In the end, the Manager was brought in, and they all agreed that if, by giving Tommy a small grant to get his equipment, they could reduce the problems he caused, everybody, including Tommy would benefit. It was within the remit of the local Manager to make an ex-gratia payment of up to £25, a reasonable sum in those days, and he agreed to do this providing the Rector would take, and spend, the money on Tommy's behalf. Nobody felt Tommy could be trusted not to spend it on alcohol if the payment were not supervised in this way.

The first item, a trolley of some sort, was in fact free, as an elderly parishioner remembered that at the back of her shed was an ancient ice cream cart, the sort familiar throughout the country between the wars as a "Stop Me and Buy One". The vicar took this to Tommy, who proceeded to restore it, and alter it so that the window cleaning equipment could be in the front box, originally used to keep ice creams cold, and the ladder attached to one side allowing enough space to pedal the cycle part which pushed the box. With one large wheel at the back, and two smaller wheels under the box, the whole was a fairly stable form of transport.

To everyone's amazement, Tommy took to the task with great enthusiasm, and within two weeks he had a gleaming, virtually new window cleaner's trolley complete with a sparkling new bell the Rector had purchased with the balance of the grant. A young Welsh singer had, at that time, started to become very popular in Britain, one Tom Jones, and

Tommy, displaying hitherto hidden sign-writing skills, painted the words along the side of his machine:

Tom Jones. Your Swinging Window Cleaner

The machine he referred to as "the company van", and from that moment on he never again attacked another car!

The Rector had purchased absolutely everything he needed, and Tommy had found an old, large pair of Wellington boots, which he cut off at the ankles to enable him to slip them over his shoes to keep his feet dry. This footwear became his trademark!

Tommy never made a fortune on his round, for in fact he was far too slow. At each customer the first question was:

"Have you got a cuppa, Mrs?" which led to a 20-minute chat before the ladder went up. Even then, if he spotted somebody he knew as he was climbing the ladder, he would scurry down again for another chat.

His drinking, other than on Saturday nights, descended to reasonable proportions. His custom on Saturdays was to sink as many pints as possible, and follow this with a big bag of chips, vinegar, but no salt, which he would consume on the way home. On one particular Saturday, after a session lasting from three in the afternoon until ten at night, he was clearly the worse for wear in the chippie, and on being served threw the bag of chips all over the shop and stomped out. The owner was furious, and indeed spent a great deal of time clearing up the mess, including scraping chips off the wall.

The following Saturday Tommy, as usual, ordered his bag of chips. The owner could not believe his eyes;

"You've got a bloody cheek, Tommy. Can't you remember what you did last Saturday?"

Tommy looked him between the eyes and quietly responded,

"But, you put salt on!"

The whole situation was so ludicrous that the owner burst out laughing, served Tommy anyway, and life went on.

Indeed life for Tommy in Ashthorpe Magna went on with little change until he was taken ill over 25 years later, and eventually put into a nearby hospice. A friendly local farmer had taken away Tommy's "company van", and agreed to store it carefully in his barn. The next time it was seen was at Tommy's funeral where it led the coffin, the Rector and a large number of mourners into the church. Several times in the years that followed, friends of Tommy had tried to locate the "company van", but without success. It had completely disappeared. Perhaps, if there is a special place for window cleaners, then they can take their "company vans" with them?

For the latter part of the 20th Century, Tommy's place was taken by Bryn O'Dell, a very different character, but equally an eccentric. It seemed that Bryn had started his adult life at a major Art School in London, and his works showed a very high level of artistic talent especially with still life and portraiture. His problem was, partly that he only painted what he liked rather than what the public required, but also, that he was so desperately shy he was almost incapable of promoting himself or his works. Although in the last few years of his window-cleaning career, he had had a series of ailments, and was unable to do the upper floors of the High Street, he lost no customers. His charges, and therefore income, came down to recompense for the single level cleaning, but his customers did not have the heart to dispense with his services.

Bryn had successfully replaced Tommy as the Ashthorpe Magna window cleaner but years after Tommy's death the scruffy little man, his cut-down Wellingtons and his "company van", were all remembered with great affection.

Anybody involved with breeding or training horses, in any way, will agree that the successful birth of a new foal is an exciting, and almost miraculous occasion. Paddy Black, the

Head Boy at one of the most prestigious stables in Newmarket, had seen hundreds of such births during his 25-year career, firstly as a 15-year-old stable lad fresh in from Kerry in South-West Ireland, and for the last ten years as Head Lad at Sir Guy's stables.

As the beautiful, black, glistening, male foal emerged from the mare, Paddy realised that here was something very special. The Hermit, for that is what Sir Guy had decided to name the foal, for historical reasons, was to affect Paddy's life in a most amazing way.

With millions of pounds, swilling around as cash in the system, and spent throughout the year in the horse racing industry, it was perhaps inevitable that the crooked elements in life were attracted to its fringes. Gambling stables, of which Sir Guy's was definitely not one, bent bookies, dodgy jockeys, Far Eastern gambling syndicates and money launderers were all to be found at race tracks up and down the country. The criminal elements were attracted not only to the major venues such as Epsom, Newmarket and Cheltenham, but also to the less famous tracks such as Wincanton, Towcester and Stratford-upon-Avon. Although Sir Guy, as a member of the Jockey Club, was both publicly and privately vociferously against any form of corruption, his Head Lad, Paddy, as a lowly paid member of staff, was not quite so clean. Over the years he had done little, but well paid, favours for the criminal community and had amassed a considerable hoard of cash in many small accounts, never holding more than £2,000 in each. Like so many of his fellow Men of Kerry, what Paddy lacked in intellectual ability, he more than made up for in pure native cunning, and never once did Sir Guy have any inkling that anything even slightly suspicious took place from his yard.

During the first year of The Hermit's life, he was being closely observed by both the Trainer and his Head Lad, and they were both in total agreement that here was a horse with the greatest potential either man had ever seen. On that basis

Sir Guy entered the yearling in a number of major races over a year in advance, including the Tote Ebor, and the bookies started to offer huge odds on the unknown entry. This was the opportunity Paddy had been seeking, and he started off on a campaign of ante-post betting, never more than £500 with one bookie, nor with bookies anywhere near Newmarket, and never more than one bookie in a town. On the first ten bets he received the staggering odds of 500–1!

Soon the bookies realised that something was happening, as not only was Paddy's considerable money being invested, but his crooked partners were also betting heavily on The Hermit. The odds, still far in advance on an unknown horse, quickly tumbled, and eventually, despite all the stable's efforts at secrecy, those shady experts employed by the bookies, the Gallop Watchers, reported back on this wonderful new horse. The odds fell to 10–1, and fell even further on the day of the race with The Hermit starting his first race as the third favourite. March had been a wet month leaving the track with fairly soft going, which suited the youthful muscular limbs of The Hermit, and even the most inexperienced punters on the course were impressed by the star newcomer.

It was not an exciting race, even for a Classic, and The Hermit, despite his inexperience, came out of the stalls like a rocket, settled into an early lead, and remained there until he crossed the finishing line. Paddy's dream, of owning his own stables, became a reality, and although he handed in his notice to Sir Guy, he did stay on for three months with his old mentor, until the new Head Lad was ready to take over the post.

Paddy had, at the suggestion of one of his less than salubrious friends, deposited his winnings with a South African bank in London, and he visited the capital for a meeting with a small group interested in investing in a new training stable. Whilst the others continually referred to the venture as "Paddy's Stables", the Man of Kerry did not seem to realise that, as he was only to have 49% of the company for his £490,000 investment, he would actually not have a controlling vote. They showed him the details of a rather run-down farm near somewhere called Ashthorpe Magna, which was within the total budget, and they all set off the following day for Gloucestershire.

The farm was about 3 miles out of the town, just past the vineyard on the other side of the road. Whilst the house was rather modest, it was adequate for Paddy and his wife, and the buildings were ideal for conversion to stables. Mary, Paddy's wife of some 10 years standing, was not that interested in horses, but having been brought up on a farm, also in Kerry, she loved growing vegetables, and was delighted with the new prospect opening up to her.

Paddy was dressed in the gear he felt most suitable for a trainer; heavy Harris Tweed checks, check Viyella shirt, knitted woollen tie, brown brogues and a red spotted handkerchief dangling from his breast pocket. A brown trilby hat on top of his thinning sandy hair, and even his ruddy, weather-beaten face fitted the overall picture. A permanent fixture was a cigarette permanently clamped between his lips.

Within weeks a deal was struck, and refurbishment of the farm buildings to accommodate some 20 horses commenced, along with provision of the gallops, which are such an important part of the training regime. Between the group, they were able to provide the requisite 20 horses required for Paddy to apply to the Jockey Club for a training licence. As he had no police record of any sort, had 20 horses under training, and probably as he had worked for Sir Guy for such a long period, the licence was readily granted. The first months were somewhat hit-and-miss, with only very occasional successes both on the flat and National Hunt, but eventually, with a great deal of advice from his backers, Paddy learned the tricks of keeping back more promising horses, and letting outsiders win. The betting department at the Jockey Club were a little concerned at unusual betting patterns exhibited when Ashthorpe Stud horses were racing, but nothing concrete could be identified.

The swarthy visitor to the stables, a tall Afrikaner, was to be the first indication of something sinister. Although he travelled on a Zimbabwean Passport in the name of Mills, he was referred to as the "Needle Man". Paddy learned that he was in fact a top pharmaceutical chemist from Cape Town, who had been banned from his profession in South Africa for devising drugs for doping horses. For all Paddy's faults, he loved horses dearly, and was very much against this activity, but he was shouted down by his partners;

"Paddy, if you want to keep your bloody stables, you will do whatever the Needle Man tells you!"

"Why the focking hell should I; it will damage the horses," came the response in a thick Irish brogue.

"You have no choice, Paddy."

The Jockey Club became more and more interested in the Ashthorpe Stud, and could prove nothing despite horses winning races as outsiders, backed to lower odds on their next outing, and losing. Several times they called for dope tests, but could find nothing. Despite an extensive list of prohibited drugs, the samples taken at the racecourses were sent back to the Equine Research Centre at Newmarket for testing, but still nothing showed up. The Needle Man had done his job well, and the backers were making a fortune. During the next two years things went well for the group, and the number of horses under training increased to 30, but Paddy was increasingly under instruction from his shady partners. Whilst he, as the trainer, had to send off the race entries to Wetherby's, he was always told where to place each and every horse. The stables became a very unhappy place to work, and such was the secrecy required that the stable lads and girls were all housed on site, and were provided with a small bar and social area as they were banned from socialising in Ashthorpe Magna.

The Needle Man was a regular visitor, too regular in Paddy's estimation, and the Irishman constantly questioned him;

"Why the fock are you doing this, the horse can win anyway!"

"Paddy, the bosses want a guarantee, I can provide this," was the reply from the sinister South African.

Paddy tried to explain that he was becoming worried about the condition of the horses, and although he could not explain scientifically, his experience told him that far too many of his charges were developing infections, usually of the upper respiratory tract, which led him to believe that their immune systems were breaking down.

Paddy confided in his wife, Mary, who flew into a mammoth rage. She, like most of the stable residents, felt more like internees, and hated Ashthorpe Magna. On occasional visits to the town shops, the occupants of Ashthorpe Stud were treated like some form of alien. They were generally very short of stature, ruddy complexioned and the majority spoke with a thick Irish accent, and really did stand out as being very different. The only reason that Mary did not leave her husband there and then was that her vegetable gardens were doing well, and she was looking forward to stretching her limited budget by selling her produce at the Farmers' Market.

The stable jockey, Bertie Devlin, was equally worried, and like his trainer, his major concern was for the welfare of the horses.

"What the fock can we do to get out of this, Paddy?"

"Notting I can tink of," was Paddy's depressed reply. "I checked the agreement with the partners, and it seems that I can only sell my share of the stud with their agreement – and they don't!"

Paddy and Bertie spent long nights discussing the situation, becoming more and more depressed, and sinking voluminous quantities of Irish Whiskey brought in, usually in horse-boxes, direct from a small distillery in Kerry.

The whole dream came tumbling down at the last major race of the flat season, the Caesarowitch, at which Ashthorpe Lad, the stable number one horse, ridden by Bertie, was the favourite. As always, the beautiful black stallion, half brother to The Hermit, was first out of the stalls, but unusually had to be ridden very hard to maintain a position in the field from which he could win. Bertie Devlin hated strong use of the whip, especially on Ashthorpe Lad, but on this occasion, for the first time, he had to really fight to achieve a short head victory. The race goers were ecstatic, until a couple of hundred yards past the winning post Ashthorpe Lad stumbled and fell. Soon the race officials, and the course veterinary surgeon, were on the scene and a blue plastic screen was raised around the poor animal.

Eventually the dreaded announcement was made; Ashthorpe Lad was dead, but as there was no immediate evidence of wrongdoing, the win was allowed to stand.

The heavens opened. The horse's body was taken away for autopsy, and the Jockey Club, having again noticed unusual betting patterns, called for a full enquiry. In the meantime they closed Ashthorpe Stud.

Paddy and Bertie were absolutely distraught, and each morning they telephoned Newmarket to see if the test results were through, but the first indication came when two veterinary surgeons arrived at the stables to test all the other horses. The cause of death was declared as a rare virus, which could only have been exacerbated by the misuse of an unknown drug, and as, by now, the Jockey Club had identified gambling winnings well in excess of £1 million by the partners, the Police Fraud Squad was called in. Mary's sister, Colleen, arrived from Ireland via Bristol, packed her sister's cases and confronted Paddy;

"Paddy Black, you're focking mad to have been mixed up with that bunch of crooks. You'll end up doing time for this, and I'm getting Mary away from all your rotten dealings."

Colleen was a horse lover, and she twisted the final knife in the wound, "The Hermit would be alive, and winning, today if you had not been so focking greedy."

Mary and Colleen departed, and despite Paddy's shock and disappointment, the whole situation did not sink in. There were just too many people around; police, Jockey Club, veterinary surgeons and perhaps worst, BBC Panorama to make a programme on unscrupulous racing trainers. The bent partners seemed to have disappeared, and despite full co-operation with the Fraud Squad, handing over all contact details, agreements and bank accounts, there was no sign of anybody, particularly the Needle Man.

The greatest shock followed a night of drowning sorrows. Bertie Devlin was found next morning hanging from the beam of the food store, stone cold dead. Paddy's world had truly collapsed.

The Coroner's Court was a sombre affair, and eventually Bertie's body was released and shipped back to Ireland for burial. Paddy pleaded with the police to be able to go back to Ireland with the body, and stay for the funeral, but permission was refused.

The Hermit, and the other horses, were to exact their revenge, and on the day of the funeral in Kerry, Paddy Black was admitted into Cirencester Hospital with a serious chest infection. Over the next few days his breathing declined, his limbs became weak and his heart began to beat at far too high a rate. He was transferred by ambulance to Queen Elizabeth's Hospital in Birmingham, and later he died. The cause was a rare virus that could be transmitted from horses to human beings.

Carole Lamb was the Vice-Chairman of the Ashthorpe Magna Chamber of Trade and Commerce, and she owned a well-established gift shop just off the High Street. An attractive lady, perhaps in her early to mid forties, she had split up with her husband about a year earlier, if there was any criticism to be made, it was probably that her dress sense was more applicable for a younger woman in her twenties!

It was always suggested, that her main reason for her enthusiasm in the Chamber, was the attraction of the Chairman, Melvyn Hughes, and the fact that he was a single man. Indeed it was suggested, without any real proof, that for several months she was actually having an affair with Melvyn, although this rumour ceased when Lauren took over as the Chairman of the Farmers' Market. To say that Carole was disappointed was a total understatement, and people were quietly laughing behind her back at her discomfort. When she learned of the Sonia incident, if the fathering of a child can be called something as trivial as an incident, Carole was almost in tears each occasion she met with Melvyn. This made the weekly Chamber meetings somewhat uncomfortable, but Melvyn stuck to his guns and carried on as if nothing had happened.

"This week is the first Farmers' Market, and I think it is important that the Chamber is seen to support the venture. I have posters, and would be grateful if as many of you as possible could put them on your windows and notice boards to try and encourage visitors," the Chairman proclaimed.

There was a general agreement, except for Carole who continued to stare at her notebook!

"We know that Dave Lounds, the Witches of Upper Church Street and the Bailiff are planning some sort of demonstration against the market, and we must do everything possible to keep the media away from them." Melvyn continued, "We also know that the Mayor and Town Council, the Rector, half the Court Leet, the Chamber, the Ludcolmbes and even the Vineyard are all supporting the market. Despite all the wretched Charity Shops who seem to be taking away so much business, we must show the region that Ashthorpe Magna is a great place to both shop, and undertake business," Melvyn explained.

"But, what's wrong with the Charity Shops?" asked the butcher.

Carole stepped in to answer, "They were fine when they were selling second-hand goods donated by their supporters. Ninety per cent of their goods are now brand new, and mainly from China. Because they rely heavily on volunteer shop workers, and they get a rebate from the District Council on their business rates, we cannot compete on prices with them."

"All we can do to compete with this, is to build up business in the town for conventional shops, and gradually reduce the numbers of Charity Shops," answered the Chairman.

In the end, they agreed to put up posters wherever possible, and for as many members as were able, to attend the opening ceremony.

In the meantime, somewhat surreptitiously, Dave Lounds was giving out the placards to the witches!

Damien and Jocelyn, after their early introductions to the Rare Breeds Survival Trust, worked hard and enthusiastically to set up the Farm Park. They both worked as builders to build the arcs in the field to house the breeding pigs, the enclosures for the cattle and sheep, and fox-proof pens for the rare breed chickens. One of the locals had suggested that the finest protection against foxes was a llama! Somewhat unconvinced, the brothers decided to go ahead and buy one anyway as it would certainly look unusual in the Gloucestershire countryside regardless of foxes! At every stage, the brothers tried to give their buildings, however utilitarian, a rustic look and as they neared completion they certainly achieved the desired effect. In fact, most of the buildings were made from timber from the estate, and compared with many others on the market looked of a very high quality, good design and excellent materials. Jocelyn really did seem to have found a niche, which would stand him in excellent stead for years to come.

As a starting point for any catering venture, they erected a log cabin to serve teas, coffees, cold drinks and snacks to the hoped-for hoards! The same flair that they found for the agricultural shelters, they put into the design of the cabin which they named "Uncle Tom's".

"Hey, Damien, your chum, Sir Thomas, will think we've named it after him!"

"Why not? We can get him to open it, and hope that he brings his merchant banker, Patrice Finville, with him. We are going to need both those guys," replied Damien rather eagerly.

Although Damien had given the responsibility of the Farm Park to Jocelyn, they both scoured the advertisements, visited Rare Breed Sales and numerous Rare Breed breeders to establish the livestock on the embryo park. They had made a conscious decision, advised by the RBST, to stock a mixture of breeds falling into different categories; critical, endangered, vulnerable and just traditional; and initially they had decided not to stock horses, donkeys or goats.

The first of the livestock started to arrive, and both the boys, and their parents, were most excited when they travelled to Honeybourne to collect the first of the hens for the new enterprise. They had selected six pullets and one cock of the Old English Pheasant Fowl variety (critical), the same numbers of the wonderful Scots Dumpy breed (vulnerable) and a last minute impulse purchase of four hens and one cock of Bantam Silkies, which were really purchased for their fluffy, white "boots"! By the end of the day they were all firmly established in their individual pens and coops, and within an hour they were blessed with a little Scots Dumpy egg!

"Well, it's a start, Damien," the younger brother excitedly laughed.

During the following weeks the ginger-haired Tamworth weaners arrived (endangered), joined shortly later by a small herd of the traditional, local Gloucester Old Spot breed they had purchased as a job lot from a farm sale. Jocelyn had rather more difficulty in getting them settled into their new living quarters, and had to effect many repairs and alterations to the fencing which was under a constant burrowing attack from the snouts! Within a total of three months the Gloucester (vulnerable) and Red Poll (at risk) cattle had arrived, along with the Hebridean rare breed sheep, the North Ronaldsay (critical), and the Soay (vulnerable). The Scottish sheep, even though very small in stature, needed increased fencing height due to their remarkable skills at flying through the air! The final sheep was the larger, but much more cumbrous, traditional Cotswold variety that had brought so much wealth to the area throughout the Middle Ages.

About one month before the following Easter the sign appeared at the front entrance lodge:

SEAGRAM HALL FARM PARK OPENING EASTER

RARE BREEDS CATTLE, SHEEP, PIGS AND POULTRY

UNCLE TOM'S CABIN – REFRESHMENTS

On Easter Saturday the Farm Park was opened by Sir Thomas Louis Bt, who was indeed accompanied by Patrice Finville, and the media turned out in force. The cars queued to enter the drive, all happily paying £5 per car entry fee, and they ate and drank Uncle Tom's Cabin dry causing PJ, who was still at home, to rush off to the Cash and Carry for more supplies for Easter Sunday and Bank Holiday Monday.

Even Nick and Mary Darling arrived from the Ashthorpe Court to wish them all luck.

"Just checking out the opposition," joked Nick, but his wife added,

"Not really. It will be a great help to us all; the more tourists we have in the area the better for us all."

Seagram Hall Farm Park, the first part of the restoration process for the Ludcolmbe family and their home, was firmly on the map.

George's Corner

"Well, well! Fancy old George finding a girlfriend – he says he enjoys going to bed with a woman he doesn't have to inflate!"

"Did you know, on top of everything else, the poor old bugger is colour-blind! He can't tell the difference between red and blue and once walked into a police station instead of a brothel."

"At school, George was teacher's pet – she kept him in a cage at the back of the class."

Chapter 9

There was no real reason for the Farmers' Market Committee meeting, in the Old Bull, the night before the event. Lauren was right, however, in assuming that her committee would be suffering from a level of nervous anticipation, and every detail, already planned meticulously, was gone into again, and again, and…

The official opening was due at 09.00, but the committee agreed to be there from about 07.00 to ensure that everything was in place when the stalls and Farmers arrived. At the end of the meeting they distributed, for the third time, leaflets under car windscreen wipers around the Town Hall, asking people not to park there on Farmers' Market Day after 07.00 that morning.

The morning was warm, bright and sunny, in fact everything for which they had hoped. Only six cars had been left in the designated area; two belonging to the Witches of Upper Church Street, two to Dave Lounds and his wife, one which looked as though it had been there for weeks, and one which was finally removed by a rather dishevelled young lady who offered her embarrassed apologies. Despite the deliberate nuisance value from cars parked in the most difficult places, the 20 stands were set up, working around the offending vehicles, and the produce loaded onto the stalls. The farmers' vehicles were driven round to their allocated places at the Council Chambers for the remainder of the day.

Mickey Carruthers, his wife PJ, and their two sons arrived at the designated area, walked round introducing themselves to the farmers, including Mary Darling from Ashthorpe Vineyard, who, of course they all knew, and they awaited the procession.

At the other end of town the procession gathered in the Post Office car park, and Lauren managed to get them more or less in the pre-arranged order. First Rory on the pipes, then

The Mayor and Town Clerk in their ill fitting robes, Lauren and Melvyn behind them, followed by the majority of the members of the Town Council. Behind them came, true to their promise, nine of the Court Leet Officers with the wily Marshall, Ray Spicer, leading his group, uniform and united in their town blazers, ahead of representatives of various local organisations, and finally the Morris Men playing their accordion and drums far enough behind the piper as not to confuse the sounds.

The Junior School, High School and Catholic School had all allowed staff and pupils to start assembly late so they could see the parade, and the Farmers' Market. Interestingly the vogue for teaching the subjects of environment and ecology had created a situation where, at all levels, students were using the market as an example to do a school project showing the benefits of fresh local produce and lack of food miles. Certainly Ashthorpe Magna, and more importantly the outlying villages and small towns, had turned out in force to see the parade. They were certainly not disappointed. It was colourful, noisy, enjoyable and an archetypal English country-town scene.

The parade processed up the High Street, applauded by children and adults alike, until they swept around the bend into Upper Church Street, and into view, clutching the placards provided by Dave Lounds on behalf of the Bailiff, came the three Witches of Upper Church Street; the fourth had decided not to join in. Rory almost spluttered into the chanter of his bagpipes as he saw them in front; it was not fear or hesitation, but merely deep amusement at the sight. These most unattractive women were all dressed in a similar fashion, and wore, despite the warmth of the day, faded pink or beige topcoats almost of an anorak style. Several people took photographs of them, and as the large parade gradually passed the women, everybody turned to look, and to laugh! This was the protest; once more the Bailiff, his Reeve and the self-interested Dave Lounds had failed.

The Press and local Radio were all waiting in the area at which the Earl of Ludcolmbe and his family stood, and they missed the protest. The Mayor and his clerk beamed as Mickey Carruthers praised them as a Council, the Chamber of Trade and Commerce and, of course, Lauren le Noir, for creating the first Farmers' Market in Ashthorpe Magna. As always the short opening speech was amusing and concise, but the real stars were the farmers. The 20 stalls, with their colourful blue and white striped canopies, looked resplendent, and even the air was scented by the "bap" stand cooking organic, free-range local pork, sausages and bacon served on home-made baps. Already that stand had a long queue, which seemed to remain for the next five hours.

The vegetable stalls, their produce picked on the previous evening, displayed fresh, healthy-looking wares a million miles away from the insipid, lank, uniform-shaped goods offered by supermarkets. Everything seemed to be available, a huge variety of locally produced cheeses, free-range chickens, ducks and eggs, a variety of plants, home-made jams and honey of every conceivable flavour, samples from a new micro-brewery, and, of course, the Ashthorpe Wines. The only slight sadness was the bare stand booked and paid for by Mary Black at the now closed Ashthorpe Stud.

The committee and supporters were delighted, the protestors crestfallen. It could not have been a better start.

Ashthorpe Gazette

SPECTACULAR SUCCESS FOR THE FARMERS' MARKET

The 14th Earl of Ludcolmbe opened the new Ashthorpe Magna Farmers' Market in a blaze of colour and pageantry. A piper, Morris Dancers, Council Members in robes and representatives of many organisations gathered together for the opening of the first market in Ashthorpe since the 19th Century. The Town Hall area is reputed to have been the site of markets since Anglo-Saxon times, and the bright and sunny scene showed that the confidence shown in bringing it back is well placed. It was a wonderful occasion enjoyed by all.

The first two pages of the newspaper carried several colour photographs of the parade, the ceremony and a number of stalls with local dignitaries such as the Earl, Lauren and the Mayor buying produce. Unfortunately for the calm of the Bailiff, the shot of the parade on the front page clearly showed the Court Leet Officers in blazers, which Andy had not previously heard about, with the Marshall leading the section. To all intents this was an official Court presence, but without the Bailiff, the Reeve or their rather disgruntled supporters, many of whom turned up in a private capacity both to look and to buy!

Lauren noted, with some pleasure, that two of the three witches, minus placards and anoraks, actually visited the market and made purchases. One rather clever stallholder, having recognised them, gave them each a small jar of lavender honey as a gift, which both accepted!

It is not recorded if Andy Gross uttered his, by now oft used, expletive when collecting the *Gazette* from his doormat,

"FARMERS' BLOODY MARKET!"

It is probable!

The problem with many of the buildings in the Old Town of Ashthorpe, is that, whilst they are all in a designated conservation area, and many individual buildings are in fact Grade II Listed, with one having the nightmare of Grade I Listing, only half are individually owned. The remainder predominately belong to four landlords, each with a different perception as to their responsibilities for the condition of the buildings they own.

It is almost possible to identify the owners when walking around the area concerned, and often a smart shop front, will have an unpainted, second, and sometimes third floor where the brickwork is desperately in need of repair. The Ashthorpe Magna Civic Society had spent years fighting with one landlord in particular to try and get him to pay attention to his three major buildings on the High Street he leased out, plus the double fronted building he occupied, but despite their protestations nothing seemed to transpire!

This particular owner, Dick Gowan, third generation of purveyors of drapery and fabrics, was a single man in his mid-sixties, who lived a solitary and frugal life. He certainly was never seen socialising in the area, nor did he ever use his car to leave the area. The rickety wooden garage doors had a variety of vegetation growing over, and through them, suggesting it was months, or perhaps even years, since he had moved his car. Apart from occasional trips to various food stores, a weekly trip to the bank to pay in his takings, and on Sundays, dressed in a once elegant suit, his visit to the Quaker Meeting House at the bottom of the High Street, he was never seen out.

Mr Gowan was generally well liked, and his shop was something of a time capsule taking the visitor – or even customer – to a gentler, more polite age.

"Good Morning, Madam, is there anything I can show you," was the shopkeepers general greeting.

Although Dick wore an old, rather shabby, brown, shop coat, estimates of buildings he owned, in and around Ashthorpe, suggested that he was worth several millions of pounds in property alone. His shop was an Aladdin's cave of stocks, many of which seemed to have been there for years, and people came from miles around to purchase items which had long ceased to be readily available elsewhere. Muslin was high on this list!

Each of the adjacent three High Street properties he owned, and leased out had, for reasons of style, an overhanging solid canopy about a metre wide, presumably to protect the shop windows from rain. Originally they had been covered with felt and bitumen, but this had long since peeled back over the majority of the area, leaving it exposed to the elements, extremely unsightly, and probably dangerous. Ashthorpe Magna, due to its geographical location, rarely experienced harsh weather but the previous year there had been a short, sharp period of frost along with a metre or so of snow, which unusually lay on the ground for two days.

The three shops involved were a Chinese take-away, an Estate Agent and the newsagent, and none were prepared for what happened. Melvyn Hughes saw the whole incident in slow motion from his own shop opposite. Each of the canopies was connected, and Melvyn realised that something was untoward when the snow from the right hand shop started to fall off the end, and that on the left-hand side had moved down to the right. What started slowly increased in momentum, and a loud, rending crack disturbed the quiet bestowed upon the High Street by the thick covering of snow. The laden canopy was gradually tearing away from the wall, and crashing to the ground. An elderly lady, who had been struggling rather unwisely through the snow, was unable to jump out of the way, and was engulfed in snow and rubble.

Melvyn immediately called 999 and asked for Fire and Ambulance to come urgently to Ashthorpe High Street. The traders had all rushed from the warmth of their shops, and were clearing away the covering of the old lady with their bare hands. The sheer numbers of helpers allowed them to work quickly, and by the time the emergency services arrived the victim was fully released from her prison, sitting up and covered in a heavy woollen blanket. She was whisked off to hospital immediately, and despite being in a state of shock, was only kept in hospital for one night.

The three traders were not in the least happy; the Police had arrived, told them to cease trading and cordoned off the area. The following morning was still cold, and the snow still fully around, when the workforce from the District Council arrived.

"Mr Gowan?" enquired the young council official.

"Yes," replied Dick Gowan.

"I have an enforcement order whereby the council are going to make safe the canopies and brickwork to the front of your shops. This will be charged to you. When that is completed, we hope later today, the Conservation Officer will be attending to inform you what requires doing before the shops will be allowed to re-open," the council-man informed him.

His day became worse; a Police Inspector arrived to inform him that he had called for a full report on the accident, and it was possible that further action may be taken due to the danger caused to the public by the state of his buildings.

The Conservation Officer was his final visitor;

"Mr Gowan, we require that the canopies are replaced, identical to the originals, and complying with current Building Regulations."

There was some feeling of relief on the High Street, that at long last Mr Gowan would be forced to repair and make attractive, his properties. Sadly for Ashthorpe Magna, this never actually happened. Dick Gowan was, indeed forced to spend a great deal of money, and lost rental income which the three traders hit by the accident refused to pay for the period they were closed, but at the end of the day, whilst the replacement canopies were done to a safe standard within Building Regulations, Gowan refused to decorate the frontages of his buildings. They were still a blight on the generally very attractive High Street.

Not that all landlords were the same, indeed probably the largest property owner on the High Street, John, known as Jack, Sparrow, pursued improvement on all his properties with a great zeal. The difference between he and Dick

Gowan was that Jack seemed to be a member of every organisation in town! In the past he had been Mayor, President of Rotary, Worshipful Master of the Lodge, and a founder member of the Civic Trust, and whilst he certainly made a considerable income from the leases on his commercial properties, he was always perceived as putting Ashthorpe first. Many thought the difference between the two landlords was sad, for they were both from long established Ashthorpe families, both were third generation shopkeepers in the town, and both were essentially very engaging people. It is most probable that the ethos of Dick Gowan regarded money spent on maintenance as a waste, whereas Jack Sparrow regarded it as protection, and even enhancement, of his investments.

The only lady owner was the feisty widow of a local farmer, who, when she married late in life, let out the property she had previously used as a florist's shop, with a three bed-roomed flat above, realised that this was a good way of making money, and soon swallowed up three more properties coming to market. She fell somewhere between Jack and Dick in terms of maintaining her properties, and while there were times when they could perhaps have done with a lick of paint, in general they were kept in reasonable order.

The one landlord who was disliked by virtually the whole town was Don Plaice, recognised generally as being, at the best, sharp, and by most as a bully. A stocky, muscular little man, he stood at no more than 5 foot 3 inches high, and seemingly the same width! His bulbous eyes were covered by what appeared to be two bottle-end spectacles, and he had grey thinning hair and a ridiculous looking appendage on his chin, supposedly a beard. To make matters worse he wore clothes, so outrageous, that people laughed as he walked by. In the winter, shorts of the type favoured by Adonis-like surfers on Bondi Beach, colourful vests, and perhaps the worst, when the shorts were abandoned, colourful baggy trousers which had the appearance of ill-fitting pyjama pants. This comic appearance was enhanced by a variety of shoes, built up to give him the appearance of more height, known as "stackers" or "platforms", the effect of this type of footwear on his gait was to give him a swaying, rolling motion reminiscent of a feminine drunken sailor!

Like many little men, indeed like many little dogs, Don was aggressive, arrogant and downright unpleasant. The visual effect was worsened by the pebble glasses, and the slight squint caused by childhood strabismus, but the overall effect of meeting the man was amusement, tempered with the veiled threat from his demeanour and personality.

Since he had inherited some money, he had invested in residential letting properties, and unfortunately in the past five years his search for more property had brought him to Ashthorpe Magna. He claimed to have a portfolio throughout the South West Midlands and even into Wales. He was a difficult man both to buy from and to sell to, and to achieve the two letting buildings with which he had ended up, he had bought, over a three-year period, four properties, and subsequently, after a minimal amount of work, sold two for a modest profit. Buying from Don Plaice took all the skills of an Arabian Market trader, with months of dealing, brinkmanship, withdrawals and certainly very suspicious financial wranglings. On his last property sale, the deposit was paid in a series of small bank drafts to a variety of recipients, including his ex wife, two lady friends, a French property developer and a couple of unknown beneficiaries; the buyer supposed all this to be a mixture of tax evasion, coupled with the desire not to pay his ex wife her lawful due from the divorce settlement.

Threats were implied at every stage in his dealings, both buying and selling, and on one occasion he pointed out to a tenant, who he was encouraging to leave before the end of her lease, that in the past when he had problems, as he had with a Chinese Restaurant tenant, he used the services of a tough group from Manchester. This may have been true, he was certainly unpleasant enough, but it may also have been his typical form of bluster and showing off. One thing that was agreed was that Don was certainly a hard worker, and usually recruited the able assistance of one of his girlfriends to avoid using professional tradesmen. What he did not do was spend money unless he was forced. All fittings in his properties were of the cheapest quality, and he paid no regard for any regulations, even planning permission in Grade II Listed buildings, and to avoid the costs involved with replacing rotten windows with hard wood, he ripped out the old items replacing them with ugly, and illegal, UPVC. None of the studio apartments, nor one bed-roomed flats, in his buildings had the necessary items to comply with Fire Regulations, such as extinguishers and fire blankets in the kitchens, and once his tenants got to know him they realised what a shady, unscrupulous character he was.

The second of his buildings had once been an elegant family home, on three stories, with beautiful gardens leading down to the River Dart. One family, the Longvilles, had lived there for many generations, until in the 1970s the last member of the family had died off at the age of 80. Johnnie Longville was a great loss to Ashthorpe Magna; he and his father before him had been, from a very early stage, keen amateur photographers and as Johnnie had no descendants to whom to leave his possessions, the two historic photographic collections were left to Ashworth Civic Trust. Even as a confirmed bachelor, Johnnie had played an active part in every aspect of the town's social, civic and charitable life, including a period as Mayor, and shortly after the war a spell as Bailiff. Not only did he leave the wonderful collection of photographs, but his friend, Jack Sparrow had tape recorded many stories of life in Ashthorpe from shortly after the turn of the 20th Century. One such tale was the general introduction of electricity to the town, which Johnnie recalled as being as late as 1947. The Electricity Company visited all houses to work out what was needed, but Johnnie's ageing father wanted nothing to do with this newfangled, magic energy. Johnnie pleaded with his father, and eventually he agreed to allow just two light fittings; one on the landing outside Johnnie's room, and the second in the room itself. It was to be a further four years, with the gasometer threatened with closure, that the father eventually agreed to full installation. In fact, the father became such an enthusiast that he ordered the first television in Ashthorpe, and it was not long after that the great and the good of the town gathered in the house, now belonging to the ghastly Don Plaice, to watch the Coronation of Queen Elizabeth II.

Tenants of Don's came and went. Generally for the 6-month short tenancy, but the braver ones sticking it out for a whole year. Gradually they began to realise a common factor whenever one left, that Don Plaice never returned the significant deposits to his tenants.

"Listen, mate, you've smoked in the flat, and I have to employ decorators before I can re-let it!" was Don's regular opening gambit, or,

"You've done nothing in the garden, and I have to bring in gardeners."

There was nothing in the contracts which mentioned either of those items, nor indeed did Don ever do any of the things he said were needed. At the most he would get a girlfriend in for a day to clean and occasionally slap a quick coat of paint onto the walls, or have a couple of days trimming the garden. In most cases the tenants were young women, and gave in easily, but in the case of big Paul, a great friend of Firtle at the Old Bush, he did not give up easily. Knowing Cliff Vintner, the local solicitor, to be the one working for Don Plaice, he appointed a larger company of lawyers in Cirencester to advise on his behalf.

It was not a question of the £700 involved, although that would be useful, but the principle that Don was effectively cheating his tenants, which Paul could not tolerate. The solicitors recommended the Small Claims Court at Gloucester and Paul, supported by Rollo Firtle, presented the papers and attended Court.

The business of the Court that day was largely taken up with tenant/landlord disputes, some on behalf of the owners trying to recover rental arrears or goods from rogue tenants, and about an equal amount of tenants trying to obtain their rights from rogue landlords. On the advice of the solicitors, Paul presented his own case to the Circuit Judge, who appeared to listen intently, interjecting a couple of times with a pertinent question, and his whole deposition cannot have taken more than seven or eight minutes. The Judge spoke again, addressing the Clerk to the Court;

"Is Mr Plaice present?"

"No, Your Honour," replied the Clerk. The Judge scowled.

"Every week in the Court, I see greedy landlords using the deposit system to bolster their own income. Will the plaintiff please come forward."

"Yes, Your Honour," Paul came forward to the bench, and listened to the Judge.

"In my book, what Mr Plaice did comes very close to theft, and what you told me of other cases suggests there is an element of coercion to get the departing tenants to go quietly. I hope as many people as possible will take heed, and never give in quietly if they feel there has been wrongdoing. I am ordering the full deposit to be returned to you through the Court, and on top I order Mr Plaice to pay Court costs of £250, along with a further sum of £250 to compensate the Plaintiff for the distress he has been forced to accept. Mr Plaice has 28 days to pay the Court the total figure, or to appeal for a longer period in the unlikely event he is unable to pay immediately. Case concluded."

The Clerk explained the procedure to them, but added the caveat that in many instances payment takes a considerable time when the Defendant decides to be difficult.

The *Ashthorpe Gazette* went to town on the case;

Rogue Ashthorpe Landlord Guilty

The whole case was reported in detail, and names printed. It had taken over as the town gossip, but this time it was done with malice. Don, of course, did not care, and continued to strut around on his platform heels, treating everybody in his normal arrogant manner.

True to form, Don Plaice received the letter from the Court, for which he had to sign, but threw it to one side on his desk with a look of disdain. As predicted, Don, after 6 weeks, had not paid up.

Paul, and his chum, Firtle, were in the pub one evening discussing the whole matter, when grumpy, (but not really!) Peter said,

"Look, we know where the little rat has his studio nest, the back of the bottom floor of No 27, so why don't the pair of you go and ask when the money is going to be sent?"

"Yes, but you know his reputation for violence!" replied Firtle, slightly nervously.

"He is five foot nothing, and you two are both well over 6 foot and 16 stones each. He won't try anything on! As long as you don't start anything," came Peter's sensible advice.

"But he is such a liar, he could claim that we went round to cause trouble," observed Paul.

"OK, I'll come with you purely to act as a witness," Peter agreed.

The strange trio set off up the road, two very bulky young men flanking the diminutive octogenarian. They reached the gate and the passageway leading to the apartment, and seeing the light on inside, knocked heavily on the door. It swung open slightly, and they called out Don's name. There was no response, so Paul knocked even harder and the door fully opened.

They stood in stunned silence. The whole interior was pink, and they could see a clothes rack, to the left, full of ladies dresses, with, beneath it, a row of garish stiletto ladies shoes. They edged further in and saw a drying rack with all manner of "ladies" underwear laid out on it. Peter picked up a silver framed photograph from the hall table. There in a gold lamé dress, bouffant wig and Dame Edna glasses was a fully dressed transvestite, but clearly Don Plaice. They, both sheepishly and jubilantly, left the apartment, closing the door fully behind them, and headed back to the pub.

The news hit like a bombshell. That evening the discovery spread through the pubs like wildfire, and the grapevine continued through the shops next morning. By ten o'clock it was common knowledge that Don Plaice was a transvestite. Don himself, unaware that he had foolishly not closed his door properly, drove into Ashthorpe and parked in his usual spot. He did not understand why everybody was looking at him and laughing, until he parked the car and stepped back to avoid a group of about six teenagers on bicycles;

"Got any spare lipstick?"

"Can I borrow your handbag?"

"Hello, Sweetie."

Gradually, what had happened dawned upon the odious Mr Plaice. He dashed into his studio, saw the light on and saw it all!

The bullying, arrogant little man, could stand violence, verbal abuse or unpleasantness, but the one thing he was unable to accept was people laughing at him, and they did. Everyone did. As he drove along the High Street, his belongings loaded into his Estate Car, people pointed and laughed. As he turned onto the Cirencester Road, people pointed and laughed, and wherever he passed youths, male and female, he was greeted with obscene gesticulations. Don Plaice was finished.

The following week, Cliff Vintner, his solicitor, paid the £1,200 to the County Court, and instructed the agent who handled more commercial properties, to put the two houses immediately onto the market at a very reasonable price. This time there was no haggling!

Jocelyn was thrilled with the first few months' activity at Seagram Hall Farm Park. He found that he wasn't on his own to do the work, for a regular group of rare breed enthusiasts would turn out on weekends and holiday periods, as volunteers, to help get the attraction established. They were dedicated and hard working, refused any form of payment, and even, during busy periods, shared their packed lunches with Jocelyn! They were all thrilled when, after about a month, Jocelyn arrived with a cardboard box containing Seagram Hall Farm Park sweatshirts; dark green with the Ludcolmbe crest silk-screened in gold. The volunteers, mostly retired couples, were happy to look after the animals, show visitors around, and even man the small, but very tasteful, gift shop Jocelyn had recently completed.

The unexpected bonus of the free volunteer labour, was to allow Jocelyn time to build more housing for new stock, and increasing progeny from the original animals, and to enable him to make a start on the Adventure Playground which he had not anticipated being possible until much later in the year. Perhaps the greatest early success was that of Uncle Tom's Cabin! Lady Ludcolmbe, PJ, trained and experienced in hospitality and catering, had set the operation up and trained Jayne, a buxom and attractive twenty-year-old from a nearby village, who had taken to her duties like a "duck out of water". Damien, typically for an elder brother, felt that Jayne's motives were more personal to Jocelyn than to the cause of trade and tourism, but they both seemed happy with whatever arrangement they had established!

Nobody, not even PJ, had realised quite how beautiful the views were from the cabin; to the front the glorious Tudor mansion, Seagram Hall, was just far enough away not to see the amount of restoration still required, and to the side of the balcony area where 5 tables accommodated 30 visitors, the rather rickety bridge leading across the small lake to the overgrown island on which stood the mysterious Saxon Chapel, reputed to be the oldest in the county. There was something about the light at various times of the day that gave the whole vista a totally magical atmosphere, and this was appealing to the visitors. It became quite clear to Jocelyn, Jayne and indeed the volunteers, that what they were developing was not an attraction to be visited on a one-off occasion, or even once a year, but somewhere that people would be attracted to on many occasions throughout the year. In the few short months they had been operating, many visitors were becoming regulars, some coming twice a month both to observe the developments with the rare breed stocks, but also to look at the ever changing views altering with the passing of seasons, and with the vagaries of the English climate.

Jocelyn decided that for the following year they should introduce an annual family ticket, and market this heavily for the Christmas Gift trade. Sadly for Mickey, who had become used to his wife being around again, PJ had returned to New York for the Autumn, but, both the Earl and his eldest son approved of Jocelyn's scheme, and they jointly started discussions on how best to market the product.

They decided to make the whole thing as personal as possible;

"Our Park is your Garden," suggested Damien.

"A Visit for Every Season," countered Father on a rather literate note.

"Make ours Yours," from Jocelyn, less literate, but more succinct!

By the end of the school holidays during the second week in September, they had produced fliers advertising the Family Membership Scheme under the banner "*Make ours Yours*", and over 1,000 had been given out to the summer holiday visitors, with a further 2,000 to distribute over the next 2 months to visitors, and a further 10,000 to go out with the, Lechlade and Cirencester editions of the *Gazette* in early December. An incentive was designed to help cash flow in the anticipated poor months of December and January, and they had fixed the annual charge at £50, but with a special price for bookings made, and paid, by the end of December of £40, and £45 by the end of February. The park was open throughout the winter, but visitors were far higher than anticipated, Uncle Tom's was kept open, and an analysis of the Family Membership Scheme showed a total of nearly 4,000 season tickets sold, bringing an immediate income of in excess of £150,000, and on an assumed 10 visits per ticket, and 2.5 visitors on each visit, this should mean 100,000 people coming the next year to spend money. Jocelyn's venture was destined for success.

George's Corner

"Where you here last night when a little boy came in crying?" He exclaimed through his tears, "I've lost my daddy!"

The lovely Amy behind the bar patted him on the head, and asked "What's your daddy like?"

Quick as a flash came the response, "Beer and women."

"George claimed his teacher said he would be famous one day. Not true – what she really told him was that if he didn't improve dramatically he would be history!"

Chapter 10

Nobody quite remembered when the plan to develop the River Dart first came about, or who first had the idea. It was first recalled, about the time of the millennium, when the River Authority for the Thames and the Inland Waterways Authority, approached the District Councillor, "Sleepy" Honey. The purpose was to see if, in his opinion, Ashthorpe Magna would be interested in a funded project to widen the river and put in locks, to allow cruisers to link with the main navigable river.

This was further enforced when the Tourist Board had a meeting with Mary Darling, wife of the ex-porn baron, Nick, to see if a river scheme would assist her with the development of her tourist site at Ashthorpe Vineyard. Of course, the river had been used by locals for generations, and the current excavations of the Saxon remains of the earliest identified settlement at Ashthorpe were taking place on the field to the south of the old bridge over the River Dart.

Councillor Honey took advice from his Liberal masters, and all of them felt that support of such a scheme would gain them considerable public support, so the word went round on the grapevine that the idea may have emanated from Sleepy, and, however unlikely, many did believe this. The Town Council also decided to get on the bandwagon. Mayor Sparrow, the best of the local property landlords, declared, via the *Ashthorpe Gazette*, the support of himself, and of the Town Council, for the Ashthorpe Dart Access Scheme, to be known as ADAS! Gradually support poured in from most other groups, including the Chamber of Trade, Court Leet, Market Towns Initiative and, most importantly, Gloucestershire County Council.

An Area Co-ordinator, the beautiful Val Sanderson, was appointed by District Council to look at the methods of financing the initial engineering survey, which would be required, and Val appointed a steering committee to look at the feasibility of ADAS. Her first task was to ask the Charitable Trust, who had the responsibility for the Upper Thames Navigation, to use their experienced team to produce an initial document for debate by the newly appointed ADAS committee. This was done in a remarkably short time, and ended up as a 12 page document including detailed maps of each section of the river, suggestions as to where locks, weirs and moorings could be introduced, and quotations from three specialist engineering companies to undertake the initial survey.

Val called the first committee meeting, and waited anxiously to see who would be sent to represent each body. At the meeting, held at the Council Offices, far too many people, all with their own agenda, sat around the large table to undertake their first job, appointment of a Chairman.

The Court Leet had sent along their Brooklooker, at that time Major Andy Gross, as their representative, and his large frame and booming voice made him a natural for the post of Chairman of ADAS. Some debate took place, but in the end he was elected unopposed. His Deputy, the Treasurer and Secretary soon followed and the meeting got down to business.

"Ladies and Gentlemen, you all have a copy of the Trust's excellent report on ADAS. I thank them for such a detailed work produced in such a short time frame," announced Andy.

"May we first go through this together?" he requested.

There was an overall consensus of agreement, until the point at which the quotations, all at a figure of £25,000, were reached.

"The Town Council cannot consider this sort of cost for a survey," put in Mayor.

"The District Council has some discretionary funds, but nothing of this order," added "Sleepy" Honey.

And so they went on!

"Please will you stop this bickering," Andy ordered rather than asked!

Val charmed everybody, and smiled at the group, "May we first go around and see how far away we are from the total, and then we can look at completing the funding?"

Andy went round the group.

"Providing you are prepared to use English & Co, with whom we have worked in the past, the IWA (Inland Waterways Association) would almost certainly be prepared to consider paying 20% of the fees, or £5,000," came the first offer.

The representative of the Countryside Agency, who financed the Market Town Initiative, agreed to a contribution of £10,000.

A timid little elderly lady, not known to any of the others, stood up sheepishly;

"I can pledge £2,000 on behalf of Small Grants for Regeneration Projects," she murmured. Nobody had even heard of this grant, but they all clapped politely and smiled at her.

"Providing we can first obtain the outline approval of the Environment Agency, the Upper Thames Trust will contribute £5,000, plus, of course, provide our staff and equipment if the project goes ahead," came the generous offer from that body.

"We are already up to £23,000; where can I look for the final £2,000?" Major Gross enquired in the manner of an auctioneer working his audience.

Several hands were raised. Mary Darling was the first to speak,

"Ashthorpe Vineyard would be pleased to provide the remaining £2,000."

Damien, who was representing Seagram Hall, looked rather pleased that Mary had spoken first, thus avoiding the need to admit to his father that he had committed their limited funds!

"Thank you all. Shall I now contract English & Co to undertake the initial survey?" Andy asked.

The only question came from the Mayor;

"Shouldn't we have a public consultation meeting before placing the contract?"

"No, I don't think so," responded the Chairman, "it will only delay matters."

The vote was unanimous in favour of signing the contract.

The incident of the Court Leet Officers, and the pissoir, created a change in Ashthorpe Magna. For many years past, coaches, loaded with tourists, had passed by the town on the way to Stratford, Burford, Cirencester and even farther away. After the articles comparing Ashthorpe with Clochemerle had appeared in French newspapers, some tour operators were being requested to include the area on their itineraries. This, coupled with the now successful coach visits to Ashthorpe Vineyard, caused a new interest in this little-known edge of the Cotswolds. The two attractions of the vineyard, and Jocelyn's rare breed farm, when added to the pissoir story, gave the town a renewed life.

Carol's coffee shop boomed to the extent that she only occasionally counted the sugar lumps, and even Jamie, at The Firkin, reputedly smiled at a group of tourists refreshing themselves in his pub! Carole at the gift shop had taken to stocking somewhat tacky Ashthorpe memorabilia, but perhaps her greatest success was a pottery facsimile of the pissoir, created rather cheekily by a group of students at the High School, with the words "The Ashthorpe Pissoir" written along the face of the trough. They left her with the first batch of 10 models, on sale or return, and promised to return the following week to collect a £4 payment for each one sold. Carole, really to be kind to the students, put them on display with a price tag of £8 each, but by the end of the day they had all sold – predominately to the French! For the first time in his life, the Craft teacher at the High School received a call from a student requesting the use of the studios at the weekend to do extra pottery work. They soon built up a thriving little cottage industry.

Melvyn, in his capacity as Chairman of the Ashthorpe Chamber of Trade and Commerce, was delighted with the newfound commercial success in his town, and even happier when people were giving him some of the credit for the success.

"But, Melvyn, we should find somewhere in France for Ashthorpe to twin with," was Lauren's suggestion over dinner; now a fairly regular occurrence.

A brilliant idea flashed through Melvyn's mind. Pétanque. Boules to most people. Many years before, Melvyn had visited Brittany, with friends, and they had spent a very jolly week at a campsite with a "*Terrain de Boules*".

The word "boules" is in many respects similar to "football". The latter encompasses Rugby Union, Rugby League, Aussie Rules and Soccer. Boules embraces *Jeu Provençal, Lyonnaise, Bocce* and the most popular, and international form, Pétanque. As a formal sport, the latter was only started in 1911 when the local champion at Lyonnaise was taken ill, and confined to a wheelchair. His friends felt sorry for the fact that he could not join in with the game, as it required taking steps, and a violent throw of a large metal ball over quite a long distance. Eventually Jules le Noir, for that was his name, produced some smaller balls which fitted into the palm of the hand, and he and his chums devised rules that involved drawing a circle from which to throw without moving the feet, and playing over the short distance of between 6 and 10 metres.

They were in the village of La Ciotat, near Marseilles, and they name the game in the local dialect "*Pieds Tanquées*", or feet together, which became contracted to Pétanque.

Lauren was amazed at Melvyn's knowledge of, what is regarded by some, as France's national sport, and she did not even know that her namesake, le Noir, was honoured as the sport's founder. It transpired that on the French camping holiday, Melvyn and friends had met up with the Founder President of the British Pétanque Association, and author of *The Pernod Book of Pétanque*. At the time, Melvyn and his current wife were living in Hampshire, and going home with a signed copy of the book, he joined a local club, eventually captaining the Southern Region Championship Team.

"Lauren, why don't we start a club here in Ashthorpe, and twin with a club in a similar sized town in Brittany?" enquired a rather excited Melvyn.

"Darling" – it was the first time Lauren had addressed him as such.

"Darling, it's a wonderful idea, but where would we play, and would we get enough people?"

"Well your chum Ludcolmbe at Seagram has a perfect area to the side of the Hall; an undulating, light sandy gravel surface, and plenty of it! As far as enough people are concerned, so many holidaymakers have seen the game in France, and wondered about it, and I am sure they would be interested," Melvyn replied.

He continued, "and don't forget Pétanque is a year-round sport. In Hampshire many of the summer players were from the local Rugby Club, and the winter players from the Cricket Club. I am sure we could do the same."

After a night of passion, which had a frisson Melvyn had never before encountered, they visited Mickey Carruthers at Seagram Hall.

"You don't have to explain Pétanque to me," said the Earl, "wait here."

Within minutes he returned clutching an enormous leather bag, and wearing a rather faded, light jacket bearing the words "*Club de Pétanque – Antibes*".

"We used to play virtually every night, often for money and always with huge quantities of Pastis!" Mickey explained.

171

After they had finished their coffee, and, then, joined by Damien, they went outside to the side of the Hall; Melvyn had been correct, the surface was perfect. For the next hour they played – Lauren could not believe the skills shown by three Englishmen!

Mickey, more animated than his son had seen him for years, exclaimed,

"We must have a Club. We'll base it here, and I want to be the Patron!" the middle-aged aristocrat pleaded.

They all agreed. The two residents felt it would bring visitors to the Hall and Jocelyn's Farm Park, and Melvyn and Lauren knew that it would help with tourists to the town. Melvyn also guessed that it would provide him with the opportunity to take the lovely Lauren to Brittany, thus sealing their relationship in public.

"We could start with an open day and friendly competition for beginners. We can invite as many as possible, but I do remember seeing a veteran Parisian bus used by Pernod as a promotional tool," Melvyn suggested.

"I sold a house in Belgravia to a delightful French aristocrat, Compte Claude du Nord, who was the UK Director of Pernod. I am sure I can locate him," the Earl contributed.

Over luncheon they divided up the duties. Melvyn would contact the British Pétanque Association, the BPA, to register the new Club, Mickey would contact Pernod to see if there were any dates when the bus could be available, and when a date was fixed Lauren would contact all the media, and Damian the local clubs and organisations to invite them to the occasion.

"Don't forget, that rogue at Ashthorpe Vineyards should be good for some sponsorship. PJ is coming back home this week, and we did promise them dinner, so perhaps if you two could join us we can get moving," Mickey shrewdly suggested.

"One problem is providing enough boules for people to try out. I will see if the BPA have some they can provide, or perhaps the importers of the main brands of boules can assist. It may also be a good idea if the BPA could organise members from clubs not too far away to come and help with the instruction," was Melvyn's next idea.

The first call was to the Secretary General of the BPA, whose name and address Melvyn obtained from a friend in Hampshire, and he was delighted to confirm almost instantly that the Ashthorpe Pétanque Club was to be affiliated. He did have a number of ulterior motives; unfortunately the BPA Patron, since their formation in 1985, had been the delightful Countess of Loudoun, who had, unfortunately, died the previous year at the age of 83. They had, to that point, found no suitable replacement, but Melvyn assured the official that he would arrange a meeting with the Earl of Ludcolmbe who would undoubtedly look favourably on the request. The other reason for his enthusiasm was that, whilst there were many affiliated clubs in Oxfordshire, Warwickshire and the South West, there was a dearth of clubs in Gloucestershire. Several pubs were known to have introduced the sport, and built terrains over the previous decade, but perhaps due to the rather insular nature of the locals, they had never expressed a desire, despite many approaches, to join in with the governing body.

Lauren, with Mickey's permission produced headed notepaper for Ashthorpe Pétanque Club, with the Ludcolmbe family crest at the top, with the wording underneath:

Ashthorpe Magna Pétanque Club
Seagram Hall
Ashthorpe Magna
Gloucestershire
Patron: Rt. Hon the 14th Earl of Ludcolmbe

The bottom of the page stated proudly:

Affiliated to the British Pétanque Association

Two days later, Mickey came through with the news that his old contact, Compte Claude de Nord, was back in London, having spent five years in the USA, as President of Pernod in that country, and was spending his last year before retirement back in his Belgravia home. He needed a boost to their publicity, and saw the inaugural event at Seagram Hall as providing just such an opportunity.

Less than two weeks from the initial idea, everything was in place. A date was booked one month ahead, the Parisian bus would be present, all the local media was informed by Lauren, and the Pernod publicity machine had issued Press Packs to all the UK National Press, plus most of those from Paris and the North of France. Damian had written to all the local organisations, and followed this up with phone calls and visits, and the BPA had unleashed its own publicity upon the press, affiliated clubs and local non-registered clubs announcing both the event, and also the fact that the Earl of Ludcolmbe was the new Patron of the British Pétanque Association.

Three locals contacted Melvyn, the Club Chairman, and stated that as devoted Francophiles, they were keen players and would be very happy to help with the playing organisation of the day, and in particular marking out some 10 "pistes", or lanes, prior to the event. They were to become three of the keenest committee members of the new club.

"Mrs Darling?" PJ asked on the telephone having again returned from New York.

"Yes."

"Hello, Mary, Lady Ludcolmbe here – PJ. We were wondering if you and your husband may be free on Friday to join us for dinner?"

"Yes, PJ, we would both be delighted. I was going to contact you all anyway to see how we can help with your Boules thing. We have four students, from the Wine Institute at Bordeaux, doing work experience up here, and they seem to spend hours each evening playing on the drive," replied Mary enthusiastically.

"That's super, Mary. We look forward to seeing you both at about 7 pm," said PJ.

The dinner party had expanded a little to include Mickey and PJ, their two sons along with one unknown sundry girlfriend; Melvyn and Lauren; the current BPA President, Chris Jarrett and his wife who were visiting to finalising playing details; and, of course, Mary and Nick Darling who arrived complete with a case of six of their best whites, and a case of reds. PJ, as a professional, coped well with the numbers, and was well helped by the girlfriend, who as it transpired was the new cub reporter on the *Gazette*.

Whilst the food was excellent, the wine flowed copiously and conversation was unstilted, the subject was constantly brought back to the matter in hand, the Open Day. Nick Darling had, early in the evening, handed Melvyn a sealed envelope,

"This may help get the thing moving, Melvyn. Keep it quiet this evening, though," Nick requested.

Sheer curiosity led Melvyn to sneak a look at the contents when he had visited the toilet; it was a cheque for £1,000 made out to Ashthorpe Magna Pétanque Club. They now had one of the most prestigious venues in the country, a senior Earl as Patron, and money in the bank. It was quite clear from the conversation around the dinner table, which lasted well after ten o'clock, that they also had a huge reservoir of enthusiasm and support, but more importantly they had a group of individuals with a vast knowledge and experience.

The day drew near. All the local hotels, inns and B & Bs were fully booked, indeed one commented that it was just like the Cheltenham Festival Week, but this time most of the visitors were French rather than Irish! Other Pétanque players had come forward, and under Melvyn's guidance, games were arranged and league tables prepared, but clearly the numbers were getting slightly out of hand. The saving grace to their plans was the space available; whilst singles and doubles are regularly played, by far the most popular competitive game is trebles. The 10 pistes, each holding a game of three against three, would allow for 60 players at any given time, and one expert player would be needed for each piste, both to advise the less experienced or to act as a referee when required. It was decided to limit the numbers to 60, with each paying a nominal £5 entry fee, which would provide 3 prizes for the 1st, 2nd and 3rd teams.

The final accolade bestowed on the event was an announcement that the Président of the FIPJP (*Fédération Français de Pétanque et Jeu Provençal*) and his deputy would be arriving on the morning flight from Marseilles to attend the Open Day. Not for the first time in his life, the French love for an English "Mi Lord" was to prove a positive benefit to Mickey Carruthers. Fortunately protocol, so much loved by the French, dictated that the BPA President should collect his much more important French counterpart from Heathrow at the crack of dawn.

The day dawned. Although the official opening was at 9.00, by 7.00 the Pernod bus was in place, the organisers were getting things arranged, and checking in players, the TV cameras, at least three from France, were setting up in the best places, and Uncle Tom's Cabin was doing a roaring business in selling Full English breakfasts crowned with bacon from Ashthorpe Park Farm Gloucester Old Spot Pigs!

"*Pas des croissants,*" complained the French Crews, but as they had been on the road for several hours, they all tucked into that truly great English meal, the breakfast!

In Tudor times, especially during the long and prosperous reign of Elizabeth 1st, the High Street of Ashthorpe Magna, began to take the shape that remains to today in the 21st

Century, nearly 400 years later. The woollen industries, notably dyeing and weaving, were booming in Ashthorpe, and the residences of the merchants and tradesmen, opening onto the muddy thoroughfare of the High Street, all had little industrial units at the back of them, often housing a workman and his family along with the machines or vats required to do the work.

The stench in the summer must have verged on the intolerable, and the conditions in winter, a much harder season than it is in modern times, led to a situation where only the fittest, or wealthiest, survived. In 1684, Charles Adams and his family were no exception. His wife had borne nine children over the past 11 years, but only four survived, the eldest girl of eleven, Helen, and one other girl and two boys. He was a dyer, and the whole family lived in a building, accessible through an alleyway, at the rear of Number 8 High Street, which housed the dyeing tanks and the cooking area on the ground floor, and the sleeping area for them all on a mezzanine floor overlooking the vats. The winter of 1684 was especially harsh, and due to a poor harvest the previous autumn even basic foods were scarce. The wife, and mother, Elizabeth Adams, was yet again pregnant, but due to a severe bout of influenza which developed into, what today would be recognised as pneumonia, became feverish and in much pain. Local ladies came to try and look after the unfortunate woman, but there was nothing they could do to stop her going into premature labour. Charles was sent out to the nearest alehouse, no great difficulty as there were then ten such establishments on the High Street, and by the time he came round from his drunken stupor it was all over.

Elizabeth had not survived the ordeal, and the child was stillborn. With little fuss their remains were buried, and such was the normality of such an occurrence in that era, life for Charles carried on much as before. Life did not much change for the eleven-year-old Helen, for with her mother being,

177

either pregnant or nursing an oft sickly infant, most of the bare household duties had fallen upon her previously. Despite this, Helen was a happy, and somewhat precocious child. She looked older than many others of her age, and already the signs of maturity were developing; her young breasts were clearly visible, her hips had widened to accentuate a waistline, and her legs were becoming a feminine shape. Her blonde hair, always grubby from the conditions in the cottage, fell below the level of her shoulders in ringlets, and often covering her heart-shaped face.

She was also the only child of the working families in Ashthorpe who had any ability to read; this anomaly had come about from the fact that she had a beautiful little voice, and had for three years been the youngest member of St Osmund's Church Choir. To enable her to read from the Hymn Books, the Choirmaster, himself a teacher, had enrolled her for reading classes in his little school, without making any charge.

One fateful, winter night, her father returned home to the dark, cold little building they occupied, in a typical drunken state. He climbed into the bed next to Helen, and probably in a habitual manner after twelve years of married life, he rolled over and groped for the youthful breasts of the shivering child. He climbed on top of her, forcing her legs apart with his own strong limbs, and despite her growing screams, roughly entered her. By then, the bed, the rough woollen blanket, and his own chemise were covered in blood, and all the children had joined in with Helen's screams. The sexual act was over in seconds, but it must have seen an eternity to the child, and he roughly put his hand over her mouth. Within a short period both the screams and the shivering had stopped.

He climbed down the unfinished, wooden steps to the main room, and collapsed in a heap at the bottom, unaware of the continued shouts from the three remaining, stricken children, nor of the beating on the door and sounds of commotion in the dingy alleyway. One of the neighbours had wisely brought a tallow torch, and another had had the presence to wake the Steward of the Manor, a lawyer by profession, who also brought a lighted torch. It was immediately obvious what had happened. Helen was laying in a supine position, legs still apart, with copious amounts of blood continuing to pour from her body – although clearly dead, the look of horror remained on her beautiful face.

Within minutes the Steward had summoned the Constable of the Court, and the staggering, inebriated Charles was taken to the Town Hall, which housed the Ashthorpe jail cell. It was rarely used, and in any case only would have been able to house three or four prisoners, but on that night was empty. The wretched Charles was roughly thrown in, and the door locked behind him. He was not to remain there long, as the Steward had already been informed that the new Assize Judge for the Western Circuit, one Sir George Jeffreys, was to pay his first visit to Ashthorpe Magna.

George Jeffreys (1645–1689), himself a grandson of a judge, was educated at Shrewsbury, Cambridge University and the Inner Temple, and used his personal wealth to buy an estate in Buckinghamshire, and befriended the newly-restored King Charles II. Jeffreys was always a staunch Royalist, as were so many of the families from Denbighshire where he was born and brought up, and more especially he was a great supporter of the Stuart cause. He is recorded as having drinking sessions with the Merry Monarch, some suggested to curry favour, which was probably untrue, but it was certainly correct that he befriended the King's younger brother, the Catholic Duke of York who later became James II.

Regardless of the motives, Judge Jeffreys was awarded the post of London Recorder and Chief Justice of the King's Bench, which involved him in the trials of high profile treason cases, notably Algernon Sidney of the famous Rye House Plot. The soubriquet, "Hanging Judge Jeffreys", was not brought in until 1685, a year after the events in Ashthorpe Magna, when he supervised the "bloody assizes" used to try, and convict, the failed participants of the ill-fated Monmouth Rebellion, and many other innocent bystanders who had incurred Royal displeasure.

It was well known in the Royal Court, before the eventual death of Charles II in 1685, that a challenge was likely to be mounted against his Catholic successor, James II. Largely rumoured to be centred in the West Country, the rebellion would come from Charles' illegitimate son, the Duke of Monmouth, who still at the time lived in the fiercely Protestant Holland. In these seriously troubled times, the West Country was always a potential problem, and was very cut off from both London and its judiciary system.

So it was that George Jeffreys, by then Sir George, was appointed in 1684 as the Assize Judge for the Western Circuit, to establish the judicial rule of London on these outlying areas of the country. The Judge threw himself into his new job with a great passion, and as there were few courthouses extant outside the major conurbations, he set up the assizes in hostelries in the towns. It was well known that he was almost permanently inebriated, and he often slurred his words when pronouncing a death sentence on some unfortunate wretch. He is recorded as having said, in rather lengthy religious form, on many occasions,

"I hope to God that he does not try and plead innocence, for this will waste my time, and guarantee the ultimate sentence on the miscreant."

In a number of cases he did allow the defendants to keep their lives, but sentenced them to the current popular punishment of deportation to the West Indies.

There are suggestions that the Judge's first assize at Ashthorpe Magna was not his only one, and that one of the later trials during the "bloody assizes" took place there to convict the stragglers from the Monmouth Rebellion. There were gaps in the judge's history after the major trials in

Dorchester, where there would certainly have been time, but there is no existing evidence.

Nor is there real evidence of which hostelry in Ashthorpe was used for the first trials. Over the centuries virtually every building on the High Street and Church Street had been recorded as an ale house, but whilst large Tudor buildings did exist, especially at St Osmund's end of the street, most were either knocked down, fell down or partially destroyed and given a Georgian façade. Several make claims to have been the hostelry used that day, but none have been able to prove it as an historical fact.

The Steward would have been responsible for arranging the Court, and on most such occasions the Judge and the Steward, along with the head of the small militia travelling with the Judge, were seated at a table on a balcony overlooking the main alehouse which was used as the Court Room. The defendant, flanked by the Constable and a Serjeant-at-Arms from the militia, would be at a bench to the front, just under the Judge, and the public behind them. Ominously, the hangman would have set up his noose on a suitable beam, with a large wooden block as a step on which the guilty party would stand in his last moments. In his alcoholic haze, Judge Jeffreys rarely allowed time for the prisoner to make his peace with God, and to expedite matters would raise his hand, in the manner of a Roman Emperor, well before any prayer could take place.

George Jeffreys was horrified at the statements from a neighbour of Charles Adams, and the brief statement from the Steward. It was a case with no doubt, and the Judge pronounced a sentence of death by hanging. Within minutes the act had taken place, and after a period of time, during which the body thrashed about at the end of the noose, the remains of the man who had raped and killed his daughter hung lifeless beneath the beam. Judge Jeffreys, under the influence of the local ale or no, was so enraged at the crime that he ordered the body to be dismembered and impaled upon the railing of St Osmund's as a warning to others with similar tendencies. This was a technique he was to use widely the following year during the "bloody assizes".

There is no record as to what became of the remaining children, but certainly the cottage industry in the building continued for many decades, until industrialisation and mechanisation, largely in the North of England, coupled with the introduction of the railway systems, made such activities unviable.

It is recorded that the building that was their home, stood derelict for many decades, until it was extended in the early 1930s, and converted into a two bed-roomed residence with a small walled garden. The census records and County Archives, indicate that many different families lived there, none it would seem for more than a year, and even the introduction of a light in the alleyway was unable to dispel the gloom seeping from the building with such a terrible history.

George's Corner

"You know George does have a problem with understanding many things, but that really is his sheltered upbringing. Air-raid shelters, bus shelters, taxi shelters…"

"Had my flu injection today. Naturally it was a sterile needle, but tell me why they use sterile needles in the US when giving lethal injections?"

Chapter 11

For the first time ever, Jocelyn had queues forming at the entrance to the Farm Park. The French visitors had arrived in force, and, although some rare breed establishments do exist in France, they are few and far between compared with Great Britain, and the tourists seemed fascinated with the very concept.

Uncle Tom's Cabin continued to sell the Full English Breakfast, which was fast making French converts, and Mickey had even managed to find a slightly moth-eaten French Tricolour, which was flown opposite the Ludcolmbe Family Standard, each from one of the two towers of the gatehouse at the main entrance. Even before the opening ceremony the Pernod bus was giving away small glasses of pastis with one lump of ice, and topped up with cold water changing the clear, slightly oily, liquid into the wonderful milky drink. It has to be said that the British did not relish the idea, especially at 8.30 in the morning, but the French, predominately from Normandy and Brittany, accepted the offer with alacrity! Nick Darling had arrived with a huge box containing 250 flags bearing the Ludcolmbe Coat of Arms, and the words Ashthorpe Magna Pétanque Club; Mickey expressed a little doubt as to their ability to sell such a quantity, but his mind was eased by Nick's comment;

"Don't worry, they were a donation from a friend who has made squillions from flags and banners; we can sell these for at least a fiver with all the money going into the Club." He carried on, "Let's use ten to decorate the area around the terrains, the cameras will love them, and we can sell the rest!"

The morning was, luckily, sunny and clear, and the Earl busied himself organising the opening ceremony. As the owner, and Patron of the new host club, he would normally have conducted the formalities himself, but on this occasion he felt it was more diplomatic to invite the Président of the FIPJP to undertake the welcoming speech. It was Damian's new girlfriend, the effervescent Claire from the *Gazette*, who suggested the whole event would gain greater coverage on the French TV Channels if the speech were in French, and Lauren agreed to translate for the benefit of non French speaking visitors.

The President of the BPA arrived with his French guests, who had landed at Heathrow at 7.00 local time. At that time of day the journey was almost exactly an hour, and the visitors were obviously enthralled with the countryside and the little villages en route. The BPA Vice President called Melvyn on his mobile when they were about 10 minutes away, and the welcoming party assembled in front of the entrance to the Great Hall; at the centre were the Earl and Countess with their two sons, plus the gorgeous little Claire; Melvyn and Lauren were to one side, and the Darlings to the other. Even the Mayor and Clerk had turned out in their robes, prompted by the fact that the Bailiff and Reeve were also present in their colourful dress.

The excitement shown by the Gallic Media had for once rubbed off on the English contingent which, unusually, did not display their normal look of a cross between boredom and disdain. Within the main welcoming group, only Melvyn was not a fluent French speaker, but he knew enough to conduct the pleasantries, and as President of the home Club, carried out the introductions with some panache. Prompted by some of the French press, the FIPJP Président asked if there were time to sample the English Breakfast, and to Jocelyn's delight, the two new arrivals, accompanied by Melvyn and Lauren, sat down to the truly great platter. The cameras, TV and still, followed them in, and photographed them from every angle, and did not seem to realise that the advertising banners on the walls behind each shot they took carried the new web-site address for Ashthorpe Gloucester Old Spot Sausages and Bacon. By the time of the opening, success was guaranteed.

The organisers had allowed a mere five minutes for the opening speech, but the honoured guest was so overwhelmed by the whole affair, that he went on for a full quarter of an hour, even praising *Le Bacon* by name – although his interpretation of the pronunciation of Gloucester left a little to be desired.

True to their promise, the pistes were well laid out each of a width of 3 metres, and length of 14 metres, which was quite enough for the game, which starts at a length of 6 to 10 metres. Each indeed had an expert to advise and judge, and more than enough boules for the mostly novice players had been provided by existing BPA members, BPA stocks and the major supplier, Boules JB.

They soon realised their first mistake in the organisation of the competition. The tournament was a knockout so the twenty teams in the first round were whittled down to ten, then to five. It took considerable mathematical abilities from the BPA to solve the dilemma, and Melvyn then realised he would have been better to either go for 32 teams or restrict the entries to 16 teams, which would have allowed a straight run down to quarter finals, semi finals and finals. However, most of the entries were virtually complete novices whose enjoyment was not marred by the internal confusion.

All in all, the day was a spectacular success, and Melvyn, in particular was pleased to have met the Présidents of three Breton Clubs, all of whom had invited him over to discuss closer participation between their own Clubs, and the Ashthorpe Magna Pétanque Club.

Not a single participant was disappointed; the Ludcolmbes had achieved everything for which they had set out; the Darlings, had been allowed to both give samples, and sell bottles of Ashthorpe Wines, both of which proved a great success – their staff had been summoned down on at least three occasions during the day to replenish the stocks. It was a particular pleasure for them to see the numbers of bottles purchased by the French visitors. The BPA was delighted with the publicity generated, and the town dignitaries of Ashthorpe Magna were ecstatic with the international media coverage provided. All Nick Darling's flags had been sold! Perhaps, most importantly, the visitors and new players had enjoyed a magnificent day out. Ashthorpe Magna Pétanque Club had acquired over 30 new members, including several Family Memberships, making them, not only the newest, but also one of the largest Clubs in the Region.

Ashthorpe Magna had well and truly launched itself onto the tourist map, without changing anything whatsoever of the nature of the town. So many similar towns, in and around the Cotswolds, had lost their "heart" – in some, the traditional shops had given way to antique centres, London-based Estate Agents and upmarket art galleries at the cost of butchers and grocers. Not so Ashthorpe.

Excitement was mounting with the Chairman of the Chamber of Trade and Commerce. Melvyn was poring over small-scale Michelin Maps of Brittany to locate the Clubs by whom he had been invited, searching the web for attractive little hotels liable to attract Lauren, and checking with Brittany Ferries on the availability of Commodore Class Cabins on the Portsmouth to St Malo route. He remembered, from earlier trips, that this was probably the most luxurious standard of accommodation across the Channel; the cabins were all outside ones, with picture windows; had a good sized bathroom; complimentary chocolates, fruit, coffee and breakfast; and the special attraction to Melvyn, two large beds rather than bunks! He planned on using this latter facility to its full! All he now needed was Lauren's final agreement, and indeed the dates she could come. With a dedication, comparable with Casanova himself, he put everything in place before mentioning the subject again to Lauren.

"I've found a lovely little Hotel, part of the *Logis de France* Group, which are always good," announced Melvyn.

"I know them well, we used to stay in them when I was small. What I remember is that they were all privately owned, and therefore different, and most of them have excellent restaurants," Lauren enthused.

"We're meeting Clubs in Paimpol, Plouha and St Brieuc, and there is the lovely little *Logis de France* Hotel in Paimpol, so I thought we could stay there for a few days, rather than have a night in different places. They're less than half an hour from each other so it should be easy enough." By the very expression on Lauren's face, Melvyn knew he did not need to enquire if she was going to come with him.

"I can get away at any time, but when would suit you?" Melvyn enquired.

The response came quickly, without hesitation, "Sooner the better."

The following morning Melvyn was on the telephone. The crossing and the Commodore Class Cabin on the Brittany Ferries *MV Bretagne* was booked, as was the *Hotel du Port* in Paimpol. He made the booking for six nights. He was lucky to get hold of all three Club *Présidents* on the telephone, and make appointments, one each on the Friday, Saturday and Sunday – the Club in Paimpol was actually based at the *Hotel du Port*, that of St Brieuc in the *Café du Marché* overlooking the market place which only operated as a market on Mondays, and in the village of Plouha, the Pétanque headquarters was in the *Bar du Commerce* by the main car park.

"Major Gross, it's Val from the District Council here."

"Yes, my dear, what can I do for you?" enquired Andy.

"We've had a few letters of complaint from the anglers. They claim that they should have been consulted in the first instance, and are fuming that we still have not called a public meeting. Councillor Honey feels that we must do something quickly; have you any idea when the report is due out?"

The future Bailiff felt a little guilty that he had not replied to a call from the Consulting Engineers, English & Co, which he had received three days earlier.

"Val, I am still waiting to hear from them. I'll call them immediately and get back to you. What we will need to do is to call a Committee Meeting as soon as possible after that, and then arrange a public meeting," responded Andy Gross.

It transpired that the call was to let Andy know that the report had, in fact, been finished the previous week. They agreed a Committee Meeting for its initial airing.

Despite the fact that it was a brilliant, informative and colourful report, the news was a staggering shock. Whilst the initial survey had suggested that five normal locks would be adequate to cover the fall between Ashthorpe and Lechlade, this had not made allowance for the fact that the tributaries feeding the River Dart, in the summer virtually dried up, meaning the main river would not have enough water for the boating envisaged. The only solution to this problem would be to build more expensive locks, with accumulator reservoirs to store the additional water required, and the five locks originally envisaged would have to increase to six. In addition, large stretches of construction of straight stretches would be required, due to the meandering nature of the river in many places. This sent the initial cost estimate of £5 million soaring up to a massive MINIMUM of £8.3 million!

The report had included effects on employment, and, somewhat dubiously, came up with a figure of 26 new jobs, and also an even more optimistic figure of tourists on cruisers being brought to Ashthorpe from the Thames. Even at £5 million, Andy Gross could only just, in his most optimistic mood, see the justification for the project. At the minimum of £8.3 million (probably meaning £10+ million) there was no possible financial justification, and Andy could not see any possibility of raising such a figure from the many funding bodies.

"I cannot see either County or District Councils supporting a plan at this cost," opined Val.

As the group gradually absorbed the information, and the figures, it became quite obvious that the only body that may still be interested, were the IWA, but perhaps they were the organisation most likely to gain from increased licence fees.

"I think we must look for a smaller scheme. I don't think we can drop it altogether, but we will end up with egg on our faces if we go ahead with this," said Chairman, Andy.

That night, Claire the *Gazette* Cub reporter, was staying up at Seagram Hall with Damian. To the delight of his father who enjoyed her lively and witty company, but not so much to PJ, who, like so many mothers never approved of girlfriends brought home by their sons – especially heirs to an Earldom.

The following morning, Claire knocked on the oak door of Ashthorpe Manor, and was greeted by Major Andy Gross.

"Please come in, my dear, what can I do for you?"

"Major Gross, as Chairman of ADAS, can I ask you a few questions please?" Claire flashed her brilliant smile whilst asking the question.

"Of course, fire away," responded the Major.

Three days later the *Ashthorpe Gazette* carried the headline:

RIVER PLAN SCUPPERED BY SHOCK OVER COSTS

Ambitious plans to open up the River Dart to pleasure boats were blown out of the water this week – but there is still hope for Ashthorpe's tourism according to a leading member of the navigation committee.

Major Andy Gross, Chairman of the Ashthorpe Dart Access Scheme (ADAS), told the Gazette that, in his opinion, there was no way their proposals to open up a 10 mile stretch of the river between north Lechlade and Ashthorpe Magna for boating could go ahead due to the cost of the project, some £8 million.

Claire's article went on to describe, most accurately, the work proposed, and the reasons for the staggering cost estimate increases. She concluded;

But Major Gross said there were now other project ideas in the pipeline, which would only cost about £1 million and would have just as positive an effect on Ashthorpe's tourist economy.

He told the Gazette: "We've found there used to be a canoe festival on the Dart as recently as 1982, and the Victorians had punts on the river – so the report doesn't mean nothing can be done. The river could be made usable again for these kinds of purposes just with a bit of dredging, tarting up the riverbanks and installing a weir. There will also be similar benefits to the town, improving tourism and still providing opportunities to develop footpaths and cycle ways."

Major Gross now plans to take a canoe himself down the river to assess the possibility of opening it for minor navigation.

Claire resisted the temptation to add " if they could make a canoe big enough to convey the Major!"

Many townsfolk, even those not specially interested in the river, one way or the other, could not help laughing at the prospect of Andy Gross in a canoe. Legend had it that, when the Major first became a Court Leet Officer, the robe had to be remade to allow for the expanse of stomach. When asked, as he was on many occasions, he would never either confirm or deny! The real truth was that the majority of the people of Ashthorpe were somewhat apathetic about most changes, hence the same people appeared on committees of different organisations, but they all liked to either criticise, or poke fun at those who did the work for the town. Most public meetings were poorly attended, and often by the same active group. But, the meeting called by Andy to present the English & Co Plan was different. The anglers arrived!

The venue for the meeting was, as normal, the Council Offices on New Town Road, but on that particular occasion the room was packed, all the chairs taken, people sitting on the window ledges and standing all round the room. Even the door leading from the corridor was propped open, and people were crushed into the space trying to hear what was going on.

How it was possible to identify the anglers? Who knows? At least 80 of the 100 visitors cramped into the room were obviously from that fraternity. Perhaps it was the sun and wind gnarling of the faces? Perhaps the faraway expressions from too many hours sitting on river-banks, watching a float bobbing up and down? Whatever the reason, identifiable they were. If the occupants of the top table – Andy Gross, the Mayor, the lovely Val from District Council, and the scholarly looking engineer from English & Co – had any concept that anglers were a quiet, thoughtful bunch of people, they were wrong!

Val was shouted down when she tried to welcome people on behalf of the district council; the Mayor was barely heard when he did the same on behalf of the Town Council, and the barracking started when Mr Denton from English & Co set up his lap-top for the Power Point presentation. Major Gross stood up; his powerful voice boomed out:

"What the bloody hell do you think you are playing at?" The room fell silent as he continued, "You have been demanding consultation for months, and now you have it, you behave like a bunch of unruly school kids," he continued. "Either you give Mr Denton the courtesy of your attention, or I will close the meeting immediately." He won this first little battle, and the engineer presented his case.

As with the report, it was beautifully executed, and those at the top table could see that some were being won over by the sheer graphic and photographic skills; they felt a little easier. A slightly muted ripple of applause went around the room, and Andy Gross stood again:

"Now it is your chance for comment and questions, but I warn you once more, one person at a time."

A gentleman at the back stood up. He would normally have been described as "large", but when Major Andy Gross was present it was difficult to regard anybody else as "large".

His modulated tones reached every corner of the room, without shouting, and Andy, in his own mind, identified the newcomer as an Old Harrovian or an Old Etonian. His appearance, his bearing and his dress, pointed to the fact that this, indeed, was a man of substance.

"My name is Ian Campbell-Templeton, and I have purchased the old Ashthorpe Stud. My main reason for this is the attraction offered by the fishing on the River Dart. I would like to read out a letter, with your agreement, Mr Chairman, I received yesterday from a fisheries expert. I think you will find it very appropriate to the meeting, and the report."

"By all means, Mr Campbell-Templeton, please carry on."

The newcomer to the area took out a paper from the inside pocket of his gilet, placed his reading glasses, dangling around his neck on a string, on the end of his nose, and commenced:

"I am strongly opposed to opening up the River Arrow for navigation in respect of narrow boats and cruisers; I produced a twenty-page document in opposition to the original plans which used the existing channel in its entirety. The purpose of the document was to advise the layman on the impact it would have on a river of riffle and pool regime on which ninety-five per cent of the native fish and invertebrate species depend.

"I was the district Fisheries Officer, covering the whole of the Upper Thames and its tributaries, for the Environment Agency and its predecessors for 37 years and one of my tasks was to rehabilitate the fisheries.

"As yet I have not seen a definitive statement that states categorically that the opening up of the Dart for navigation has been disbanded. This is an issue of importance to a considerable portion of the residents Ashthorpe and district and should be addressed without delay.

"My informal conversation with Major Gross suggests that the proposals are no longer considered viable and that you were looking for other options, one of which was canoeing. You may recall that I mentioned there are three kayaks on a rack at my home and my daughter is a level 2 Kayak coach. I have been known to paddle an open boat and, whilst my daughter was a member of the Lechlade Kayak Club, my wife implemented a series of courses and training for those who wished to progress. The efforts of my wife resulted in an influx of new members and the club has continued to flourish after we ceased to play an active part.

"I am not an angler but naturally I am well versed in angler requirements.

"I am aware the B.C.U. (British Canoe Union) are endeavouring to get all waters opened to canoeists, I believe the government favours access by arrangement. There are, quite naturally, statements from both the B.C.U. and the angling fraternity fighting their respective cases.

"It is a sad fact that canoeing and angling on the smaller waters cannot co-exist without conflict irrespective of any future legislation."

Andy Gross interrupted; "Mr Campbell-Templeton, I apologise for interrupting, but I think the meeting should know that we have tried, as yet without success, to make direct contact with the B.C.U. I have sent e-mails, and left telephone messages, but no response. I was hoping to have somebody here tonight. Please carry on."

"Thank you, Major. The letter continues:"

"Contrary to a comment in this month's *Canoe Focus*, stating that the current open house is working well in Scotland, there are numerous organisations and individuals who will tell you otherwise. A former factory owner from Ashthorpe can no longer run his salmon fishing business on the Tay as a direct result of rafters and groups of Kayaks.

"The River Dart is currently classified as non navigable, and anyone wishing to paddle it legally must gain the permission of all riparian owners and angling clubs. As I understand the law a formal lease or deed is a temporary transfer of ownership!!

"Again in this month's *Canoe Focus* reference was made to an Environment Agency investigation that states canoeing will not have an impact on the spawning areas. They failed to mention another R&D report on The Effect of Canoeing on Fish Stocks and Angling. Briefly the 72-page report concludes that canoeing has no detrimental effect on fish stocks but is in conflict with angling. It suggests the way forward is by dialogue and mutual arrangement. The report in its entirety is being made available to me should you require it.

"The Dart is of riffle and pool regime where dismounting on the shallows would be a normal occurrence in normal flow conditions. It can often take several hours, in a four-hour contest, to bring the fish on the feed; canoes travelling through the swim on such a narrow river puts off the fish for some considerable time, and they may never start feeding again for the remainder of the contest.

"If you managed to paddle the river as you suggested you will have noted that to remain buoyant you have to follow the main channel irrespective of width, and on the Dart there is every chance the route would take you through the anglers swim.

"Conflict is assured!

"So what are the options?

"In my view canoeing will not bring business to the town, it will only open up an amenity.

"Paddlers will have a change of clothes, flask and food in the boat or the support vehicle. They often launch and paddle straight through to their destination where they are reunited with the support vehicle.

"The Dart will have little charm to many paddlers except in high water conditions, the process of dismounting/remounting adds little to the enjoyment. Until such times as legislation comes to be, paddlers need the co-operation of the angling fraternity; the only way I can see canoeing and angling co-exist peacefully is by agreement. I feel sure that a series of specific paddles could be arranged at mutually convenient times, and only then. Ad lib paddling would not be tolerated by angling clubs. If for example a charity paddle was organised during the closed season I cannot see the clubs refusing access, the coarse fish close season is from midnight on the fifteenth of March to midnight fifteenth of June."

The speaker concluded; "This letter is from the nearest we have to a genuine 'expert', and not only is he violently opposed to the full ADAS but he suggests that agreement between canoeists and anglers is most unlikely. I support what you have said on the feasibility of the full scheme, but I would ask you to consider any alternative most carefully."

"Thank you for these most valid points," responded Andy, "next question please". A sea of hands rose.

A scruffily dressed character rose to his feet. He was the last remaining member of a family which, for generations, had woollen-associated industries in the town. Although most of their land and property had long since gone, it is certain that Bill still owned some stretches of the riparian rights near to the town centre.

"First we are told that we are having bloody great narrow boats and cruisers running up and down the river. Then, after a hugely expensive report, we are told that this is economically not feasible. Anybody could have told you this without spending all that money. No bugger asked me!"

The Chairman looked a little flustered "Now, Bill, moderate the language a bit! In any case, I know that you were sent at least two letters, and didn't reply to at least two phone calls."

"Yes, but I know at least two other riparian owners who have had no contact from you. But it probably doesn't matter now the thing has been dumped," replied Bill.

The Major replied, a flush on his cheeks suggesting that he was getting somewhat angry with Bill's attitude;

"I don't think dumped is the right word. We, and all three councils, were advised by professionals that the scheme was a possibility, and as such could produce jobs, tourism and trade. Surely you, of all people, should see that this is a benefit?"

"Yes, but it is our lifestyle that is threatened. It is our property values that will tumble if we have hoards of yobs paddling up and down the river. It is our fishing rights that will become meaningless. Be advised that I, and at least three other Riparian Owners, will not be granting you and or your associates permission to come on to our lands in order to activate any suchlike scheme that you may have in mind for the future." Bill sat down with a gesture of finality.

Andy had noticed that a number of heads were nodding in agreement with Bill and proceeded carefully;

"Can we take some questions on the actual feasibility study?" he said, diverting any further debate on personal issues. A string of questions followed, some from anglers, who were clearly not going to change their opinion, and others from local tradesmen who were, naturally, very keen on the proposals. A few stories came from older residents who recalled their youth when many local young people would have their canoes on the river.

"Are there any further questions?" Andy felt he had earned a couple of pints!

"Yes, I'll be quick. I must point out to the earlier speaker that river development does not have an adverse effect on property prices, in fact in my experience quite the reverse. It is wrong to use this as an argument against any project. Whilst I have already stated that I am worried about the interaction between canoeists and anglers, I do feel that something could, and should be worked out between both groups." The tenor of Ian Campbell-Templeton guaranteed that, even at this late stage, the audience listened to him. He went on:

"Rather than, unlike some, merely being a complainer, I am willing to join your group to try and achieve a negotiated agreement between both parties. I have worked in many troubled countries around the world, and feel that our local anglers and canoeists are no more difficult than the Arabs and the Americans!"

They later learned that he was in fact Sir Ian, and had been in the Diplomatic Service ending up as Ambassador to an infamous Middle-Eastern State, before receiving his "K" and retiring to Ashthorpe Magna.

Bill had the final word from the floor; "Don't forget to announce in the press when Major Gross is undertaking his canoe ride. There will be many wanting to see this!" A laugh went around the room, even from Andy's supporters.

Andy Gross, with some relief, thanked the flock of visitors, and closed the meeting.

"May I call you Ian?" the Major asked.

"Of course, Andy," came the response.

"Would you care to join me for a pint at the Old Bush?"

"I'd be delighted. We've spent so much time working on the house since we moved in that I have had no opportunity to investigate the local taverns." They had started the evening on opposite sides of the argument, but finished off as pals, helped on by Rosie's Black Sheep.

A week later Andy received a call from local botanist, and photographer, Robbie Muggeridge, who was an avid supporter of the river development plans. He was also a keen canoeist.

"Are you OK for next Tuesday?" he enquired.

Andy replied, "Yes, but only if it is good weather!"

"Can you meet me by the archaeological dig site, next to the Old Bridge, at 10.00?"

"Yes, of course," came the moderately enthusiastic response.

"OK, I'll bring cameras and anything else we may need. I'll have a couple of chums with canoes joining us."

What Andy did not realise was that the word was out. The *Gazette* would be sending Claire, plus their house reporter, for the occasion, and the anglers decided to protest on the New Bridge.

The day turned out to be Andy's worst scenario; it was windy and wet, but what was even worse was the fact that, although planned as a private viewing to assess the river at this point, it had now become a public spectacle. Seven canoeists had turned up with their craft, and dozens of spectators had arrived to see the unfortunate Major loaded into Robbie's boat. They were rewarded for their efforts by a sight worthy of the London Palladium, or a Carry On Film! The task of squeezing Andy into the craft took over half an hour, during which time the canoe had to be baled out on several occasions. The Extra Large Life Jacket which had been provided would not do up around the waist, and Robbie was worried about the whole thing sinking under the excessive weight.

Claire's photographer was in his element, and clicking away happily at every misfortune, but eventually Robbie climbed in behind the Major and they drifted out to the centre of the river. Two experienced canoeists stationed themselves like outriders in a Presidential cavalcade, but were there in case of any accident. They eventually headed downstream, and everything seemed more peaceful and orderly; until they rounded the bend above the New Bridge.

The structure was thronged with anglers, all wearing heavy protective coats against the blinding rain. They had a banner stretched across the bridge proclaiming "KEEP OUR FISHING", but in the rain nobody saw the pockets filled with bags of flour. As the canoes approached, the bags were opened, and at the appropriate moment they were emptied onto the craft navigating beneath them. The combination of the rain, and the flour, which covered the boats, the occupants and the river surface, was to make the targets look like some mad aboriginal tribe going into battle with full war paint.

They may have thought the worst was over as they passed the bridge and moved slowly downstream towards the weir below Seagram Hall. Andy Gross was manfully battling away with his paddle to maintain the straight line of the craft.

"Andy, harder on your side!" came a gentle request from Robbie.

Then, "Andy, HARDER, we're heading for the weir!"

Only metres away Robbie changed sides with his paddle, at which point the boat swung erratically around, crashed into the reed bed, and turned onto its side. The photographer, who had been running down the riverbank, was still photographing like mad! The canoeists clustered around, several jumping out of their boats to help Robbie and Andy, and other spectators rushed to help. It was reminiscent of a beached Great White Whale stuck in the mud-banks of the

River Humber. When eventually the Major emerged from the reed beds, he was covered now in water, mud and a liberal layer of flour. Still the camera rolled.

The front-page photograph said it all. Andy Gross had never looked so miserable in his life.

George's Corner

"See old Jamie's glasses? He must have good eyes to see through those lenses! Mind he swears that when he's reading a road map he sees people waving back at him."

"Peter drinks to make other people more interesting."

"Yes, but he's showing the classic signs of senility. Firstly forgetting names, then forgetting faces, after forgetting to do up his trouser zip, and finally forgetting to undo it!"

Chapter 12

"Melvyn, " Lauren could never quite pronounce the name as it is said in England, which made it sound even more charming: "Melvyn, it would be more sensible to take my Renault. If anything goes wrong, there are far more garages for Renaults than your Alpha Romeo."

"But, Lauren, we are only travelling a hundred or so miles in France, and my Alpha is only a couple of years old and unlikely to break down. Even if it did I am a member of the RAC!" Melvyn need not have bothered.

The truth then came out as Lauren replied; "Yes, but I know my people, and they would prefer us to be in a French car rather than an Italian one!"

So now Melvyn saw the reality, and gave in. He phoned Brittany Ferries, just to let them know the change of registration on the booking for the next evening. A young man at their booking centre, with seeming disinterest, recorded the changes and put down the telephone without even wishing them a good journey.

"I'll bring my car round to you at about three tomorrow afternoon, and we can load my gear into yours, if that's OK?" suggested Melvyn.

"Yes, darling, that's fine," replied Lauren, "I'll see you then," she added, and bent forward to administer the formal Gallic cheek greeting. There was a definite electrical charge between them, and the formality of the farewell only added to this. Both knew that the other both felt, and desired, a more passionate embrace, and both were visibly trembling with anticipation when they parted.

At a few minutes before three Melvyn arrived, and by three thirty they were heading south in the Renault. The journey took them over the Hampshire Downs, near where Melvyn had lived many years earlier, and they stopped for a while at the misnamed Sam's Hotel in Shedfield near Wickham; it was owned by Bernard, and had never, to anybody's knowledge, been an hotel! What Sam's certainly was, was "The Birthplace of British Pétanque", for in 1982 it was where the BPA was founded, and the site for the first, tiny, British Championships.

"Hello, Melvyn, back again?" asked Bill, the local vet doing his paperwork at the window seat over a pint.

"Hi, Bill, good to see you. This is Lauren, we are on our way to Brittany," replied Melvyn, amazed, but pleased, that he had been recognised, as it was nearly 15 years since his last visit.

He showed Lauren the well established terrains, and they said their farewells in the pub before setting off for the final half hour drive to Portsmouth Ferry Terminal, to the North of the City.

They passed very easily through the check-in desk, and were directed to the head of Row 1; in fact they were still rather early, and there were only a few cars in the departure queue. Usually the ferry company left everything until the last minute before loading, but on this occasion the freight traffic was already being loaded, and Melvyn observed,

"Bloody stupid if you ask me. They should load as quickly as possible so that the punters can start spending in the shops, bars, restaurant, and cafeteria."

"I remember that the standard in the cafeteria used to be quite good?" more of a question than a statement from Lauren.

"Yes, but the problem is that if you don't get in quickly to the cafeteria or bistro, the chefs down tools, I think at 9.30, and only cold dishes are available," Melvyn went on, "What I want to do is to book a table in the restaurant as soon as we board which gives us chance to have a drink and relax first."

"Ou, quelques choses," she replied with a decidedly wicked expression on her beautiful, moon-shaped face.

They were unusually lucky that evening. The freighters were all on board, and the cars were summoned up the metal ramp leading into the very bowels of *MV Bretagne*. Lauren and Melvyn were the first at the accommodation desk to pick up their cabin keys, and Melvyn carried their overnight bags to the Commodore Class accommodation.

"I'll just nip up to Deck B to book our table for dinner."

On his return Lauren was in the bathroom, and Melvyn hung up his coat. He looked out of the metal-framed window across at the Naval Gunnery School, *HMS Excellent*, when he heard the bathroom door open. Lauren stepped out, completely naked. She had let down her hair, normally in a formal style, and walked towards him. He could not help revelling in her sheer beauty; the beautifully formed breasts with large, but pert and slightly brown nipples, the shapely, still flat stomach, and slim indented waist leading down to the golden triangle of hair.

She pressed her naked body hard against his, and her tongue darted in and out of his mouth seeking out his. Her hand stroked his still clothed crotch until she was confident that his manhood was aroused. With an, almost, indecent haste the couple stripped off his clothes, and she pushed Melvyn onto his back on the bed. Indeed his manhood was aroused, but to incredible limits as it was taken between her red lips, tongue still darting.

Lauren was clever, and she managed to keep up the up-and-down motion whilst keeping him just below the explosive limits. All the time Melvyn was running the back of his thumb up and down her, by now hardened and engorged, clitoris, and the dripping entrance to her area of ecstasy. They moaned together with the sheer sexual pleasure.

Suddenly Lauren mounted Melvyn's writhing body, grabbing his manhood with both hands to place at her entrance, and with an almost aggressive force impaled herself upon him.

"*J'arrive, j'arrive,*" she squealed.

He continued to thrust to the "thud, thud" rhythm of the ships engines, idling to provide power for the floating hotel, and again Lauren screamed with a great intensity. The thrusting increased, and in seconds the shouts from both were in unison.

They both realised that the ship was leaving its berth, and they had to forcibly get themselves off the bed to shower before dinner. The heady scent of their strenuous sexuality would not allow them to sit in public without bathing, although anybody seeing the couple walk into the restaurant, hand-in-hand and fully flushed faces, could have guessed what had happened in the Commodore Class Cabin!

"*Deux grandes Gin Tonic*" were requested whilst they studied the menu.

Lauren chose a duck paté to start, followed by *Sole Bon Normande*, and Melvyn went for the French Onion Soup, with a veal steak as the main course – he felt he needed the energy. He also ordered a bottle of last year's *Muscadet Sur Lie, Sevres et Maine* as the wine. The *Bretagne* rounded the Martello Tower, far out in the Solent, built to defend the entrance to Portsmouth and Southampton from the Napoleonic fleets, as the food was delivered, and as darkness surrounded their vessel the twinkling lights of the Isle of Wight shone on the starboard side of the ship.

They both declined dessert, but had two coffees with a large Calvados, the fiery apple brandy from the Calvados region of Normandy. By the time they had finished, the lights of the island were disappearing behind them. The throbbing of the engines, and the gently swell of the channel, had a highly soporific effect on the couple who felt that each sense in their bodies was satiated. They slept well!

Phil and Lesley Durban were not an extraordinary couple in any way, rather they may well have been described as "ordinary". The only organisation to which they belonged was the PTA of the local Ashthorpe Technical High School at which their only child, Helen, had recently become a pupil. Their greatest sadness in life was that they had not been able to produce a sibling to Helen, and despite several years of tests, including a visit to the National Fertility Clinic in London, they could not conceive another child. As Lesley had not become pregnant until they had been married for nearly five years, the impression she got from the fertility experts was that they were rather lucky to have conceived even one child.

With regrets, they settled into life as parents of one child upon whom they devoted all their interest and energy, without running into the danger of spoiling her.

Lesley kept her professional skills honed by working as a supply teacher at primary school level for Gloucestershire County Council, and she thoroughly enjoyed the variety of schools to which she was allocated, especially those occasions when she worked in the City of Gloucester itself, her hometown. She admitted to herself on occasions that, whilst she enjoyed Ashthorpe Magna, she did miss the hustle and bustle of even a small city such as Gloucester, and when working there she took advantages of many amenities offered such as the Museum and Art Gallery, concerts in the glorious cathedral, and even the shops! Whilst Lesley envied those forty-somethings who were able to wear stylish and trendy clothing, she was never tempted to emulate them, and stuck to her own, rather nondescript, style.

Husband Phil had, what perhaps could be described as, more bounce than his teacher wife. In their sixteen years of marriage he had never strayed once, but it was certainly not due to lack of offers. Phil was a good-looking man, tall and with rugged features, and a long mane of shaggy sandy coloured hair. If it were not for his London accent one could be forgiven for thinking he could have been an itinerant Celtic balladeer. He had started his working life as an apprenticed cabinetmaker, and had developed a great love, and knowledge, of restoration of antique furniture, which became his greatest hobby. After he had completed his apprenticeship he went on to join a local building company, and quickly picked up all the other skills required; bricklaying, plastering, electrics and plumbing. His happiest job with the company was the restoration of an old farmhouse, which took over six months, where the building was virtually stripped to a bare skeleton, and every feature lovingly replaced. His boss was so pleased with his work that when he received payment he gave Phil an amazing bonus of £6,000, which was used as the deposit for a pleasant three bed-roomed semi-detached house on the Wimpey Estate off New Town Road.

Word soon got around that the company, especially Phil, were terrific at restoration of cottages, and soon Phil and his boss formed a joint venture company, Cotswolds Restorations, to specialise in just such work, and the only condition imposed was that the fledgling company would sub contract its labour from the original firm. Phil worked long and hard to develop the business, which he did with great speed, and he concentrated on training two young employees in his own skills and standards. The work, and money, came pouring in, and within a year Cotswolds Restorations employed some dozen staff, including two very promising young women, and Phil's life should have been content. At home, in their new house, Phil, Lesley and Helen were superficially very happy, but the contrast between their "nice" suburban home, and the characterful, and often spectacular, houses on which he worked gave Phil a different perspective, which he found difficult to accept.

Phil's evenings were spent in the workshop he had built in the garden, restoring pieces of smaller furniture which he purchased from local farmhouse sales. The original idea was that he would sell them on at a profit, but having invested so many hours of his own time into a project, he could not bear to part with a single item. Daughter, Helen, seemed to understand this, and would spend many hours in the shed with her father touching the pieces under restoration, and making up little stories about the people who may have used whatever it was, centuries before.

Her mother did not comprehend;

"Phil, the attic is now completely full of your second-hand goods, and now you're starting on the garage!" she would complain,

"And anyway Helen is supposed to be doing her homework."

"But, Mum, I finished hours ago!"

Like so many teachers' children, Helen was way ahead of her class, and because it all came very easily to her, she was bored at school. The only days which she enjoyed were when the school choir was at practice, or the Drama Society was rehearsing. Although she had only been at the school for a few days, she had auditioned for the choir, and was readily accepted. She had been thrilled when, after only a couple of weeks, she was asked to sing solo a song, written for a boys voice, "Oh for the Wings of a Dove" made famous in the 1920s by Ernest Lush. The Choirmaster, also the music teacher at the school, had marvelled at the quality, tone and sheer beauty of Helen's voice, and concentrated on refining those very few bits he thought could be improved.

Phil's only personal indulgence was, on a Friday evening, after tea, to take a ten-minute walk into the centre of Ashthorpe Magna, and enjoy a few pints of Hobsen's best in the Firkin. It was never more than two or three pints as he always worked on Saturday mornings, and occasionally on Saturday afternoons, although this annoyed Lesley who felt this should be family time.

One of the Friday evening regulars was Steven Wooley, the Estate Agent on the High Street opposite the Firkin. Steven was a chubby, amiable person, who, despite his occupation, was well liked by the town, unlike his opposite number at the other end of the street who was considered by some to be something of a crook.

"Phil, do you mind if I talk a little business?" Steven enquired.

"No, fire away," responded Phil.

"I've been asked to value a derelict cottage at the back of the High Street, but I really need to know how much it would cost to restore before I can even hazard a guess as to the value. I will probably suggest, with something as unusual as this, that it is put up for auction, but even then the owner needs a guide price, and probably a reserve."

"Absolutely no problem, but I'm working in the morning tomorrow. How about two o'clock tomorrow afternoon?"

"That will be great, Phil, and I'll make sure you get the restoration work when it is sold."

The two men met as arranged, and they went down the passageway at the side of Number 8 – the building to the left had been generously described by Steven as "derelict", but it was a disaster! The first part of the building, clearly Tudor in style and age, had bulging walls, the guttering was hanging down and many tiles were missing from the roof. The brickwork, filling in what was obviously the original front door, was so bad that the gloomy interior could be seen from the passage. The newer part of the cottage, built onto the back, was probably Victorian, and in a little better condition, but still needed a great deal of work, and the garden further on still was completely overgrown, but nevertheless quite large, and enjoyed a rear access which was most unusual for such properties in Ashthorpe.

"This is the front door," said Steven battling with the key to get in.

They spent nearly an hour looking around the property, Steven with some disgust, and Phil with growing pleasure as he envisaged the restored item.

"Do you need to sit down first, Steven?" enquired the restorer, going on without awaiting an answer.

"First, it will need an architect to draw up the plans prior to making a planning application. Not only is it Grade II Listed in a Conservation Area, but also everything must comply with Building Regulations. This alone is going to take two months minimum, and probably cost some £5,000. As far as I can see only the roof on the Tudor end will need replacing, but the wall on the passage side will certainly have to come down and be rebuilt. Wall, £6,000 and roof £20,000 including all new timbers. Then everything will need to be replaced; plumbing, electricity, gas and central heating installed. The windows and doors will all need replacing in hard wood, and a damp-proof expert will have to undertake chemical damp-proofing."

He produced the pencil, which like every other tradesman in the land was kept behind his ear, and started writing down numbers.

"Steven, with the best will in the world, I cannot see this being done for less than £90,000 and then there is the garden, the brick-build shed which is falling down, the rear access gate, and the wall on the left which goes with the cottage and needs some work. That all adds at least another £10,000. Realistically you would have to quote £110,000 to be on the safe side."

"How would it look with all that done?" asked Steven.

"Absolutely bloody marvellous!"

The two returned to the Firkin, the first time Phil had been into a pub on Saturday afternoon for at least two years, and then it was Steven's turn to produce pen and paper. Jamie Rivers looked at them very suspiciously, over the top of his glasses, as they sat in the quietest corner.

"OK. Here is my idea. A three bed-roomed fully restored Tudor cottage, off the High Street, with rear access, a garage and a good garden would go on the market for somewhere in the region of £350,000. People are willing to pay for character. If I put a price guide of £150–180,000 with a reserve of £150,000, after restoration costs of £110,000 it would leave a profit of between £60,000 and £90,000. I think this would attract bidders."

"Sounds about right, Steven." Phil was not thinking of other bidders.

Lesley was especially grumpy when Phil returned; she could smell beer on his breath. Undeterred, Phil blurted out everything.

"You want to do WHAT?" A challenge as much as a question.

"I don't want to tell Helen until I actually own the property; you know how excited she gets."

"Don't I get any say in the matter?" an increasingly petulant Lesley asked.

"NO. Your husband is offering you the possibility to live in what will be one of the most beautiful homes in Ashthorpe. It is up to you whether you show an interest or not. I'm going to see the Bank on Monday to raise the funds."

They spent a rather quiet weekend, and Phil spent most of it working on a Victorian, Sheraton-style corner cabinet in the shed. By Monday, the Bank had agreed to finance the venture, and Lesley had accepted that it could happen. The auction was planned three weeks ahead, with exactly the figures, worked out in the Firkin, quoted in the details by Steven.

The Estate Agent spotted Phil on the High Street, a couple of days before the Auction, and dashed over to join him.

"I'm not sure how this is going to go, Phil. There hasn't been much interest, and most of those who have seen it felt the work was too much." He grumbled, seeing his commission disappearing if it did not reach the reserve, he went on, "I've managed to get the vendor to agree a slightly lower reserve of £130,000 to give it a better chance. It really is worth much more than that for the land alone, but nobody could get planning permission to demolish and rebuild bang in the middle of a Conservation Area."

Lesley, who still had doubts, came around slightly when Phil took her around the derelict property and explained what he wanted to do. She was entranced by the possibilities in the walled garden, and by the time they had fought through the brambles she was already telling him how she would lay everything out.

"I've arranged slightly different cover at school on Tuesday, just so I can come and keep an eye on you!" Her voice was no longer harsh, and Phil knew he had won the battle.

There were three properties in all to be auctioned, but even then the seating Steven had arranged in the Town Hall was only about one quarter full.

Phil and Lesley had positioned themselves at the front. They later realised this was a mistake as they could not see any other bidders from their position.

Steven started the proceedings, and the cottage was the first on the list. He read through the details calmly;

"A unique opportunity to obtain a Grade II Listed building, part Tudor and part early Victorian. All of you who have seen the property know that there is a complete renovation to be undertaken, but I am sure it represents the chance of a very good investment."

"Who will start me at £150,000?" Absolute silence.

"£120,000?" Still no response.

"OK, don't be shy, I'll accept an initial bid of £75,000. No less."

"Thank you, it's the lady at the back."

Several other bids came in, but Steven was having to go up in increments of only £1,000 as it slowly reached the

£100,000 mark. Still Phil, who had been to many auctions with clients, did not bid. One by one the bidders pulled out, and as it crept towards the £120,000 mark they seemed more reluctant to stay in the bidding. Steven was using all his skills to squeeze out the extra £1,000 from them. At this point Phil, with the offers teetering at £122,000, put his hand up, and indicated with a single finger on his left hand, and three fingers on his right, a bid of £130,000.

"Thank you, Phil, £130,000. Any advance on this. I still think it is far too cheap," called the auctioneer.

The two final bidders shook their heads, and there was no other voice forthcoming.

Steven picked up his gavel saying, " For the first time", looked around the audience, then "For the second time" and finally "for the third time." The gavel came down with a thump on the oak Town Hall table.

"Sold to Mr Phil Durban."

That evening they told a very excited Helen who demanded to see the property immediately.

"We can't, darling, cos we won't get the keys for a little while," said her mother consolingly.

Dad chipped in "I'll tell you what, I'm sure Steven will let me have the keys for a while, I'll see if I can borrow them on Saturday and we'll all go and look around."

For the rest of the week Helen could talk of nothing else, and although she knew her father would not be back from work until midday at the earliest on Saturday, she was ready, dressed and waiting by ten in the morning!

True to his word, Phil arrived complete with the keys, and as it was a lovely warm day they walked down to the High Street and entered the gate to the alleyway at the side of number 8. Helen was, by now, in a state of total excitement and screamed with delight at the overrun garden, and laughed as her father struggled with the key to open the door. Once in, she looked, first, puzzled and then when they entered the Tudor section her puzzlement turned to worry. Neither parent, too absorbed with planning the restoration, noticed Helen's growing distress.

They went up the stairs, which had been constructed between the two ages of building, and her distress worsened.

"My God, Phil, it's gone icy cold," Lesley cried, noticing Helen for the first time, "poor little Helen's frozen."

They reached the top, turned first into the Tudor section, and Helen let out a ghostly, high-pitched scream. She called out something, but in a voice neither parent recognised, and collapsed in a heap on the floor.

Phil picked her up, and carried her limp body downstairs, and laid her gently on the tiled floor. Lesley called 999 on her mobile, and despite all the criticisms of the Health Service, an ambulance arrived in a short space of time.

The rest of the day seemed hell for the parents; they were all taken to the A & E Department at Cirencester Hospital, where Helen was checked over thoroughly, but with no signs of any ailment showing up from either physical checks or scans. The duty Casualty Officer, nervous at disturbing a Consultant on Saturday afternoon, called the Neurologist and explained the situation.

"I'll be with you in 20 minutes, Patrick, you did the right thing in calling me."

The Neurologist arrived, spent 2 hours examining Helen and going over the details provided by the Registrar on duty in A & E, and agreed that he could find nothing physically wrong with her. The fact remained that she was in some sort of coma he had never seen before. He spoke to several colleagues on the telephone, but none were able to help or even advise. In the end all he could suggest was transferring the patient to the John Radcliffe Hospital in Oxford, which had some of the most sophisticated brain scanning equipment in Europe.

The next week was a nightmare for Phil and Lesley. Helen remained in what was described as a light coma, occasionally opening her eyes, but obviously had no awareness of who, or what, was around her. Despite the high level of both equipment and staff at the John Radcliffe, nothing could be seen to explain the extraordinary condition of the patient. Helen was visited by a great number of Consultants, including Neurologists, Psychologists, and even academics from the little known Department of Paranormal Psychology. Both parents took time away from their work so that always one could be with the child in case there was any change, but none came.

One evening, Phil was at home, trying to catch up on his VAT paperwork, when the phone rang;

"Hello, Phil, Mike Shaw here from St Osmund's." They had got to know each other since Helen had joined the church choir. Fr Mike went on,

"I was horrified to hear of your problems with Helen, it must be dreadful for you, and of course for little Helen."

"Thanks, Mike, the worst thing is that nobody can work out what is the matter, what to do or what is going to happen." Phil's voice was wavering, "We're at the end of our tether and just don't know where to turn."

"Phil, can I come over to visit her please. There may be something I can do to help."

In his state, any offer would have been accepted by Phil, but he replied graciously;

"Thanks, Mike, as long as you realise that she doesn't seem to hear anything, and just lies there on her bed."

"Of course, I understand. Would tomorrow afternoon be OK?"

"Sure, Lesley will be on duty by the bedside. I'll let her know. Best to avoid three o'clock as the Consultants are having a strategy meeting in her ward then."

"OK, I'll be there at two," replied the priest.

At two o'clock, sharp, Fr Mike arrived and spent a few minutes in the corridor consoling Lesley, who was very clearly distressed, run-down and extremely tired. Her face had aged ten years in such a few days, that Mike was now as worried for her health as for that of her daughter.

"Lesley, can I have half an hour on my own in the room with Helen, you go off to the canteen and have a break and some lunch?"

Lesley had been ignoring her food intake, but somehow the calmness of the priest made her feel hungry, and she readily agreed. Clutching what looked like a bible, Mike entered.

On her return she sat on the seat outside the private ward, and waited for him to reappear. When he eventually came out, she was quite astonished at the look of shock on his, normally unworried, face.

"What has happened, Father, please tell me."

"Here come the consultants, can I please see you all together and just tell the tale once."

On this occasion the medical party included the Psychologist and the Para-Normal specialist along with the neurologist and some other University scientist. They took ten minutes first to visit Helen with Lesley. Fr Mike Shaw remained in the corridor with his head resting in the palms of his hands. When they returned they were introduced to the cleric, and explained to him that they could see no change, and that they continued to be completely flummoxed.

"I think, gentlemen, and, of course Lesley, that I might be able to come up with some new thoughts on this," the priest said, in an almost casual voice.

"OK, Father, let's use the meeting room down there, it's not being used this afternoon," suggested one of the party.

All faces were turned to Fr Mike, with an expectant air. He started,

"What I am going to tell you is, to many, unbelievable, but I must ask you to give me a hearing." He did not wait for their acquiescence before continuing,

"I am the only priest in the Diocese licensed and approved by the Bishop to conduct Exorcisms, in fact I am referred to as the Priest-Exorcist. I have held this roll for nearly 10 years, and I promise you that I have seen things, which I almost cannot believe myself.

"Nothing to do with this aspect of my work, I took in a prayer book to pray for little Helen. I apologise, but there was nothing else I could think of doing," and with a grin on his, by now much more relaxed face he added, "and, anyway, that's what a priest is expected to do!"

"The ward suddenly went cold as I addressed her as Helen Durban, and she opened her eyes and spoke.

"'But I'm Helen Adams,' she said firmly and clearly, but in an accent which I certainly did not recognise. She closed her eyes again, and no further words came.

"It instantly fell into place, and I recall reading, all those years ago when I first came to Ashthorpe Magna, the story of an 11-year-old choirgirl raped and murdered by her drunken father. My predecessor at that time, Father Wilson, even wrote in the parish register that he refused to give Last Rites before the man was hanged, as he believed God would wish to see him rot in hell for such a heinous act."

"When I first read this awful entry, I visited the property in which the murder took place. It was the cottage you have purchased, and the murdered child was 11 years old and called Helen Adams."

Lesley looked ashen-faced; the others stunned. Nobody spoke, so Fr Mike continued,

"I believe that our Helen here, when she went upstairs in the cottage, saw what had happened and collapsed, and that the still-present spirit of the old Helen, by some mysterious satanic intervention, entered the body of Helen Durban. They are now two persons in one body."

The Neurologist spoke, "But, Father, if, and I only say, IF, this is correct, it flies against all medical knowledge and evidence, and what, anyway, can we do about it?"

"I understand your scepticism, but if I am right, then there is nothing medical science can do about it. Only one person can treat this case; God."

The Para-Normal specialist was by now looking at the priest in awe, and nodding his head.

"I agree with Father Shaw, and I think that in my experience, not certainly as great as Mike's, this diagnosis is a real and genuine possibility. I can see no other course."

Mike concluded his argument, "Assuming I get specific permission from the Bishop, and I think I will, then I would like to take Helen back to the cottage and conduct a service of exorcism on both her and the cottage."

One by one the others capitulated, but all said that they would wish to be present. The person most in favour of this action was her mother, Lesley. The paperwork to allow Helen to leave the unit was quite extensive, and had to be signed by two Consultants, and countersigned by both the Hospital Manager, and the parents, who accepted full responsibility. As Helen was able to sit up and support herself in bed, even though only rarely opening her eyes, and then only for a few seconds, it was decided to drive her to Ashthorpe in a car, and take her in a wheelchair to the cottage.

Father Mike Shaw had spoken with the Bishop, and whilst he did express some reservations, he finally approved the exorcism. He and Mike had done battle on several occasions on the form of service for exorcism, but in the end the Bishop, he claimed after consultation with Canterbury, had agreed on the new Catholic version. *"De Exorcismus Supplicationibus Quibusdam"* had been approved by John Paul II on October 1st 1998, and pushed through the Vatican early the following year. The document was 84 pages long, totally in Latin, but within six months it had been translated into the vernacular around the world. The probable reason for agreeing to a Roman form was that the powerful, right wing,

Anglican Bishops in Africa had already decided to adopt this as their standard service.

The little party of patient, priest, parents and three doctors from the John Radcliffe, travelled on foot the short distance from the Rectory, where they had met up, down to the cottage, pushing Helen in her wheelchair.

Father Shaw entered first dressed in his surplice with a purple stole, and carried with him a container of holy water, his bible and a crucifix. The bible he placed on a dusty old cupboard, and he walked around the house deep in prayer, and sprinkling holy water liberally. At each point he made the sign of the cross, and in Latin said the words *"In Nomine Patris, et Filiis, et Spiritu Sanctis"*.

He beckoned the party in and gave them a copy of the service, which he had printed out the night before.

Again starting with the sign of the cross he addressed the group;

"Please take the Order of Service, and follow it carefully. It is important that you all make the responses clearly. These you are making, as a group, on behalf of Helen."

He then sprinkled the body of people, including Helen, with holy water, and gave the now familiar sign and incantation.

The service started; it was much like the Service of Baptism, familiar to all, and with the questions and responses.

"Do you renounce Satan?"

"Yes, I do."

This well-known supplication and response went on for some time, and was followed by a lengthy Litany of the Saints calling upon many known saints, but a number of which even Mike had not heard. Helen remained sitting in her wheelchair, face not moving. He then moved to the all-important rendition of Psalm 53:

P.   "God by your name save me, Helen, and by your might defend my cause."

ALL. "God, hear my prayers, Helen hearken to the words of my mouth."

P. "For haughty men have risen up against me, and fierce men seek my life, Helen, they set not God before their eyes."

ALL. "See, God is my helper, Helen, the Lord sustains my life."

Psalm 53 continued for another fifteen minutes, and concluded:

P. "Save your servant"

ALL. "Who trusts in you, my God"

P. "Let her find in you, Lord, a fortified tower"

ALL. "In the face of the enemy"

P. "Lord, send her aid from your holy place"

ALL. "And watch over her from Sion"

P. "Lord heed my prayer"

ALL. "And let my cry be heard by you"

P. "Dominus Vobiscum"

ALL. "Et cum Spiritu Tuo"

Father Mike continued with a reading from St John, 1, 1-14, and then from St Mark 16, 15-18. He again signed himself, and the forehead of Helen, and entered the final phase.

"I command you, unclean spirit, whatever you are, along with all your minions now attacking this servant of God, by the mysteries of the incarnation, passion, resurrection, and ascension of Lord Jesus Christ, by the descent of the Holy Spirit, by the coming of Our Lord for judgement, that you may tell me by some sign your name, and the day and hour of departure. I command you, moreover, to obey me to the letter, I who am a minister of God despite my unworthiness, nor shall you be emboldened to harm in any way this creature of God, or the bystanders or any of their possessions."

Father Shaw again made the sign of the cross on Helen's forehead, placed the crucifix first on her head, and then laid it on her chest. He bent his face close to her, and breathed on her as he said,

"May the blessing of Almighty God, Farther, Son and Holy Spirit, be upon you and remain forever."

Concurrently with the response "Amen", a rush of warm air, as powerful as that created by an express train passing through a station, but with no noise, swept through the cottage. The warmth remained, and the air was heavily scented with a sweet rose odour.

"Mummy, Daddy, what's happening?" Helen had fully awoken, regained her colour and her voice.

She, aided by the priest, got out of the chair and rushed into the waiting arms of her parents. The deliberations of the medical witnesses went on for weeks, and the whole incident was reported in a number of scientific journals.

For Phil and Lesley, they were only happy at the outcome, and at Helen's insistence work commenced almost immediately on the cottage. Helen spent as much time as possible playing there, and the whole atmosphere was changed forever. Helen never spoke again of the matter, nor of what she had seen.

George's Corner

"Poor old Harry sitting in the corner – he seems to be weeping into his beer. His first wife died, and his second wife won't!"

"See moneybags is in again – he'll probably tell us how much his houses have gone up since yesterday. Mind you he even wrote to Santa Claus telling him to just let him know if he needed anything for Christmas."

Chapter 13

Many good things can be said about Brittany Ferries – good routes, modern and high quality ships, excellent accommodation – especially Commodore Class – and decent food, outside the heights of the tourist season. The entertainment in the bars and "night club" is tolerable and whiles away time. But what misguided planning allows them to totally ruin the morning arrivals?

Those first-time users of the Portsmouth-St Malo service would be forgiven in thinking that the schedule gave them time to have a meal, a bit of shopping, a couple of drinks and a full night's sleep. The official arrival time is stated as 09.00, French time, but for some inexplicable reason at six o'clock, which is, of course, five o'clock UK time, comes the first "DING-DONG", the announcements that the vessel is nearing St Malo, and that breakfast is being served in the Cafeteria. And repeated every five minutes thereafter. Rarely do the first cars disgorge themselves from the bowels of the ship before 08.30, but even then the occupants have been left in the hold with their vehicles for, often, half an hour or more. In Commodore Class, at the earliest possible opportunity, the Stewards drop in with the complimentary continental breakfasts. The fruit juice is welcome, the croissants inedible and the tea or coffee had clearly been made some considerable time in advance!

Those brave enough to push their way down to the Cafeteria have the dubious pleasure of trying the French interpretation of "Full English Breakfast". Hard, shrivelled, fried eggs, pasty-looking bacon swimming in grease in a stainless steel dish, kept warm under a heated light, and baked beans looking as though they had been in their basin for several days. It was no wonder that the French visitors to Seagram Hall had revelled in the breakfast provided there!

Eventually, all the commercial vehicles do leave, and the cars quickly depart and speedily go through customs, and onto the French roads exhorted by signs in English to "Drive on the Right".

Lauren and Melvyn, despite the morning irritations from Brittany Ferries, were still in euphoric moods, and had already agreed to spend a couple of hours in the beautiful, walled-city of St Malo, having a real French breakfast rather than the version provided on *MV Bretagne*. They left the car outside the walls, and walked through the main entrance into La Ville Intra-Muros.

"Oh, Melvyn, it is so peaceful when you get inside," said Lauren, beaming ear-to ear. They crossed the square opposite the Hotel de Ville, sat at a table in front of a café, and settled down to a slow breakfast accompanied by the ever-popular pastime of people watching.

St Malo was a small defensive town in pre-Roman times, but had grown over the centuries to a thriving population of over 50,000 in the *sous-préfecture* of *Ille-et-Villaine.* It was originally an island guarding the entrance to the River Rance, now famed for the *Barrage de la Rance,* and the road across giving speedy access to Brittany. The city, as we know it, was founded as a monastery in the 6th Century by Saints Aaron and Brendan. From the 15th Century onwards St Malo was famed for its corsairs, a population of reputedly pirate-mariners, but in fact they were far more official than the word "pirate" suggests. They were actually either approved of, or appointed by, the French King as *"Courses au Large"* with the responsibility of accosting enemy ships and imposing charges, or especially further afield, capturing enemy vessels and bringing them back to France. The proceeds were shared between the crown and the corsairs.

A strange, and warlike people, the *Malouins*, the French word for the inhabitants of St Malo, actually declared themselves an independent republic in 1590, a situation that lasted for four years, but amongst these early warrior seamen, many became famous for maritime exploration, always in the cause of financial gain. To this day a French child is taught that Canada was discovered by a sailor from St Malo, Jacques Cartier (1491–1557), who ventured up the St Lawrence River stopping off at areas later becoming Québec and Montréal. A modern Englishman, who for years knew nothing of the Falklands Islands, only learned from the conflict with Argentina, that their name for these pieces of rock was the *Malvinas*. This name was derived from *Malouins,* after the explorer from St Malo, Jacques Gouin de Beauchene who had discovered the group during his exploration of South America. Later, but equally famous to the French, *Malouins* were René Duguay-Trouin (1673–1736) a naval hero and subsequently, Admiral, and a descendant of his mother's, the privateer Robert Surcouf (1773–1827).

Lauren and Melvyn, hand-in-hand, walked the full circuit of the ramparts, going down occasionally to look at certain shops and galleries, and to visit the magnificent cathedral of St Vincent where many of the corsairs had been buried. They decided to take an early lunch at the *Ajoncs d'Or* Restaurant, and again enjoyed the pleasures of Brittany shellfish. Early in the afternoon they left St Malo, in a due south direction, on the main road towards *Rennes*, turning off after 16kms on the N176 towards *Dinan*, and decided that, rather than take the scenic coastal road, they would carry on along the main road to *St Brieuc*. Shortly after this town, they turned towards the coast on the D786 and drove through the tiny, but characterful, fishing villages of *Binic*, *Etables*, *St Quay-Portrieux* and *Plouha*, so loved by tourists from Northern Europe, especially campers, who flocked here in July and August. The locals maintained a constant barrage of protests against the summer influx, but in their hearts realised that with their beloved fishing industry all but destroyed by the factory ships of Spain, Russia and Japan, plus EU mishandling of fisheries policies, there was, in reality, no viable alternative for a livelihood.

At about four o'clock in the afternoon, Lauren and Melvyn drove on the winding road through the rocky landscape, down the hill and into the glistening port of *Paimpol*. They had both visited this little town in the past, but neither had remembered quite how beautiful it was. Finding the *Hotel du Port*, right on the quayside, was very easy, and they had no difficulty in parking immediately in front.

"Bonjour m'sieur, dame," came the greeting from the elderly receptionist.

As is often the norm in family-owned hotels in France, the receptionist insisted on showing the couple their room, before returning to the entrance hall, completing the paperwork and handing over the keys.

"Ah, m'sieur, dame, il y'a un message."

A note, written in beautiful English, welcomed them to *Paimpol*, and asked them to be his guest at dinner that evening, stating that he would be at the *Hotel du Port* at 19.00. It was signed *"Jean Junter, Président – Club de Pétanque – Paimpol"*.

The room was best described as one of "faded elegance", but the large windows opened onto a slightly rusting balcony in front of which was the road, bordering onto the main quay, lined with recently painted bollards, more for decoration than practicality. Even at that early hour in the afternoon it was a bustle of activity with the larger vessels leaving the port for their overnight activities, and the smaller lobster vessels already unloading their day's catch. All the time, the yachts were going in and out to the inner harbour, which had become the *Port du Plaissance,* all powered by their motors, some inboard, but many on the smaller craft, outboard, and those going in for the day were busy furling their sails, while those heading out for an evening's sail would be busy getting the mains and jibs ready to hoist.

Lauren and Melvyn had drawn the two slightly shabby chairs to the open full-length windows, and for an hour had sat, not talking, merely enjoying the peace and tranquillity that the scene of such busyness induced.

"Darling, thank you for bringing me with you. I did not remember how perfect is was here."

Melvyn did not even reply, merely smiled.

They decided to wait, with a glass of pastis, at one of the tables outside the hotel, and next to the main entrance to the main downstairs room, which provided the little bar, one end of which doubled as the reception area, and the main *salon* at which visitors and residents alike enjoyed breakfast, lunch and dinner. A short, portly man walked across from his car, came directly to their table and said,

"You must be our visitors from Ashthorpe Magna; I am Jean Junter." He offered his hand in greeting as Melvyn offered him a chair at the table.

"I heard so much from our national *Président* about you, and your club, that I have been looking forward to meeting you. Welcome to Paimpol."

"It is a pleasure to meet you," said Melvyn sincerely as they shook hands, and almost shyly Lauren too offered her hand.

"Enchanté, Monsieur Junter."

"Please, Lauren, do call me Jean."

There was something about the man's character, which was quite irresistible. He could not have been much above 5 feet, 4 inches in height, and he seemed almost as round as he was tall. He had a beaming smile, which encompassed all who saw him. His age was probably as much as seventy, but his podgy, round face had smooth, translucent skin, and although his hair had clearly been more voluminous in an earlier age, he was certainly not bald. Jean Junter exuded a genuine charm, and was warmly greeted by every passer-by.

Although they had only just met, conversation flowed freely from the moment he joined them. He asked if they minded eating at the *Hotel du Port*, which he explained was the best restaurant within twenty kilometres, and his guests were delighted to accept.

"Jean, I have lived in England for about 20 years. How is it that your English is better than mine?" and Lauren added, in a humorous vein, "and probably better than Melvyn's!"

"No. Not true, but thank you anyway."

He explained that after the war he was old enough to join the Merchant Marine as an Engineering Apprentice, and stayed there for 15 years ending up as Chief Engineer on the "*France*".

"Then I decided to marry," he added, with a shrug suggesting that this was another story in itself.

"After I left the Navy, I joined a marine paint company as a representative covering the West Coast, but soon progressed and became the National Sales Manager, based in Paris. The company was a subsidiary of a British marine paint company, and with my new job came the responsibility for liaison with Head Office in Newcastle-upon-Tyne, and I spent two or three days there each month. The language was not really a problem; I had learned reasonable English during the war, and my time at sea was largely on passenger ships who carried predominately English-speaking guests." He grinned and expounded, "If you include American as the English language."

Melvyn interrupted, "Hang on, Jean! You said you had picked up English during the war, but you told us you were only 15 at the end of the war?"

"Ah, if you want me to bore you with a rather long tale, let's order dinner first, and carry on when we have finished. I don't want to detract from the delights the chef will produce!"

They decided it was not quite warm enough to eat outside, and they moved in to a table, just inside but protected from the chilly north-easterly breeze. For the first time they discussed the very reason for their being there, Pétanque. Jean explained that he had arranged an evening gathering on the Friday, as he had already spoken to his opposite numbers in Erquy and St Brieuc, and they had organised events on the Saturday and Sunday. In fact, on the Sunday, St Brieuc had laid on a friendly competition between all three clubs in honour of their visitors.

They ordered, and consumed, an excellent three-course meal, which, although simply prepared and presented, contained the freshest local ingredients imaginable, and each course was accompanied by a different wine from the area around Nantes. None could have been bettered by the finest 3 Star Michelin Restaurants, in Paris or London!

"Jean, I am still fascinated as to how you learned English during the war?" Melvyn commented, more as a question than a statement. Jean's cheeks flushed slightly as he agreed to relate the tale.

It was a tale, absolutely accurate, which would not be believed if included in an American block-busting movie on how the Americans won the 2nd World War!

"In 1943 I was 13, and we could only go to school for a few hours a week during the occupation. My father had always been a fisherman, but he was closely watched, by the Germans, and also by, how do you call them, the collaborators. He was known to be the head of the local resistance movement, but had to go to extraordinary lengths to avoid capture. In fact he was taken in on several occasions, but nothing was ever proven."

They paused whilst a fresh bottle of Muscadet was brought to the table, uncorked with great ceremony, and although Jean was asked to try it, he graciously gestured to the waiter to allow Melvyn to taste and approve.

"Naturally, whilst not at school, I would work on the fishing boat with my father, and even at such a young age, I knew the treacherous waters around Paimpol as well as anyone. It is low water at 11.00 tomorrow morning so I will show you what I mean, but there is a period two hours before low water when everything is covered by water, but half an hour later the pinnacles of the rocks break through the surface. The Germans had already lost two vessels in these conditions, and would never, by then, leave harbour at that period.

"They would not allow the adult fishermen to go out at that time of day when they could not follow, but every day or night I would take out the little lobster boat and lay the pots. The Germans were so used to this little boy that they took no notice after a while.

"My father, once he was satisfied that the occupiers were no longer interested in me, asked me to take a passenger just out of sight of the German observation post and meet with a rubber dinghy to transfer him. He told me the man was an RAF pilot trying to get back to England, and I readily agreed. My code name was Captain Bob, and the man in the black inflatable was Captain Charlie.

"In total I carried more than 200 Englishmen to rendezvous with Captain Charlie, and although we never exchanged more than a few words a tremendous bond grew between us.

"The amazing thing was to come 20 years later when I visited a boatyard in Falmouth with my opposite number in the UK Marine Paint Company, and was introduced to the owner, a retired Lieutenant Commander. We only spoke a few words before he uttered the question 'Captain Bob?'. Yes, it was indeed Captain Charlie. It was shipping those brave pilots that caused me to learn English."

Melvyn and Lauren were absolutely enraptured by Jean's amazing story, and at 11 the following morning, looking out to sea as the murderous looking rocks broke through to the surface, they could imagine the whole scene so many years before. The young man, now old, still had a look of excitement on his face as he showed his guests the route he took with escaping airmen hidden in his nets. The whole story became both a reality and recent history.

The couple became very good friends with Jean Junter, and despite the hospitality and friendship with the other clubs they had already decided that his was the one with which they would twin.

The Ashthorpe Dart Access Scheme, ADAS, had been formed over three years previously, and even the public meeting was two years before. The Chairman of ADAS, Andy Gross, still held that post, but was far more occupied with his role as High Bailiff. Effectively since the infamous trip on the river, Andy had given up on the project, and the main benefit to evolve was the participation of Sir Ian Templeton-Campbell the retired diplomat who had purchased the stables after the demise of the race-horse trainer. Even Ian, who had heard the tale of the river trip many times, could not help but laugh at the prospect of the Major stuck in the mud!

Although restoration of the house had taken much of Ian's time and energy he was now fully entering into the life of Ashthorpe Magna. Andy had become quite close to Ian after the ADAS meeting, and they had even spoken about Sir Ian joining the Court Leet, but as he had spoken to many officers, it had become clear to the diplomat that there were two distinct factions, and that scandal mongering and back stabbing were rife. He did not approve of Andy's aim to become the longest-serving Bailiff in the 700-year history of the Court, nor could he approve of the Marshall, Ray Spicer, who spent much of his spare time plotting against the Bailiff. As far as the Reeve was concerned, Ian knew full well that he would have great difficulty working with Cliff Breakshaft.

There were two pressing items of town interest, the final decision on the river programme, and the forthcoming Court Leet elections.

Andy finally agreed to call an ADAS meeting, and at the suggestion of Ian Templeton-Campbell, he booked the front room at the Old Bull to meet. Since the river incident nothing had happened, and public interest had waned – even among the anglers who assumed they had won. It was a somewhat dull and predictable meeting. Although Andy Gross and Ian presented the "smaller" scheme with a riverside walk, nature reserve and canoeing over a limited stretch of the Dart, with perhaps involvement of youth groups such as the Scouts or Sea Cadets, their enthusiasm did not seem totally convincing. The beautiful Val from the council tried to inject a bit of oomph into the proceedings, and was surprisingly backed up by John Sleight, the Mayor, but even the IWA representative did not believe the arguments of the anglers could be overcome.

It was really only the Chairman of the Chamber of Trade and Commerce, Melvyn Hughes, who spoke with any passion in his belief that the limited scheme would bring more visitors to Ashthorpe Magna, and therefore business to local tradesmen. He was proud to tell of his success in Brittany, and suggested that the town could become an attraction to the anticipated influx of French visitors. He believed that the attractions of the vineyard, Seagram Hall and the archaeological dig would be well supported by an "Ashthorpe Water Park", but the Chairman, Andy Gross, perhaps still remembering his own day on the river, did not give Melvyn the backing he sought.

"Sleepy" Honey, the District Councillor, supported by Val, did put in the request that the scheme, even if not approved by the committee, was not totally discarded, merely shelved. His reasons were, sensibly, that if government legislation in England were brought in, as with Scotland, to allow free access to waterways then the objections from the riparian owners, mostly anglers, would be largely overcome.

So it was that the vote was either to go ahead with the scheme, or to postpone a final decision until government legislation on waterways removed many of the problems. The latter won with a handsome majority showing the true English skills of compromise and procrastination. Perhaps equally English was the response to the headlines in the *Ashthorpe Gazette* stating "Committee Shelves Plan for Ashthorpe Water Park". Eighteen organisations telephoned or wrote letters of complaint pointing out that shelving the project was a great loss to the community, additionally some dozen or more members of the public acted in a similar manner. Not one of either the organisations or individuals had attended any meetings, written or telephoned to give their support when it was needed. The vociferous few anglers had defeated, at least temporarily, the silent majority who would not stand up to be counted until too late.

Sir Ian's worry about the Court Leet grew as he met more people. In his judgement it was the fact that the rather less than suitable Reeve, Cliff Breakshaft, was liable to stay in his post until Andy had achieved his ambition, which caused the unrest. The fact that the Bailiff was grotesquely overweight, and regularly suffered from different ailments, left people with the worry that if he could not perform his duties then Cliff should automatically take over. This terrified many of the Court Leet Officers, and many townsfolk, as their public representative being one so rudely spoken and mannered he was a positive danger to the reputation of Ashthorpe Magna. To Andy, this arrangement suited him, as to have such an unsuitable deputy meant that there was no pressure to finish his tenure at the appropriate time. Added to this the Mayor and his conniving Town Clerk took every opportunity to undermine the Bailiff's tenure, they claimed for the good of the town, but in reality because of the animosity between the two Senior Citizens.

Perhaps this could have continued for another two years if it had not been for the third most senior officer, the Marshall. Or rather, not because of the post of Marshall, but because of the person holding that post, Ray Spicer. On the surface a successful man in his early forties, his background betrayed only by his hairstyle, occasional lapse of accent, and the dress sense and bearing of his wife. Like so many "boys done well" Ray did not accept people like Andy as his superiors; he was envious of the public school clues, the accent, the dress sense, the bearing and ability to get along with all people, he was envious even more of the fact that Andy was a retired Major, and received a natural deference for this fact.

All Courts Leet have a "Steward of the Manor" who is the Lord of the Manor's representative on the Court, and acts as a liaison between the Bailiff and, in the case of Ashthorpe Magna, the Earl of Ludcolmbe. Historically the Steward was a lawyer and in effect acted almost as the Chairman of Magistrates, but in modern times this role has disappeared so anybody can be the steward. Stephan MacDonald had been Steward for 8 years since his retirement as an English teacher in a Gloucester Grammar School, and was well liked and respected in his post. He was scrupulously fair, and obsessively honest. By the very nature of the job it required somebody who loved ceremonial and detail, and Stephan had perhaps the greatest aptitude of all – that of being pedantic.

One evening, about six weeks before the Court Leet Elections, which were the responsibility of the Steward, Stephan MacDonald was surprised to receive a telephone call from Ray Spicer, the Marshall.

"Stephan, I am rather concerned about some aspects of the Annual Court and Elections. Could we possibly meet up in the next couple of days?"

"Yes, Ray, when can you come round to my house? I don't like discussing Court business in public."

Two days later Ray sat in the ample conservatory of Stephan's home, overlooking the fields with the river Dart in the distance. Stephan brought in some coffee, and opened up the discussions;

"Well, Ray, what's all this about?" The Steward admired his Marshall for his drive and energy, but certainly did not like many of his attitudes nor what he considered to be an over ambitious or even "pushy" approach to the Court.

"Mr Steward, I and a number of other officers on the Court are very worried about the health of the Bailiff, and the fact that if anything should prevent him from carrying out his duties, Cliff Breakshaft, the Reeve, would take over."

The Steward thought for a considerable time before responding;

"But, Marshall, the Bailiff and the Reeve are elected by the men of the town who have taken the Frankpledge and become Jurors. How can we do anything against this?"

"Steward, I am not suggesting we go against the will of the Jurors, but merely offer an alternative if Andy insists on he and Cliff being offered as a package."

Stephan MacDonald interrupted, "Anyway I consider myself a friend of Andy Gross and would be very loath to be involved in anything that seemed like a plot to remove him. He has done a great deal for this town, and I am not sure how many other people would be willing to stab him in the back."

Ray Spicer responded swiftly, "Precisely, Stephan, as a friend it would naturally be important to explain that it is for his own benefit. The people would support this, although Andy does not have the following he had in the past after the fiasco of the Disco in the Town Hall, the humiliating events on the river and his opposition to the Farmers' Market."

"How do you think we could effect this, as you say for Andy's benefit, and who would be Bailiff and Reeve?" asked the Steward.

"I think the obvious choice would be for Sir Ian to come straight on as Bailiff, and to give him the help and support, I would be willing to become the Reeve."

The Steward was silent for several minutes. Ray could see that his brain was trying to work out the implications, but after a while he replied;

"There are several historical precedents for a new Juror coming onto the Court, and immediately becoming Bailiff, but I can think of none where the Bailiff and Reeve have both gone together. I need a little time to look through the records, and consult Lord Ludcolmbe, before seeing what can and cannot be done – even if I agree it should!"

Two visits to the County Records Office, and one to Seagram Hall, later, the Steward requested the presence of Ray Spicer about a week later.

"Ray, I am not at all happy about this. I don't think Andy deserves such treatment after years of service to this town, and even Cliff Breakshaft, despite all his failings which you point out so vociferously, has always served Ashthorpe Magna to the best of his ability."

"But, Steward, it is Andy's health we are all worried about, not only does it lead to mistakes an difficult situations with the Court, but it also involves duties which could worsen the state he is in. We all admire what he has done, and we all wish him well, which is why this suggestion has come up. He will thoroughly enjoy being Immediate Past Bailiff, and will in the future, if he is well enough, undoubtedly join in with the Past Bailiffs Association."

"Well, Ray, I can find nothing in the past records which preclude the changing of a Bailiff and Reeve, and his Lordship has said that we must do whatever is best for the Court. Somewhat reluctantly, and against my better judgement, I will agree to write to the Bailiff and suggest that he stands down, but only after you have the agreement of Sir Ian to take over the position."

Within 24 hours the super salesman Marshall had convinced Sir Ian that he would be doing a great favour to his friend Major Andy Gross by offering his services as the new Bailiff. He was blissfully unaware that he had been used to guarantee that Ray Spicer became Bailiff of Ashthorpe Magna a year later.

True to his word, the Steward, Stephan MacDonald wrote on behalf of the Lord of the Manor stating how sorry they were to learn of the continuing health difficulties experienced by Major Andy Gross. The letter suggested that now might be the correct time to take life a little more easily, and "in accordance with tradition" step down to make way for a new Bailiff. Andy was devastated, and if anybody had been there when he opened his mail they could well have spotted a tear coming into his eyes. Since the departure of his wife to live in Spain, the Court Leet had been a major part of his life, and now it was being taken away. He spoke to several people he knew to be friends and supporters, and whilst a couple said they would resign from the Court if he were not there, he could detect that it was signed and sealed and the best he could do would be to bow out gracefully. For a moment he had thought to round up his supporters and actually offer himself for election against the Steward and Marshall's choice, but he realised that even though many would sympathise and possibly wish to vote for him, for the sake of stability of the Court they probably would not do so, leaving him with the humiliation of being voted out of office.

So the Bailiff, Major Andy Gross, made his apologies and on the grounds of health declined to attend the Annual Court and Election of Officers. As this was the one occasion each year at which the Steward took charge of proceedings it did not really matter. There were indeed three resignations, but as always three new men were willing to step in, Cliff Breakshaft did not really understand what was going on and stayed on the Court as one of the two Ale Tasters, and Sir Ian and Ray Spicer were duly elected as Bailiff and Reeve. There were many mutterings of "stabbing in the back" and worse both in the Court and around town, but the fact that there was a real Knight as the Bailiff of Ashthorpe Magna quelled most grievances. In any case small English towns have very short memories in such matters, and St Osmund's night was occupying the attention of the population.

It is amazing that such portentous events can go on in a town, and half the population are blissfully unaware of anything. These are the people who shop in supermarkets in large centres, live on the outskirts of town, and probably work as far away as Oxford or London. Within weeks decisions had been made on the river usage that passed well over their heads, the Court Leet had broken, or perhaps bent, a tradition of over 700 years, and Fr Mike Shaw was planning an event to celebrate the Saint after whom the parish church was named, St Osmund. None of these people knew anything, or even cared. They were happy to live their own life in every respect on the fringe of Ashthorpe Magna.

The old faces were those on the St Osmund's night committee, the Immediate Past Bailiff, Chairman of Chamber and his lover, Chairman of the Farmers' Market, Lauren Le Noir, the Mayor and even the owner of Verdi's Restaurant down by the river, Claudio Bellini. The interest of Claudio was more that that of contributing to the town's efforts, as he was one of the few who benefited from, and understood the wealthy "yuppie" incomers who regularly used his restaurant. For this reason he could see an unfulfilled market for the other half of the population for a "bistro" type of establishment on the High Street, and had already approached the owners of most suitable premises to see if they were willing to sell. He gradually came to realise that properties changed hands without coming onto the market, and that he needed to become more involved with the hierarchy to "get the tip-offs".

He had been especially prompted by a comment from one of his customers one evening;

"Claudio, what's this about Melvyn Hughes and the beautiful French widow?"

"I don't understand; he just got back from a visit to France with her to set up a twinning for the Pétanque Club at Seagram Hall."

In the way that all good rumours start, the diner laid down his cutlery and spoke to Claudio in a conspiratorial whisper;

"I was told that they were looking at houses as well. It wouldn't surprise me if he sold up here, can't be making much, and went to France with the lady."

He added in rather a vulgar aside, "Don't blame him, mind, with a body like she's got!"

Claudio started thinking. Yes, what his customer had said made a lot of sense. The old haberdashery shop would be ideal for a bistro. Double fronted. Bags of space, and in need of a great deal of restoration work so probably not too expensive, especially if he could get in before Melvyn went to an agent. The following morning Claudio went to the shop, paid his £30 membership to the Chamber of Trade and volunteered to help with the next town event, St Osmund's Night.

George's Corner

To say that the grumpy old men were "bitchy" would be an understatement. One particular evening they were in full swing:

"See old Eddy is back in. A difficult guy to forget, but well worth the effort!"

"His father looked on him as the son he never had."

"He suffers from delusions of adequacy."

"He has nothing to say, but delights in saying it!"

His suits are of a good material – pity he has never been there for the fitting."

The one-liners flowed with the rapidity of the ale. The locals and even the victim loved it!

241

Chapter 14

The Farmers' Markets throughout the summer had proved immensely successful, and the first hint of any downturn came in October when the heavens opened at six in the morning, leaving stalls, produce and farmers cold, wet and very miserable. The usual shoppers at the market included a handful of people from the town centre, including most of the protestors, very few from the new estates, and the majority coming in from outlying villages – but unfortunately on this day not many had ventured out.

The end of October and early November were relatively mild and dry, but luck being what it is, the day of the November Farmers' Market was, if anything, worse than the previous month. Additionally the amount of fresh produce in November was much less than in earlier months, especially on the vegetable stalls. Very, very few people turned out to buy, and the 12 stallholders who had braved the elements spent most of the day either supping coffee from the Town Hall, or sipping pints in the Old Bull! Mike, the Chairman of the Gloucestershire Farmers' Market Group, informed Lauren that they had an emergency meeting planned after the Christmas Farmers' Market to examine the long-term future in Ashthorpe Magna.

"I have, Lauren, spoken to my members, and the poultry stall, the cheese stall, the hot sausage and home-made pork baps, and the burger stall have all agreed to turn out for your St Osmund's Night on 4th December."

In the meantime she spoke with her companion, Chairman of the Chamber, Melvyn Hughes, who wrote an impassioned plea to the public through the *Ashthorpe Gazette* on the lines of "Use it or lose it".

St Osmund's Night arrived, and as with so many events in Ashthorpe Magna, it turned out to be a mild and pleasant evening, and perhaps having a local saint on the team helped! The Rector and his committee had done an excellent organisational job. The majority of High Street shops remained open for the evening, and even the Town Clerk had organised some fifty stalls along the High Street and in the market area around the Town Hall. The only problem came with three vehicles being left by Dave Lounds, and other residents of Upper Church Street, near the Town Hall entrance, the area designated for the four Farmers' Market visitors. Unfortunately the two fresh food stalls could not get into the spaces due to the parked cars, and as both had travelled some 30 miles to be present they decided to go straight home. Other than that the event went brilliantly with early evening performances by schoolchildren, running into a "gig" in the street by two popular local groups. In the event it produced a profit of well in excess of £2,000 to be used solely for local youth projects.

The two Farmers' Market stalls that had pulled out of St Osmund's Night due to the protestors never came back. The damage had been done. The pre-Christmas market was nothing short of a disaster. The 20 stalls had dropped to 12 by November, and the December market, which the public had been asked to support, had dropped to only 8. Again the day was dismal, and only the fresh free-range duck man had any success with his pre-Christmas orders, although the bread producer did sell most of her stock, and the Chairman, Mike, had a good run on his Brussels sprouts. Again the people of Ashthorpe Magna, despite their majority demand for the Farmers' Market, had not given their support. Melvyn was bitterly disappointed that the readers of the *Ashthorpe Gazette* had not heeded his pleas to support the Farmers.

Mike moaned, "It's the only bloody time of year they buy sprouts, and I bet half of them are thrown away. The rest of Christmas veggies come either out of frozen packs or after a several thousand miles journey from Africa or South America. What's wrong with things in season – the whole world has gone bloody mad." He packed up many swedes, turnips and carrots to take back to his farm.

About three days before Christmas Lauren was not surprised to hear from Mike.

"Lauren, I am bitterly disappointed to tell you that for the time being we will not be continuing with the Farmers' Market in Ashthorpe. I would personally have tried a little longer, but the incident at St Osmund's Night really upset several traders."

"I hope you may consider coming back in the spring, Mike?" Lauren almost pleaded.

"I'll see what I can do, Lauren, but I can't promise anything."

Quickly a meeting was called before Christmas, and Lauren reported events to the *ad hoc* committee, which included Sir Ian Templeton-Campbell.

The following evening Sir Ian had been invited to join the Ludcolmbe family for dinner at Seagram Hall. It had transpired that both parents and even the two boys had mutual friends in the Diplomatic Service, and they were regular visitors at each other's homes. Damien's girl friend, the lovely reporter from the *Gazette*, was present at the gathering, and the evening became a rather jolly and boozy pre-Christmas party. The Darlings from the vineyard were also present, and Nick's past as a Porn Baron had been largely forgotten, to be replaced with admiration for his success in bringing in tourists to the area. Lauren and Melvyn completed the guest list.

It was natural that much of the discussion at table was over the demise, or possible demise of the Farmers' Market. As all the guests at table had been, and were active supporters of the market the talk was very much a feeling against the level of support from the local population.

The peaceful Christmas and New Year holiday at Ashthorpe Magna gave no clue as to the bombshell headlines in the *Ashthorpe Gazette's* first edition of the New Year:

Ashthorpe Gazette

'SELFISH PEOPLE' THREATEN MARKET

A resident of Ashthorpe Magna and former diplomat has hit out at other residents who – he claims – are responsible for putting the Farmers' Market at risk.

Sir Ian Templeton-Campbell spoke with the Gazette just before Christmas and discussed the story in the previous edition of the Gazette and a call from Melvyn Hughes, Ashthorpe Magna Chamber of Trade and Commerce Chairman, to "use it or lose it".

The Ashthorpe Knight said that overall the recent markets had been hugely successful but he felt the risk to the market was not only down to lack of support.

"Whilst Melvyn's comments are totally valid, I feel he has missed the greater problem – that of the attitude of the residents of Upper Church Street to the market in their own backyard," he said.

"Whilst they are asked regularly to move their vehicles for just one day a month, on each occasion the same five or six leave their vehicles in the most difficult positions."

Sir Ian said several residents regularly parked their cars near the Town Hall, causing disruption.

He added: "The parking of these vehicles was so bad on St Osmund's Night that two farmers, who had driven considerable distances could not set up and turned round and left."

"This is an event which has attracted up to 3,000 visitors and benefits local causes by several thousand pounds, and these

narrow-minded and selfish people are prepared to spoil even this."

He also said that a recent survey by Ashthorpe Chamber had shown overwhelming support for the market, with 96% of the residents supporting the event.

"But these few complaining residents seem to believe they have the right to park on what they consider to be their own land. It is not their land and they have no rights," Sir Ian Templeton-Campbell said.

"These events are here for the benefit of Ashthorpe Magna, the town, the traders and the residents, and a small number of NIMBYS are threatening this colourful and attractive addition to the Ashthorpe calendar."

George Higgins, one of the "grumpy old men", perhaps, at the age of 64 should not have been described as "old". However, he did live in the slightly sheltered accommodation of Weavers' Cottages, often referred to himself as a "poor pensioner" due to his army pension, and his lack of any noticeable teeth, did make him look a great deal older than his years. His doctors, who he had to visit regularly, must have despaired at his lifestyle; rising at 10.00 in the morning, a big "fry up" for breakfast, a trip to the shops to buy his evening meal, and into "George's Corner" at the Old Bull at somewhere between midday and one o'clock for his first beer.

During the afternoon he would drink steadily, pint after pint, until at about six in the evening he would announce:

"I'm going after this one!"

This did not mean exactly what it said, as it really meant "after this next few". The real sign that he was leaving was that his battered old cigarette lighter, the equally battered cigarette roller, his packet of tobacco and his cigarette papers would disappear from the bar top and into his pocket.

Perhaps due to his eating habits, maybe his excessive drinking or even his undoubted poor health, George did have one major problem. Flatulence, and the accompanying aroma! In short, George FARTED. And when George farted it was known by the whole bar – nay, the whole pub.

One day in early August a notice appeared on the pub notice-board:

OFFICIAL PUBLIC NOTICE

THE OLD BULL, ASHTHORPE MAGNA

We at the Old Bull consider the important issue of global warming, and, the consequent desire to reduce household carbon dioxide, and other gasses, very seriously.

We endeavour, whenever possible, in the interests of both public safety, and our commitment to the well-being of our patrons to act in a professional and dignified manner at all times.

Furthermore, we accept that we owe a duty of care to our patrons, and that our legal obligations under current, and planned, future human rights legislation, remain paramount in our thoughts.

We are therefore mindful of the harm that such gasses may pose to all of us, as fully advised in the recent international Kyoto Agreement.

Accordingly, in the interests of us all, we have today given George Higgins his marching orders!

Assuring you of our best attention at all times.

The notice was signed in the unlikely name of Mr G Spott –
certainly not a name anyone had heard of, despite the sexual
connotations (not spotted by any in the bar!).

Old George went into his full grumpy mode. The tongues
started to wag as to who may have perpetrated such a deed,
but the whole thing was exacerbated when, on 15th August
the dulcet Irish tones of Sir Terry Wogan read out the whole
notice on his morning radio show. Somebody not only sent a
copy of the notice, but had explained the story of George's
flatulence behind it!

Gradually a favourite emerged, one James Bond. No, not
007, but a real one. In fact James, as he was always known as
a young man, became Jimmy as soon as the Bond films
started to become famous. Jimmy Bond was a local character
without doubt. A man in his mid sixties, but youthful with it,
he had amazing skills and talents. In fact, he had spent his
working life in the somewhat boring and repetitive business
of banking, but had taken slightly early retirement to
concentrate on things he liked – painting, writing and music.
He was an excellent pianist and singer, and he turned out for
many events to entertain the public.

Probably due to his managerial and banking background
the only problem he had was that not only was he rather
pedantic, but came over as very bossy and critical of other
volunteers. Nobody could fault his energy and enthusiasm,
but people did tend to back off when Jimmy became
involved. His favourite paintings were portraits, in a
brilliantly executed style with a hint of caricature, the only
downside being that whilst they were very skilfully produced
they sometimes did not look like the sitter.

Jimmy arrived one evening in the Old Bull, and
announced to Old George:

"George, I've done a painting of you – I'll go to the car
and get it."

A crowd soon gathered as they knew that George and
Jimmy did not get along especially well.

"Here you are, George, I could not resist doing it as you have such a characterful face!"

George took the package, thanked Jimmy rather embarrassedly and opened it up in full public view. His jaw dropped, mouth opened and for the first time in the memory of most, George was speechless.

It was a lovely painting, as always slightly charicatured, but most certainly George. The item was presented in an attractive Georgian-style gold moulded frame. George spluttered:

"It's a lovely frame, but it's not me. It's Joe Stalin!! All it needs are a couple of gold stars on the collar and it would be a perfect likeness of Uncle Joe!" Those around George knew that this was not just his practised grumpy bluster, but that he was genuinely upset with his likeness to Stalin. Fortunately Jimmy did not really notice all this, and the locals made a great point of congratulating him, and thanking him for his most generous gesture. It did look like George, but it also looked like Joe Stalin! Jimmy did not hear George's final tirade:

"The only place this can possibly go in the house is the toilet!"

The original is reproduced in this book – what do YOU think?

The weeks went on, and George withstood a constant barrage of what can only be described as "Mickey taking". At every opportunity people called him "Joe", and asked:

"Have you got your red flag with you?"

Or "When is Jimmy going to the gulag?"

Even Grumpy old George tired of the attention, but his revenge was to come.

The following spring a local couple, Dave and Louise, invited most of the locals at the Old Bull to a Barbecue Party at their house off New Town Road. Included in the numbers were George and Jimmy Bond, and they both arrived fairly early, the latter with his elegant, blonde wife. The lady was

Scandinavian, certainly a great beauty in her youth, but perhaps caused by years of living with her bossy husband, rarely smiled. The night of the party was to prove different!

George had spent a couple of hours in the pub before going on, and was only on his second beer at the party. He had found a perfect corner to observe the goings-on, notably at this stage people arriving. Jimmy and his wife were mingling with the new arrivals, and Jimmy, although he may have had a couple of red wines before coming out, was certainly not under any sort of influence.

For weeks Dave and Louise had worked putting in a garden pond, not for any fish, but merely as an attraction for more wildlife and a garden feature. From his corner by the shed George could see Jimmy Bond, beautifully attired as always, on this occasion in a pale blue, silk, long-sleeved shirt and cream linen slacks. As people arrived, went inside to pour drinks, and moved out to the garden, Jimmy was gradually being moved back closer to the pond behind him. A large lady arrived and swept through the garden, causing Jimmy to reverse sharply and the inevitable happened – the back of Jimmy's knees went into the brickwork of the pond and, as if in slow motion, he collapsed backwards into the water.

As his legs slithered in behind him his torso slipped beneath the surface, only to emerge seconds later sodden with the pond water, and the contents of the large glass of Merlot spread across his silk shirt. The crowning glory was a large piece of Canadian Pondweed draped unceremoniously across Jimmy's head. Yes, George bellowed with laughter, as did most of the other spectators, but to everyone's amazement his wife's face was totally wrinkled with howls of mirth. Keeping his dignity, Jimmy stepped out of the pond saying:

"I think I had better go home and change." He squelched down the side pathway and set off for the ten-minute walk home; he must have been nearly there before the sounds of laughter were far enough away not to reach his ears.

Ashthorpe being Ashthorpe, by the following lunchtime the story had reached every corner of the town, and even out to the villages. Jimmy was re-christened James, but his full name became forever onwards, James Pond-Weed!!!

And it was Mr Pond-Weed who became the firm favourite as culprit for the notice about George's flatulence, and subsequent BBC notoriety thanks to Terry Wogan. Nobody ever found out for sure. Jimmy, or rather, James, seemed oblivious to the tittle-tattle he had spawned, but George felt honour was satisfied and a visitor to his cottage saw that the Stalin painting was now in the hallway. Life returned to normal in George's corner.

The opponents of the Farmers' Market were furious with the *Ashthorpe Gazette* reporting the thoughts of Sir Ian Templeton-Campbell without consulting the other side. Of course, the other side were unlikely to be at a Christmas social dinner at Seagram Hall. The "antis" had an informal gathering at the Firkin under the eagle eye, well at least when the glasses were clean, of Mr "Are you sure?" Rivers, and assisted by a few glasses of excellent Hobsens ale, David Lounds was asked to contact the Editor and see what could be done.

The lovely Claire was called in by her Editor – she felt sure she was going to be reprimanded for the article despite the fact that he had approved its inclusion, but in fact he congratulated her on producing a feature that was causing such a reaction. Normally the problem with anything in Ashthorpe Magna was one of apathy.

"Claire, I know you are a great supporter of the market, but these complainers must be allowed their say, however unrealistic. Get onto Dave Lounds and give him his right to reply – it could be quite revealing!"

Ashthorpe Gazette

FURY AT MARKET CLAIMS

Upper Church Street residents have reacted angrily to claims they are jeopardising the future of the Farmers' Market by leaving their cars in the road.

On behalf of residents, David Lounds said they disagreed with the accusations by Sir Ian Templeton-Campbell in last week's Gazette that residents who regularly parked near the Town Hall were affecting the monthly market.

"No one, and I repeat, no one, in Upper Church Street expressed any opposition to the Farmers' Market – many have liased directly with the company which sets out the stalls and have agreed parking arrangements with them," he said.

"Had Sir Ian consulted the market organiser or residents, he would have been aware of this."

Mr Lounds said the assertion that residents were regularly asked to move their vehicles but did not do so was untrue, adding that he had never personally been asked or reminded.

He also dismissed the claim that parking problems on St Osmund's Night had caused two stallholders to turn away and argued that there were few stalls and plenty of room for more on the High Street which was closed to traffic.

The article continued in a similar vein with the constant claim that Mr Lounds supported the market as long as it was not close to him, nor inconvenienced his parking.

Dozens of townsfolk had witnessed the demonstration at the opening of the first Farmers' Market, which showed one of Dave Lounds' claims to be a downright lie; Sir Ian, the Town Clerk and others had seen the two stallholders who could not get into the allocated space due to cars deliberately parked, and Lauren Le Noir had had regular meetings with the farmers and the company which erected the stalls. The whole response was based on total untruths, and whilst Sir Ian was in favour of writing a response to the *Gazette* effectively stating that the spokesman was a complete liar, he was persuaded that everybody knew this, so there was no point in pandering to a person already known to be a "professional objector", and one who showed no interest in the community other than to criticise.

Certainly the apathy of residents who preferred to shop in supermarkets, the popular misconception that Farmers' Market produce was too expensive, and downright laziness, did contribute to the loss of the market, but it was equally true that the attitude of a handful of objectors was the last straw in the saga.

Even the Past Bailiff, Major Andy Gross, did not gloat over the loss of the Farmers' Market, although he had originally been one of the most vociferous opponents. Of course, his motives were political and mainly to do with the fact that the Mayor and Council seemed to have usurped the authority of the Court Leet in encouraging the market. Since the effective "stab in the back" by the then Marshall, now Reeve, Ray Spicer, the ex Bailiff had retreated from public life; he refused to go to any Court functions on the basis that it was now formed on unrealistic lines, and the individuals did not have the experience to uphold the standards of the town.

He was so hurt that in fact he visited his wife in Spain for the first time in several years, and returned after six weeks rather than the planned two weeks. He did seem considerably "perkier" when he got back, and when a local commented

that it was sad the Farmers' Market had pulled out, he
elicited, probably for the final time;

"Don't talk to me about the FARMERS'' BLOODY
MARKET!"

Nobody quite remembers where the idea originated. It may
have been Dave, the owner of the hardware shop, Melvyn
Hughes stated categorically it was not him, and even one of
the "grumpy old men", Peter Epsom who had organised such
events in the past decline ownership of the idea.

It all started when the committee who organised the
Ashthorpe Magna Christmas lighting, admired throughout
the county, received a letter from the District Council giving
them the new European regulations on street lighting. It came
as an absolute blow to them as not only did it decree the
types of ladders used and training for any persons climbing
ladders, but also the "belt and braces" fixtures needed for the
strings of lights criss-crossing the High Street and the area
around the Town Hall.

The committee, known by the acronym of ABLE,
Ashthorpe Bunting and Lighting Executive, being law-
abiding citizens immediately called in the Health and Safety
Executive, who did a survey of the area concerned. To their
horror, to be allowed lighting and decoration for the
following Christmas, a total expenditure of over £2,000
would be required, over and above the several hundreds of
pounds routinely needed for replacement of bulbs and some
cable each year.

An emergency meeting was called, and, threatened with
the loss of the beloved Christmas lights, representatives of all
the major bodies, Council, Court Leet, Chamber of Trade,
British Legion, and many others turned up at the gathering. It
was at that meeting that somebody, never recorded and

certainly forgotten, pointed out that a small town on the River Avon to the north had an annual duck race which raised thousands of pounds for Christmas lights.

Melvyn, always a great volunteer, or perhaps an excuse to enjoy a day out with Lauren, agreed to visit Bidford-on-Avon to see how it was done. Whatever the reason he arrived back with a bag full of yellow plastic ducks, and the information required. Another meeting was called in the function room of the Old Bull, and again a good turn out was seen.

Melvyn explained: "The idea is that we sell the ducks' numbers. Bidford has 2,500 of the creatures and has agreed to loan them to ABLE for a race. The concept is that we make a number of posters, and with each a sheet numbered 1–99, 100–199 etc, and each of these is given to a shop or pub to sell those particular numbers. The only worry they had is that the river Avon at Bidford is wide, smooth flowing, and with most of the river bank being accessible, and they are not convinced from my description of the Gloucestershire Dart that it could work. It is important that we inspect the river carefully, hence they have loaned me a dozen plastic ducks."

John Sleight, the diminutive Mayor, put his hand up:

"Did you know that in the summer we have a fête on the playing fields near the nature reserve to try and attract the people from the New Town estate. We have some music groups, hot dog stands and various attractions on the fields which lead down to the riverbank. I think your duck races could add something interesting to the event. In any case the river nearer the old town is probably running too fast for plastic ducks!"

"Thank you, Mr Mayor," replied Melvyn, "Can I have two volunteers to help me control the 12 ducks in an experiment?" Titters ran round the room.

Peter Epsom, the octogenarian from the Old Bull rose to his feet:

"I would be happy to help. It is well over 10 years since the Lions Club used to run these races, but they finished after the winter floods some years ago when the water authority changed the flow of the river. They took two years to complete their work, and the event never got started again due to diminishing membership of the Lions."

"Thank you, Peter," replied the Chamber Chairman.

Mike stood up. A Londoner by birth, proven by his accent, he and his lovely wife had semi-retired to Ashthorpe some ten years previously, but despite an onset of cancer, hopefully cured, Mike was fighting fit at the age of sixty-eight and willing to help. He presented a somewhat fearsome figure, being large and well set, with a crop of grey hair drawn into a ponytail at the back. His working life had mostly been on the road with many famous pop groups of the 1960s where he had done everything from road manager to lighting and sound organisation. His tales included not only the performers themselves, but people involved with the industry including the Kray brothers, and Mike's very bearing indicated he was not a person with whom to trifle. The reality was that in fact he was a gentle and considerate character.

Melvyn readily accepted his offer of help, and the trio agreed to meet up the following day on the old railway bridge, disused since the Beeching Axe in the sixties, as this was about half a mile upstream from the playing fields where the race finish would be.

The Chamber Chairman at fifty-six, although looking somewhat older with thinning hair often kept far too long, was by far the youngest of the trio with Mike at sixty-eight and Peter at eighty-three; Melvyn was wearing shorts, a khaki T-shirt and new immaculate white trainers. A mistake in the event of things to come! The older two were more suitably attired with stout shoes and jeans.

They first walked the length of the river concerned, diving through the undergrowth wherever possible to survey the flow. There were quite a number of people, being a warm and sunny day, watching them warily and obviously wondering what on earth they were up to! They eventually located a suitable spot for the finishing line, across which it was narrow enough to stretch a net, volunteered by David at the hardware shop, to catch the ducks. Back up to the bridge. They decided initially to launch all twelve of the "runners" and work out what happened to them. Like young schoolchildren they took four ducks each and ceremoniously launched them into the River Dart. The plastic creatures shot off on the current at great speed, so the three men dashed down to the first access point around the first bend. As they stood and watched, the first two ducks came through, neck and neck, the third appeared from the reeds on the far bank, and three others moved into a little "bay" where they went around in circles. Eventually the seventh appeared, obviously having been delayed by some obstacle in the river; of the other five, no sign.

Melvyn, the youngest of the group agreed to wade into the shallow river to try and recover the missing ducks, and set off, fishing net in hand, whilst Mike and Peter headed around to an access point about half way down the course to watch for the remaining five participants.

Eventually Peter set off alone to the finishing point and settled in to enjoy a rest, sitting beneath a willow tree watching the river foaming down its course beneath his feet. A shallow bank in the centre of the river ensured that any ducks which may arrive, almost certainly could not get past. He reminisced that it was probably more than half a century ago since he had spent a day playing in a river, and he was thoroughly enjoying the experience. Looking at his watch he realised that he must have dozed off as over half an hour had gone by, so he scrambled up the bank in search of his companions.

Three young girls were sitting on one of the benches provided by the Town Council, their bicycles casually strewn on the grass in front of them, and Peter approached them:

"S'cuse me, girls, have you seen anyone along by the river?"

"Yes, Mister, there was one man in shorts who headed into the river over there," she pointed at a break in the foliage some 300 yards ahead, "and there was another big geezer further on round the bend in the footpath."

"Thanks, girls, see you." Peter started to walk, but was called back to a question which had him howling almost uncontrollably with laughter,

"Sorry, Mister, but are they filming *Last of the Summer Wine*?" The question from the older of the three girls, a pretty teenager, was absolutely serious. For those not familiar with the programme it is a long-running English comedy based in Yorkshire, depicting the, often hilarious, activities of three old men. The innocence of the question, coupled with the potential accuracy of the situation, caught Peter unawares – no they were not being filmed, but it could well have been one of the scenarios captured by that excellent programme.

He eventually caught up with Mike, who was directing Melvyn to a long stick with which to retrieve one of the plastic ducks. Just as he clambered down to join him he heard Mike saying to Melvyn,

"Careful, I think it gets deeper..." Too late, Melvyn stepped forward and plunged into a deep pool; already wet to his knees, the water was now up to his waist. Game to the end, he grabbed for the long stick before re-emerging into the shallows.

Mike held the supermarket bag containing plastic ducks, and as Melvyn captured another, throwing it up before struggling onto the bank, Mike counted out a total of nine ducks out of the twelve. They gave up the quest for the remaining three and set off back to their cars.

Walking again past the girls, the pretty one, obviously her mother was a fan of the programme, shouted out:

"Which one of you is Compo?"

They may have lost three ducks, but they had enjoyed the day out by the river. The sad thing was that they agreed that without many volunteers, some with dinghies or canoes, that particular stretch of river was not suitable for a duck race – not one of the twelve runners had strayed anywhere near the finishing line. When reporting back on their day's activities, to much mirth and merriment, they received many offers of assistance on the day and it was agreed that the event should go ahead. The Chairman of the Chamber, who had certainly, and literally, thrown himself wholeheartedly into the duck race, overruled the dissidents who felt that both the selected race site, and time to organise it properly, was against the event taking place.

The Rector of Ashthorpe Magna, Rev Mike Shaw, had achieved a certain amount of public notoriety since the well-publicised exorcism which he had conducted. On several occasions he had been interviewed by the press, and twice he had been a guest on one of the many TV programmes pandering to those who believed in the occult as a public spectacle.

Mike himself got into a little bit of trouble with a TV Producer when he offered the opinion publicly;

"Do you really believe that any self-respecting ghost would appear on your programme?"

Nevertheless, he was still in demand, and this on top of the ever increasing number of churches, currently eight Parishes, coming under his ecclesiastical wing, was severely tiring him. He went on a very High Church retreat in Somerset to try and clear his mind as to his future, and came back to discuss matters with his wife.

Naturally she was fully aware of his disagreements with the modern Church of England; women priests, gay priests of either inclination, fake marriage ceremonies in church of gay couples and now the possibilities of female bishops. On retreat he studied his new testament and could find no theological support for any of the modernisms, in fact quite the opposite.

Perhaps the final straw for Mike was the televising of the first lesbian "wedding". He was horrified when it transpired that one of the two ridiculous looking females in their pop star, male style clothing, was a Church of England Vicar! Or should that be Vicaress?

"Darling, I cannot keep going like this," Mike almost sobbed to his wife. "I loved my church, and I love the work I was able to do with parishioners, but I cannot take any more of the nonsense that emanates from Canterbury."

"The Grammar School keeps asking you to do more teaching, especially Latin which is gradually being reintroduced after 25 years absence. You make more money from one day's TV filming than in a month on your stipend, and your church pension starts in two years. Even though we will have to rent a house I think we will actually be better off than we are now. And…" she emphasised the word, "And, I would love to go back to work on a job for me, not just the Rector's wife. If you decide to retire early you have my full support."

Mike was flabbergasted. His wife had been the perfect Vicar's wife throughout his long career, and he had never contemplated that she may wish for something else. He hugged her, and said,

"Thank you darling. It is the PCC meeting tomorrow evening and I will tell them then, and phone the Bishop and Lord Ludcolmbe the following morning."

Melvyn and Lauren, on their return from France, had spent most of their nights together and inevitably talked of making the cohabitation a permanent situation. Melvyn's business, in truth, had not been really viable for several years. It was not his fault, but public fashion had been dictated by many gurus on style and makeover programmes on daytime television – and the fashion did not embrace the type of goods in which Melvyn had specialised for more than a quarter of a century. He only survived on a dwindling trade sale largely to hotels and restaurants, and although the property had started with no mortgage in the early days, it was now mortgaged to over fifty per cent of its value. Lauren, cleverly did not push him into any decision, but always showed her willingness to support him in any way forward he decided upon.

The visit by the Italian-born Claudio, the restaurateur did not surprise Melvyn, but his opening statements did;

"Melvyn, I had my valuer look around whilst you were away, your girl let him in, and he has come up with a valuation. Would you like to know?"

Melvyn had not yet had a valuation done, but had thought that as his last mortgage was for £200,000 that the valuation by the Bank was in the region of £400,000. Naturally he was interested,

"OK, Claudio, but you do know that I haven't definitely decided to sell up yet."

"Yes, I understand. My valuer came up with a price of £500 to £525,000, and I am willing to make you an offer, subject to survey, of the mid-point, which is £512,500. Naturally you would want your own valuation, but I don't think it will be far out."

Melvyn was stunned.

"Claudio, thanks, it does sound fair, but please give me a couple of days to get a valuation, and discuss it with someone."

The wily Italian winked and responded, "The lovely Lauren no doubt."

Indeed it was, and the next few days were spent in a riot of indecision. After all those years in Ashthorpe Magna it was not easy for Melvyn to just drop sticks and move out. There was also his illegitimate son with Sonia whom he supported both financially and on an emotional level.

It was Lauren who came out with the deciding argument;

"Darling, with the money from the shop, you could pay off all your debts, buy a beautiful property near Paimpol and invest the balance to produce some additional income. We could keep my house here so that we can spend a few weeks each year back over here, and if necessary even let it out for a couple of months each summer, and also during the Cheltenham Festival week."

The two valuations that Melvyn had asked for were identical to that obtained by Claudio, and Claudio's survey showed the main work to be done was rewiring and some plumbing. Estimates showed that to be in the region of £15,000, and a week after the first visit by the Italian to the shop they shook hands, and opened a bottle of Champagne to seal the deal.

Melvyn called an Extraordinary Annual General meeting of the Ashthorpe Magna Chamber of Trade and Commerce to hand in his resignation as Chairman.

The day of the Fun Day and Duck Race was remarkable for England – hot, sunny and a clear blue sky from start to finish. Despite the shortness of time, four of the High Street shops had had a couple of days selling the ducks, or rather, the ducks' numbers drawn on the underside by their owners at Bidford-upon-Avon.

By the time the sales sheets were gathered in it was seen that some 300 ducks had been sold, and as they had been loaned a total of 900 plastic ducks, volunteers were sent out at the event to sell as many of the rest as possible before the race at 4.30.

Although the new Bailiff did not appear at the event, many Court officers turned up in their robes and helped with the sales of ducks and raffle tickets. Perhaps due to the wonderful weather, but maybe helped by the presence of the new local brewery, the atmosphere was wonderful, and when the announcement came that the race was ready to start, literally hundreds poured down to the river bank. Rob, the gentle giant of a local retired botanist and teacher, was dressed in his wet suit and rubber shoes, and was standing in the middle of the river clutching a plastic box containing 900 yellow plastic ducks! The fact that his head supported thick locks of hair reaching down to the middle of his back, created the impression of "The Old Man of the River", but on the command he tipped the ducks into the fastest part of the flow.

The plastic creatures played their part perfectly, spreading out into two distinct groups and with one particular duck, for no explicable reason, roaring ahead of the others. The finishing line had the advantage of a garden net across the river to catch the ducks, but it was somewhat crowded with dozens of small boys there to help capture any escapees. The winner was obvious, but Rob had to make some tactical decisions on the second and third, especially as the participants were being chased by the boys!

Nobody minded, the day was a great success, and even at such short notice, and after all expenses and prizes, the ducks raised well over £500 for ABLE and the Christmas Lights. It was Melvyn's last public function before retiring to Brittany, and he was well pleased with his efforts and those of his supporters.

Life elsewhere in Ashthorpe Magna continued as normal. The Earl and his family at Seagram Hall went from success to success; the Farm Park won National and International Awards, their produce was sold in the finest restaurants in London, and after years of red-tape, the Saxon Chapel on the island, was available for both marriages and blessing ceremonies. The Hall had become a money-making venture for the first time in its distinguished history.

The vineyard too continued to bloom, despite one poor year caused by late-Spring frosts. Mary's dedication to her archaeological project had recently proved worthwhile, and teams from Bath University were uncovering the bronze-age settlement.

Ian Rose, the journalist sent by the Travel Editor of the *Sunday Telegraph*, had spent three days in Ashthorpe Magna. He had enjoyed every moment – the people, especially those in George's Corner, the stories, the history and even learning of the squabbles. Ian had vowed to himself that he would return again one day for a longer period. He pulled his battered Mini to the side of the road looking down into the valley, and he got out for his final look at this unremarkable place. Sadly for Ian, the mist had rolled back in, and there was no sign of Ashthorpe Magna.

265